PRAISE

"*Daughter of the Wormwood Star* is a book that grabs you immediately and drags you along to its wild and bloody conclusion. You don't want to look away for the whole ride . . . and you might not be able to."
—Jennifer R. Donohue, author of *Exit Ghost*

"I am not sure *Daughter of the Wormwood Star* is actually a novel—to read it is to enter a sustained and fevered dream that is not spun out of plot and characters, but instead of madness, bliss, and passion. No, this beautiful book is too weird and magical to be a novel: this book is a spell. Read it and be ensorcelled!"
—Wendy N. Wagner, author of *Girl in the Creek* and *The Deer Kings*

"*Daughter of a Wormwood Star* is a fever dream road trip through a hellish vision of America. Brilliant, blistering, and brutal."
—Jonathan Wood, author of *Broken Hero*

"[Paul Jessup] uses language to great effect to heighten the more surreal aspects of his world."
—Eric Lahti, author of *Better Than Dead*

also by Paul Jessup

Glass House
The Skinless Man Counts to Five
Close Your Eyes
Werewolves
Glass Coffin Girls
The Silence That Binds

DAUGHTER
of the
WORMWOOD
STAR

PAUL JESSUP

Underland Press

This book is published by Underland Press, which is part of Firebird Creative, LLC (Clackamas, OR).

Maybe we're all children of the Wormwood star . . .

Edited by Darin Bradley
Book Design and Layout by Firebird Creative
Cover and back art by ekosuwandono/stock.adobe.com

This Underland Press trade edition has an ISBN of 978-1-63023-113-2.

Underland Press
www.underlandpress.com

DAUGHTER
of the
WORMWOOD
STAR

For Thom, Kimi, and Pamela
The best siblings a horror writer could ask for

:episode 1:
Fear the Living

1

Have you guys seen that Angelique girl? She just moved into my dorm, right across the hall from me. Something's not right about her. Did you see how she moves? Mary, look, look at how she moves! Like an old lady, and not like she's twenty or whatever.

They say she came from a rich family.

Really? I heard she came from a poor family. Like dirt poor, old-fashioned poor, the kind of poor you read about in dustbowl history classes.

I heard her family's dead, and she's rich, and she inherited their money.

She don't look rich, look at the clothes on her back. Salvation Army's better than that garbage. Threadbare doesn't even cut it.

Yeah, she dresses like a Victorian ghost.

I dunno. I heard her family's so rich they donated a ton of money, and got one of the dorms named after them. That's why she's here, and not some other university.

Naw, she's definitely poor. Could explain how she moves, you know? Not enough food, frail, her diet's all bad. She even walks with a cane, at our age! Bet she just needs some vitamin B12 or something.

Yeah, that cane is weird. I wonder if she even needs it—it's probably for decoration.

I heard she's really sick, and she's dying or something.

What, like cancer?

Maybe. Like blood cancer or whatever.

That's a new one to me. She doesn't look like she has cancer.

What do you know? You're not a doctor.

I heard she's a vampire.

Hah, that's funny. Vampires don't exist.

Yeah, I know, but you know how it goes, someone makes a joke about her rich family drinking baby's blood for power and the word spreads.

That's crazy.

Is it, though? I heard the Clintons did that.

Next you're going to say is that she's a lizard person.

Wouldn't surprise me!

I got some classes with her, and I didn't see any scales. No fangs, either.

I guess that rules out a family of lizard vampires . . .

Could be a witch. They say witches got red eyes like that.

Naw, that's not what they say. They say it's two different colors, like David Bowie.

What do you know? You used to be a Dance major, you don't know shit.

I dabbled in that shit in high school, read up on Salem, the Witch's Hammer, all that stuff.

So? Doesn't make you an expert.

Shh, she's coming.

Hi, yeah, hi. Hi. Yeah. Hi. Hello. Okay.

That was close. You think she heard us?

Naw. Why, you scared?

I dunno. What if she is what they say she is, you know? I don't want to risk it.

I don't think she's a vampire lizard witch, that's just insane.

You guys talking about Angelique?

Yeah.

I heard she comes from a family of Satanists.

Satanists?

Yeah, and they think she's the antichrist, and raised her to believe it whole heart and soul. Can you imagine that? What a fucked-up childhood. And I thought my parents *messed* me up.

You just made that up.

No, for real, I have it on good authority, someone I trust.

Oh yeah? Who's that.

My brother knows a guy, a hacker kind of guy. He can find out anything on anyone, just give him a name and an email address and he'll work his magic. He said he found shit about her on the dark web that's all messed up.

Pfft, the dark web. That's where QAnon came from, you can't trust that paranoid bullshit.

No, it's true, I promise. Not that usual conspiracy theory stuff, trust me on that. She's adopted, and the family that adopted her has ties into everything bad about this world. Powerful rich people, politicians, that kind of thing.

I dunno, sounds like a conspiracy theory to me.

Yeah, I think so too. Get out of here, we're trying to actually figure this shit out, not run around crazy theories.

Right, so vampire lizard witch is more believable than what I told you?

Well, we didn't get ours from some friend of a friend of a hacker. These were people who met her, talked to her, hung out with her.

I talked to her.

No way, Cris. No way she would talk to you.

Yeah, she's actually really nice.

You see that birthmark she got on her forehead? Like a white star. What's that all about.

I'm telling you, antichrist.

Well, if she's the antichrist, I'm one hundred percent on board. Hail Satan!

Oh, shut it, Cris. You just have a crush on her.

So what if I do?

You're not her type.

How do you know?

I dunno. She seems straight to me.

I could turn her.

God, you talk to her just the once and already you're shouting hail Satan and acting like you can turn a straight girl on.

You weren't there when I talked to her, you don't know. I got the vibe, you know?

What vibe?

The one you get when someone's into you. You know what I mean. There is that electrical feeling, the way our fingers touched tips, the small turn of her smile. There is a connection, and it's a heartbeat and fireworks and all of that.

It's all in your head. You remember the last time you thought that . . .

Hey, it's still possible. Teach didn't say no, she just said not with a student.

That's still no.

Whatever, after I graduate, I'm taking a bus to her place and we're going to shake the foundations of the world.

I wonder if she's connected to the murders on campus.

Who Angelique?

Yeah.

What murders? I didn't hear about any murders.

You are so full of shit.

No, they're keeping it underwraps, so enrollment numbers don't drop.

I heard about them.

You did not.

Yeah, my brother's hacker friend even showed me pictures, it's really nasty.

Two murders. I wonder what will happen if it's three . . .

You think it's a serial killer?

Dunno. But I don't know anything about that kind of thing.

Wonder if it has something to do with Angelique?

Wow. Maybe. Huh. Maybe the rumors are true. She did just enroll last week . . .

Naw, that couldn't be right. They were dismembered, and both of them jocks. One on the row team, the other . . . football? Or lacrosse. I don't know, whatever. They were strong, massive dudes, and she's so frail, and sick-looking with her cane. No way she could've torn those dudes apart.

Yeah. But maybe that's a ruse . . . like Willy Wonka with *his* cane.

Shut up. This is getting silly now, vampire lizard Willy Wonkas. I'm out of here, see you guys later.

2

We all knew the murders wouldn't stop. Not even after the cops put some suspects behind bars—they just kept right on happening. Strangers started showing up on campus, too. Some of them were protesters waving their signs, blaming the police for inaction. Others were counter protesters, spitting out blue lives matter jargon, while ignoring the very same cops they were trying to uphold. Some of them were just curious and wanted to be part of whatever horrible thing was going on. Others saw themselves as white knights, protecting everyone else, while walking around in camo gear and waving assault rifles like they were cheap plastic toys.

And each of them, every single one of them, freaked us the fuck out. We started spending the nights in each other's dorms, even though that was kind of verboten. No one really called us on it, and the RAs just looked the other way. They were about as freaked out as the rest of us. Some of our clique had to go home early, with their parents pulling them out of classes or transferring them to a safer school.

The core four of us all stayed behind, though. Dunno why that was the case. I know Cris had a bad home life—her parents were uber religious and didn't like her lifestyle. Debbie's parents were off in Europe somewhere or something or another, at least that's what she said, and so they didn't even realize what was going on. Not sure why Petal's parents kept her here, and she won't really talk about it. So I won't press it.

And my parents? Well. They always acted like I was an inconvenience to their lifestyle, so it was no surprise when they told me to finish out the year anyway. Wonderful.

We were the ones left behind, and called ourselves the Orphans. I know, I know it was a jokey little name, something to lighten the mood so we wouldn't be so terrified all the time. And let me tell you, there was a lot going on to stress us out. Not just the murders, though that was also a big part of it. We all had this feeling like we were being followed, though when we turned and looked, no one was there. Cris set up a trap with a motion sensor connected to her phone, in order catch them in the act. When it snapped the picture all we could see was a misty shadow obscuring everything. It looked like smoke, or a vapor, with strange face-like patterns swirling in the mist. They seemed to be moaning, those face-shaped patterns, and whether it was in agony or pleasure it was impossible to tell.

Debbie scoffed, said that was nothing. She explained a bunch of jargon about low light and sub pixel motion capture, but it all went over our heads. We wanted to be as skeptical as she was, but it was hard. It felt like every moment something uncanny happened, and all this evidence added up. Like on Thursday, when human-shaped shadows were burned into the outside walls of the library, or the daily increase of dead birds across campus.

That one made me feel sad as well as freaked out—all those little corpses. And no matter how often the lawn crew cleaned them up, more seemed to crop up every morning. They were scattered across the pathways, discarded in bushes, or nailed to trees. One morning I found a bunch of bird skulls in a circle right outside of my dorm. Cris was with me, and she noticed it right away. The sunlight streamed in through the branches of the trees, casting shadows across their discarded skulls. It would've been pretty if it hadn't been so horrible.

Later on, I dreamt of birds tearing me apart. I did not like that dream at all. Cris and Petal were with us that night in my dorm on the sixth floor. Four Orphans sleeping on the floor together. Petal and Debbie both had dreams of this giant grotesque shadow slowly rising up and devouring everything in sight, leaving only emptiness behind. Cris had that same weird bird dream that I had.

We didn't talk about our nightmares any more after that. It seemed sharing them was not a comfort, and instead only made our unease even worse. We were so bothered by our dreams we went up the last few flights of stairs to the roof of my dorm, and laid down and watched the stars for a bit. The world slowly turned a lighter and lighter blue color, as the dawn approached. I wish I could say this was calming, but it was not. Our dreams still hung heavy in our hearts, and the murderer was still on the loose.

"Do you think he's out there right now, killing?"

"Maybe. Is today an odd number day, or an even one?"

"Even one."

"Probably not, then, he only kills on odd number days."

"Except for Babydoll."

"You mean Dora, she always hated that nickname."

"Yeah, sheesh, have some respect for the dead."

"Okay, fine, except for Dora. All odd number days."

"Some of the internet sleuths think that it's not the same killer as the others, that it's a copycat killer that killed Dora, and that's why the day is wrong."

"Oh god, a copycat killer? On our campus. That's creepy."

"Creepier than the real killer?"

"Somehow, yes."

"Why, pray tell?"

"I dunno. Just seems wrong that someone saw all this stuff and thought, hey! I want to get in on that, that looks like fun."

"Yeah, creepy, you're right."

Petal sat up, wrapped her arms around her knees. The morning light had woken the birds, and now there was a cacophony of songs rising up from the campus trees below.

"Some of the Reddit sleuths say there is more than one killer, all of them working in tandem. That's why the cops are having such a hard time tracking this loser down—they're only looking for one person."

"Huh. All copycat killers?"

"No, a group of killers since the start of this whole thing. And that some of the people put behind bars where just a part of a larger group? I dunno. It makes sense, I guess."

"Guys, I don't like this. Can we talk about something else?"

"Sure."

"Okay."

"What about?"

"Anything else, I don't care, thinking about this is giving me a stomach ache."

"At least we're not talking about our dreams anymore."

We all laughed nervously. There was some truth to that, that our dreams last night were even more disturbing than the murders we faced daily. Maybe we became numb to the killings, and now they were a part of the background hum of campus life? What a depressing thought.

"Has anyone seen Angelique in awhile?"

"No, not in a few weeks."

"Wonder if her parents called her home, like everyone else."

And then all of a sudden, the birds on campus went quiet and still. All sounds seemed to stop, no slow waking world of fresh-faced students meandering about campus, and making small talk before the day started. No alarms blaring, alerting them to the start of an oncoming class. No cars moving down Main Street toward the slow workday ahead. An eerie, unsettling silence, like the world was holding its breath, waiting patiently for something horrible to happen.

And then a scream cut the silence in half, and we all sat up, arms shaking, breath caught in our lungs. Another murder?

"Oh god, oh god, oh god, oh god . . ."

Another scream, and another. Was it coming from the same place? Maybe. It was hard to pinpoint it, the sound echoing around the campus below. If so, it would've been the first time there were multiple murders in the same day. Usually they were spaced apart, between five to nine days, in order to keep the odd numbers right and correct. Another scream, followed by *please help, someone, please!* We wanted to rush down, to help . . .

But we were so far away, and scared, and maybe that would be us next. Petal started dialing 911, as Cris paced about, dialing the number for campus police. Why did we have to go to the roof this morning? To hear such horrible sounds, yet be unable to run down and act in time? Maybe we were too late already. How long did it take someone to die from stab wounds? In the movies it seemed to happen in an instant. But real life was more complex than that, wasn't it? Bodies take a long time to die, slowly, bleeding out, shutting down. Unless it's a gunshot wound to the head, it's going to be a while.

And then, all of a sudden, the screaming stopped. Now just a restless sobbing. And then silence. The phone lines were all busy, we couldn't get through to anything. Cris kept pacing, and the rest of us joined her, moving nervously about the edges of the roof, taking turns trying to get through to any emergency line we could. My phone's battery was only at ten percent, and I didn't want it to die up here, far above the restless world. But I also wanted to help, somehow, in my own little meager way. Even if it was just asking someone else to come save the day. Petal bit on the edges of her cuticles, blood tinting the nails red.

And behind us we heard a long slow creaking sound, like the rusted hinges of a cemetery gate. We did not want to turn around, did not want to see what could be making that horrible sound. Was it the killer, now fresh and flushed with murder, coming to take us down, too? We grabbed each other's arms, trying to anchor ourselves in reality, as everything tilted sideways. More sobs from the campus beyond, and the fresh scent of fire, and it felt like the world was ending. After all this time, year after year, after all those prophetic promises of climate change and global decay, here we were at the end of time, and the world was ending . . .

A voice behind us—all raspy, raw, and beautiful. "I had a feeling I'd find you four up here . . ."

And we turned, and saw Angelique Blackthorn behind us, leaning on her cane and outlined by the red light of the rising dawn. She had just come up through the stairwell, the creaking sound the door opening behind us. *The star of morning.* That phrase from a poem rattled about in our thoughts. *Come look upon me, rebel angel, the star of morning, and see what gifts I bring to your wasteland.*

Later, we talked about the poem when Angelique was out of earshot, and Petal thought we'd overheard it in one of our classical poetry classes. Probably something by Virgil or Dante—it felt like something they would write. Cris said it sounded more like T.S. Eliot, and we argued about that for a good half hour, and then eventually just gave up. We tried finding the poem in any of our textbooks, but nothing came up. We searched for it online, and again, we got even less than nothing. The poem did not exist.

But we had to have heard it somewhere else. We had to. We all knew the next line, and recited it without even thinking. The final line of the poem, and as we spoke it all in unison, our voices creaky and broken, I got chills up and down my spine.

Love me and fear me in great measure, for I am the light that shatters the void.

3

"Now that I found you losers, we need to get to work if we're going to survive the next few days."

We all stood stunned, unsure of what to do, what she meant. The world tipped a little again, sideways, and we felt dizzy. In the far off distance, we heard sirens, and the roar of a distant flame. The smell of fire grew, little by little, ash and burning leaves. Embers tossed in the air around us, and we got that sinking feeling that we should get off the roof now, before this whole place lit up.

"What do you mean?" Cris this time, speaking up when the rest of us felt mute and tongue-tied.

Angelique walked forward, and leaned against the edge of the roof. She squinted off into the distance, and pointed her cane at Rose Hall. "There. We got to get there quick, before the cops arrive. I can push a little, give us a few moments more, but we gotta do it now."

A bright headache pulsed around the edges of our skulls, as panic set in. Each of us nodded, unsure of what was going to happen next, but knowing in our deep-down bones that Angelique was guiding us towards something *else*. It's hard to explain that feeling now, looking back all these decades later, but there it was, burning inside of us. The need to see whatever Angelique had to show us. Already, we were changing, and already she was molding us.

Everyone except Debbie. She let go of my hand, her body trembling, and we saw it in her eyes. She didn't want to go, and she pulled away from us, from the gravitational pull of Angelique. "Why are we going to Rose Hall?"

Angelique stepped forward, closer and closer to Debbie. "I can't push things until we get downstairs, you understand? So no more of this nonsense, else we'll lose the window and the cops will get there first. Do you want that? They'll rope it all up, push us all out, and we won't get to do what we need to do."

Debbie stepped back, one two, one two. We were frozen, caught between two worlds, watching this all play out in front of us. She was on the edge of the roof now, swaying over the campus below, her eyes dizzy with vertigo, as Angelique walked forward some more, twirling her cane like a circus performer.

"Please, I don't want to go to Rose Hall, I . . . I . . . can feel something terrible is going on there and I don't want to see it, please . . ."

Petal broke forward, stronger than the rest of us. "It's okay, Debbie, dear. You can stay here while the rest of us go and take a look. Isn't that right?"

Angelique lifted her cane and smacked it on the ground. She was so hypnotic in that moment, we couldn't take our eyes off of her. I often think back, and wonder if I'm seeing this memory in a different light from the present day, and seeing her as we saw her later? But I don't think that's the case. The memory is so vivid, I could show you the exact layout of the rooftop, everything. I don't think I'm wrong in how charismatic she was, even then, her gravitational pull sucking us in.

"Hush, you. It's not that easy. You don't know how this all ties together, you can't see the threads pulling at our hearts. Debbie, listen to me. If you don't come with us, they will catch you, and you will end up like the others. Understand? With me you have a possibility of survival. Out there? No chance at all."

"But why . . ."

And Debbie stepped back again, slipped a little, and then stuttered and tumbled to the side, almost falling to her death, and yet catching herself in the last moment, clinging to the edge with pink fingertips. The embers flew up around her, staining her face with burning ashes. "Oh god . . ."

"No god here, my dears, just the silence of his absence. Now grab my cane and use it to pull yourself up . . . there you go. Come on now. You know this is right, you've been one of my coven since before you were born, you can feel the truth of it in your heart."

Breathless. I tried to run forward to help, but Cris held me back. "Don't," she hissed under her breath, "You'll just get in the way, she can do this." And then we watched as she struggled, almost fell once or twice more. I didn't want to watch my friend die, none of us did. Her fingers grasped the root of the cane, and then her neck over the edge, and then her shoulders, and then her face. Elbows now on the roof, pulling the last of her body up, and then she collapsed for a moment, coughing and sobbing.

"Please," she said, "Please . . . I just want to go back home."

"It's too late for that now, isn't it? Your parents are lost out there in the world, you haven't heard from them in months. No emails, no texts, the phone calls are dead air and canceled phone lines. Do you even know if they still exist? Their house isn't even their home anymore, it has new owners, strangers in your childhood abode, giving your things away to Goodwill."

"How . . . how did you know all that . . ."

"You don't have to come inside Rose Hall with us, but if you don't, I can't guarantee your safety, understand? This coven isn't consecrated yet, our bonds are loose fibers that can unravel with one clumsy tug. We must knot and knot up soon, but we can't do that yet. It's not time."

"I don't understand."

"None of you do, and you may never fully understand, and that's okay. The universe is full of shit we don't get. Now come on already." And that frail girl with a cane helped Debbie stand up, and then turned and looked at the rest of us. "We all good to go? No more wild threads in this knot?"

Nobody said anything, we just nodded solemnly. It felt like a funeral moment, and that whatever she was going to show was going to change us forever. And yet, we had to see it, and I just hoped against hope that it wasn't going to be a dead body. I didn't want to see a dead body. I didn't want to see the killer still standing there, over the body, grinning with knife in hand. And yet, Angelique held this undeniable power over us, even then, at the start of it all, before we really got to know her and understand who she really was all this time. And so we had to see it, even if it was the worst thing absolutely imaginable. We could not say no.

"Good, good. We've wasted too much time now, I wanted to wait until we were down on the first floor before I pushed, it would've been so much easier. But things are what they are, aren't they?" She coughed into her fist and looked at us with those eerie eyes. They were a deep blood red, and had a skull shaped pupil in their center. I knew just then that they were not contacts, and shivered slightly in awe.

"Okay, losers, here's the deal. Normally I don't need this cane much, but every time I push or do a little hocus pocus, it takes a shit ton out of me. You understand? So once I do this I'm going to need your help getting downstairs, especially now that the RAs made the elevator verboten to us mere mortals."

Again, we all nodded, not completely understanding what was going on, but unable to look away or back out now. We were all in, one hundred and ten percent, caught in the tidal undertow of Angelique.

"All right. Whatever you do, whatever you see, don't move an inch, understand? Even if I look like shit, and you want to help, you don't touch me until I fall. Once I fall, then we're good and we have to get going to Rose Hall. Okay, then. One, two, three."

We all expected a flash of lightning, or her body to glow with a red aura. Something dramatic, and supernatural like that. I guess maybe our minds were poisoned by one too many horror movies, and the rumors surrounding her on campus. And the way she was acting, leading up to this moment, full of dramatic energy, like she was about to do something unbelievable. Debbie said later that she was more freaked out by how mundane it all seemed to be on the surface. When underneath, she said, something dark and violent was going on. You could tell, she said, there was an unseen energy rippling through the air. The others agreed with her, but if I'm telling the truth I don't think I'd felt it then. Not just yet, anyway. Things would change later, but you already knew that, didn't you? Of course you did.

She pushed the cane into the ground, and got into a fighting stance. Just like she was about ready to pop someone in the head. I know, it sounds silly, but that's exactly what it looked like in our memories. When she moved, her jewelry jingle jangled around her neck and on her wrists, a soft symphony of bones and gold. Her face got this intense look, as everything strained, all muscles clenching at the same time.

You ever see that movie *Scanners*? Yeah, you know the scene. Her face looked just like that. Her veins taut ropes pulled under her skin, her lips pinched tight and chapped. Her eyes rolled around until they were all just the whites with flecks of red. And everything grew more intense with each given second. There was a roar down below us, and embers fluttering around, as cries for help drifted up from the campus. The fire would be getting to this dorm soon, wouldn't it? And here we were, trapped on the roof . . . with only a rickety, rusted out fire escape to climb down.

And then the star-shaped scar in the middle of her forehead split right open. We audibly gasped, and traded looks back and forth, uncertain of what we were seeing. A raw wound now, blood trickling down her face, her body shaking as she hummed. Cris said she saw a red light inside that open wound, like a flickering candle flame, but no one else seemed to see it this time. Ghosts of memories, echoes that contradict each other.

A loud sound, like a bomb going off not too far from here, and she collapsed like a bag of twigs, her arms barely keeping herself upright with her knobby cane. "That should give us enough time to do what we need to do. Come on, let's get to Rose Hall."

"What did you do?"

"It doesn't matter right now."

"No, come on Angelique, tell us what you did. Did you do that noise?"

"I just reached out a little and pushed, that's all."

And then came the roar of sirens, as she said, "Tick tock, time's a wasting. Let's go."

A few of us meandered over to that edge and looked out across the great expanse of campus below. Fires here and there, mostly on the green and in the parks. Some of the trash cans were lit up, and only one of the dorms had caught fire. I made sure it was nowhere near Rose Hall, I didn't want to run headfirst into a roaring inferno of death. None of us did, not yet anyway.

Though I wonder what would've happened if Angelique told us that we had to do it? Even here, and now, at the start of it all? Would we have run into the flames and embraced death all for her? I wish I could say no, that wasn't the case. But already we felt that pull, that death was only an inconvenience, and that she was the gateway to something greater.

4

Running through campus had been a real surreal experience. Angelique limped behind us with her cane, Cris helping her out as best she could, trying to keep pace with the rest of us. People rushed about, helping each other survive whatever it was that was going on. Pulling people out of the buildings, using fire extinguishers to put out the small fires they could. No one was paying attention to us at all. Just four weird girls making their way to the building on the northernmost edge of campus. A squat, angry, brutalist kind of place. The sort of place that felt wrong on the inside, and invites acts of violence from time to time.

No surprise that we were heading there. At least once a week there was a fist fight in Rose Hall. Large skirmishes broke out every four or five years, scattering across the uni and getting a lot of students in deep trouble, quite a few of them expelled, and two murdered. They said that it burned down in the sixties during a protest against Vietnam, when the National Guard was called in and panicked. Several students shot dead, and in the ensuing chaos, fires started lighting up and the place became a smoldering pile of debris and ruins, only to be rebuilt a few years later.

"I really don't want to see a dead body," Debbie speaking again, as we dodged around the chaos. "Promise me that's not where we're going."

"It is precisely were we're going, but you don't have to go in with us, okay? Not if it really freaks you out. In fact, you can wait outside as a lookout, if you want. Make sure the cops don't come a little early and interrupt our seance."

A dead body. Exactly what we'd feared, and not just any old dead body, mind you, one that was brutally killed by the serial killer stalking us. Another student on campus, probably someone we knew. A weird feeling of terror and anticipation spread through us in a slow-moving mist. Nobody else said anything as we walked for a bit, our apprehension speaking for us, vivid in the nervous glances we gave each other. And we weren't just going to see a dead body, no, we were going to speak to it. I had a queasy feeling in my stomach, and I'm sure the other Orphans felt the same way. Even Petal, who knew how to act tough when she needed to, you could see that facade slip at the mere mention of talking to a corpse.

"Seance? You never said anything about a seance."

"Didn't I? I could've swore I at least implied it. Whatever, yes, we're going to talk to the dead and do a little necromancy, and that always works best when the corpse is fresh."

"Just. That. I don't know. Seances freak me out."

"Then you can wait outside with Debbie, and hope that the cops are the least of our worries."

We didn't know it at the time, but Angelique was pissed off and agitated. Her sentences changed, charged with some unseen aggression, and her movements were sharper, with more violent edges. It was probably from her recent push, whenever she did that she would get in a mood for days afterwards. That sour kind of mood that we all feared.

"Any of you other losers want to chicken out and not be part of something magical? Huh? Come on speak up, I have to know if I'm wasting my time with you four or not. Talk. Now."

A mumbled, terrified, *no, we're good, you're not wasting time with us,* was all we could summon in response, as the campus burned around us. That seemed to placate Angelique, at least for now, and that made us happy. It's so weird how quickly we changed when we met and talked in person up on that roof. Like Cris, we fell under her spell. It wasn't exactly love, but something like it, very close to it. Something perhaps more intense and passionate and self-destructive than the mere word *love* could ever contain. Worship might be a better word, yes.

We worshiped her, idolized her, and wanted to be *her.*

"Damn straight you're good, you're good as gold. Dead bodies are nothing to be afraid of. The living, yes, they're the ones you should fear."

Fear the living. Not the dead. Petal this time, raising her fist like a war cry, regaining her confidence once more. The rest of us felt chills when she said it, so we raised out fists and said it ourselves, rushing now the last quarter mile towards Rose Hall, laughing at the absurdity of the comment, the absurdity of our whole situation. It's weird how quickly the mood can change at the drop of the hat when you're rolled up in an intense situation like that.

5

The fires hadn't touched Rose Hall at all. The closest it had gotten was the two trees on either side of the front door, the leaves on top flickering with a riot of flame. They stood tall and still, giants guarding the pathway to the building with a wave of heat. The flame seemed to know of the murders beyond the doors and did not want to touch it, scared of what it saw in the hallowed halls. Oh god, we understood that fire, and understood that fear. We did not want to see what we had to see. And yet, unlike the flame, our curiosity, and the charisma of Angelique, pulled us forward under their tidal undercurrent.

Fear the living, not the dead. Fear the living, not the dead. That ran through our minds, as a collective chorus of thoughts, like whispers in the back of our skulls. Somehow, we were melding in this moment, the barriers of our mental worlds cracking just for the four of us. Angelique said it was because of our coven ties, and would only grow stronger once we knotted up completely.

I know, that sounds absurd. Maybe we were imagining it? It gets all muddled up and mixed together. Especially the moments we shared, the ghosts of our memories altering and warping. You got to feel it around the edges—that's where the truth lies. Maybe we were really all psychically connected, just like Angelique told us? Or maybe she'd hypnotized us into believing that.

Petal thought she drugged us, slipped us some acid or DMT when we were eating. I'm not so sure about that, though. Fear leant sharp edges to our experience, our minds primed at a more animal level. We all thought *too* clearly, in a way that terrified us a little.

Okay, maybe more than a little. Maybe a lot.

"Debbie, Petal, here is your point of no return. Beyond those gates you're going to see some shit you told me you don't want to see, understood? So if you need to stay behind here, go ahead and do it. If the cops come early, do a whistle. You guys know how to whistle?"

Petal stuck two fingers in her lips and let out a high-pitched whistle that hurt our ears.

Angelique smiled. "There you go! We'll hear that and get away from the crime scene as quickly as possible."

And then without fanfare or goodbyes, we braved the heat of the flaming trees and pushed those doors open. Rose Hall stretched out in front of us, a maze of staircases and long hallways. The doors shut behind, and for a moment we worried about Petal and Debbie. What if the killer went after them while they waited outside, all alone and vulnerable? No one would hear their cries for help, there was so much screaming and crying and chaos already from the fires. My stomach turned and flipflopped with that sinking sense that we left them behind to die, as we ran past a large monitor hung on the wall, blaring out the news for the day.

Nothing about the campus, yet. It seemed that everything was focused on a freak accident. A plane had crashed directly in the center of town. That was that noise we'd all heard earlier. Reports say it fell out of the sky, first the engines, then the wings, and then the massive body of the aircraft. Looking at the wreckage was horrifying, bodies twisted in metal, being pulled out by police officers and the ragged volunteer fire department. Half of downtown was in ruins now. It looked like video from a warzone, something we saw in classes covering World War II or Vietnam. It all felt so unreal.

I stopped for a moment, watched as Angelique and Cris moved ahead of me. She was using her cane less. And already she seemed less gaunt and frail, as if whatever energy she'd expanded earlier had finally returned, and she was perfectly peachy once more. Who was this Angelique? Which rumors were true? What had we just witnessed? Out there, at the end of the world? I felt a mix of terror and love and worship wash over me once more. Thrilling, yet . . .

"What are you doing?" she stopped, turned around. "We don't have a ton of time."

I pointed at the screen, my hand shaking even though I willed it to stay still. "Did you do that?"

A baby. There was the corpse of a little girl being pulled from the wreckage, a still screaming mother wrapped around the tiny dead body. The mother looked battered, burnt up, with a large chunk of metal sticking out of her shoulder. I wanted to scream and cry. Who could do such a thing?

"What are you even talking about?"

"Earlier, when we were on the roof, what did you do? Tell me exactly! Did you do that?"

Cris turned around and looked at the screen in horror. "What do you mean? How could anyone do something like that? She wasn't on the plane, she was right there in front of us."

"I know, it sounds absurd, but look at the time the plane fell. It's the exact same time we were on that roof, that was the noise we heard! The one that sounded like a bomb going off? Remember that? It was when she said she *pushed*, whatever that means, remember? What did you mean by *pushing*? Is that some kind of psychic thing? Was that how you bought us time to get down here, by dropping the plane and killing all those people? Look at the mother! The child! Did you do that? Answer us!"

Angelique frowned and scrunched up her brows, her eyes changing color to a misty grey. How did she change her eye color like that? I have no idea. Maybe my memory is all mixed up. Maybe the truth is in here, somewhere, buried underneath all of my recollections. I don't know. "How could you think I would do something like that? I'm not a monster."

"Are you, though? The moment you did whatever you did, this happened. You can't tell me that it's a coincidence!"

"I just pushed! Pushed! That's all!"

"What does that even mean?"

"You have to trust me on this, this isn't what I wanted. Dropping a plane like that? That's not part of the left-hand path."

"What are you even talking about?"

Angelique tossed her cane aside for a moment, walked up to me with her uneven gait, placed both her hands on my cheeks. She then pointed my face directly at hers, our eyes meeting. The grey misty color getting in my head, muddying my thoughts like swamp water. "I cannot explain it to you with words, it is something you need to experience, in the flesh and blood. Understand?"

I didn't want to cry, but I couldn't help myself. I couldn't get that image of the mother and her baby out of my head. The tears stung my eyes and I tried to turn and look away, but Angelique held my face still and solid in her grasp.

"It will be okay."

And then she kissed me deep on the lips and I melted into her arms, sobbing. The mist in my mind rolled over all the images of the plane crash. It seemed to wipe away the sorrow and terror of watching what I'd watched on the screen. It would be years before that memory came back to me, out of the blue while doing laundry in my own house, at the edge of the world. I'd been out of prison for a few years, and had a happy family and a new name, thanks to witness protection. Two little girls, both born a year apart.

And as I was folding their clothes, the mist of memories rolled away, and I saw the wreckage again, and another little girl wearing a similar outfit. The charred remains of her face, everything. I ran upstairs, tore open the door, and checked the beds to make sure they were all safe and sound.

6

The dead body was worse than anything we could have ever imagined. I hadn't known Sara Fisher all that well, maybe saw her in the halls every once in a while, and I think I sat behind her once during some play. She'd been a friend of a friend at that time, hovering around the outside of our little clique but never quite crossing over. I honestly thought she'd been pulled out of school and went back home to her family, like so many others. Seeing her now, like this? I wished that had been the case. No one should end up like this. No one.

It's odd what thoughts rise up in your mind when you experience horror firsthand. It's never what you would expect it to be. I guess our brains are totally random like that, and hard to predict. For example, the first thought that came into my mind the minute we stepped into the emptied classroom where we found her corpse?

Poe was wrong. There was no poetry in this corpse, no matter how beautiful she'd been in real life.

And she had been very beautiful, that strange model kind of beauty some people have. Where they don't have to really work at it, it's a natural thing that flowed from every bit of them. Their personality, the tilt of their head when they laughed, and the soft birdlike nature of her voice. The freckles on her cheek, the way her eyes lit up, all of it. And now here she was, lying on the floor lifeless like a broken doll.

Death made us all into objects of horror. That's what terrified me the most, the stillness of the body, the light sucked out of the eyes. You could tell that it was empty now, no longer a *person* but instead a *corpse*. And that it could also happen to me at any moment. One small accident, a hit on the head, a slip down stairs, a car crash, and then my body would empty itself of my being, and I would be . . .

Like that. Just an object. A corpse. A collection of cells arranged in the shape of a person. My own qualia, gone. Thinking about stuff like this was why I switched majors from philosophy to theater. I kept personalizing every theory, thinking about myself in the center of it all, and what that meant to *me, myself,* who I was at the core of everything. I'd been raised Catholic, always certain that there was some immortal thread of myself sewn into this body. In those classes I realized it wasn't true. That *consciousness* was a slippery slope, and at any moment we could be erased from this world.

And here was Sara Fisher, erased.

Her face smiling, of all things. Her eyes closed, like in slumber. Blood stained her strawberry blond hair. Her hands on her stomach, frozen mid grasp, as she tried to close the large gaping wound and keep her intestines still inside her body. One hand a fist in the wound, the other pushing some of her own viscera back inside, frozen in the moment of death. I couldn't move any further. Haunted by the scene, unable to take my eyes off her corpse. Some part of me wondered why I wasn't feeling ill or queasy, and why I wasn't vomiting or retching at the horrible sight.

Like I was looking at myself outside of myself, watching the scene unfold.

The air should've smelled rotten with decay. Or maybe other bodily smells, since I heard that we shit and piss ourselves when we die. But no. Not at all. Just the vague scent of flowers, like potpourri. It reminded me of visiting my grandma's house as a kid growing up. That same kind of smell. Lavender and roses and sandalwood, oh my.

Cris moved with Angelique toward the body as I stayed behind. Still frozen in place. My mind fractured, distant. I saw this all like an unspooling film, moving rapidly before my eyes. A play of light and sound, seemingly real but not. This was all an illusion. It had to be. I couldn't be seeing this. It's not real. It's a movie. It had to be a movie. Projected in front of my eyes like a bad dream come to life.

"You just going to stay back there?"

I couldn't speak, so I nodded.

"All right, keep watch, then. Listen for the whistle while I get to work on this seance."

Cris looked at the body, then looked back at Angelique and said, "You sure we've got to do that? What are we even going to ask her ghost?"

"I need to see who hunts us."

Who. Hunts. Us. I had this feeling that it wasn't just the general Us she was talking about—the campus students, no. That she'd spe-

cifically meant the We of our group of Orphans. That anyone outside of our little clique or coven or whatever, they were just collateral
damage. I wondered briefly if Angelique was bringing us together
because we were hunted, or if we were hunted *because* she was bringing us together.

I thought of Petal and Debbie, and nervously looked down at my
phone for any signs of life. Nothing. I felt disconnected now that we
were separated. We had spent so much time together, our thoughts
and memories intermingling, the We of our plurality a natural fit for
this narrative. And now, apart, I longed for the We of our group to
return, I worried about them, I wanted them close by. Our companionship had become like a drug, and I was going through withdrawal.

"It seems so weird, to see Sara dead like this. Like she never even
existed at all . . ."

"Hush, I need to concentrate for a moment."

Angelique knelt before the body, closed her eyes, started to hum. I
thought I saw Sara's chest move, just a little bit. Like she inhaled? And
then a twitch. Her hand pushed into her wound some more. And a
small amount of color even came back into her cheeks, just enough
to make her seem less like a corpse. I saw a green onyx ring on her
finger, and I focused on that, to keep from being overwhelmed by everything going on. It was all just too much, and I felt my mind crack
and fracture a little, and focused on that ring some more, trying to
keep it all together. Everything is fine. Just focus on the ring. Everything is fine.

Angelique opened her eyes, leaned in. "And now for the gift of
tongue, to help the dead speak once more."

Angelique grabbed Sara's head and kissed her, full open mouth,
blood smearing across her face. I touched my lips, remembered her
giving me the exact same kiss earlier. I felt no jealousy, but instead
a connection, somehow. Like the corpse and me were the same, a
thread of Angelique spread between us. Her eyes opened wide as Angelique pulled back, and Sara coughed and blood trickled down her
mouth. Her hands pushed harder on her insides, trying to keep her
intestines from falling out.

Her eyes were a weird color, now that they were open. No longer
the light green with flecks of blue and gold like when she was alive,
no. They were cataract eyes, a silver film with no pupils at the center.

"Oh. This hurts. Everything. Everything hurts. Call an ambulance, Angelique, call something . . . I don't want to die, and I'm dying now . . ."

"Spirit of Sara Fisher, we have summoned you back to the living to speak to us. We command you to speak to us!"

"I'm not a spirit, I'm dying, please . . . Angelique, call an ambulance. Please . . ."

I thought of the scene downtown, and knew there was no way an ambulance would get here in time. If Angelique had done that with her *push* she had doomed us all. Especially if that killer was still on the loose and hunting *us*.

"What did your killer look like? Tell me, I command it thus."

"If I tell you, will you help me? It hurts so much," and then Sara turned her head to look at me, so much pain in her eyes, "Please, get something. Get gauze, get some fresh water, anything. Make this stop, stop me from dying, please . . . it's not too late . . . I don't have to go out like this . . ."

Was she actually dying and not dead? She looked so much like a corpse before. What was going on? My stomach filled with ice, and everything screamed *run* and *don't ever stop running*. There was no way to fight this, I had to leave now.

And yet, the thought of separating my *I* from this *We* scared me in a way I couldn't even explain. Not even now, all these years later. It scared me more than the dead body, the dying girl, the seance, the serial killer stalking us. That fear of loneliness being alone and cut off. It was all too much to bear.

"I know this world is pain, and death is peace, I know," Angelique now speaking kindly to Sara Fisher's corpse. "But the living here, we need your help. Tell me, who hunted you, who killed you. Then I can let you rest again, in the shadows beyond the crimson veil."

"Fuck. Fuck. Fuck me. They said I had a pale shadow, that they needed to kill me, because I had a pale shadow. Three of them, each with tattoos of keyholes on the palm of their hands. And oh, the man in white. Don't look into his eyes, he has terrible eyes."

Before any of us could respond, a loud, high-pitched whistle floated through Rose Hall. Petal, warning us of the cops. I looked at Angelique and she nodded. "I heard it, too. Come on, let's go."

"Oh no, oh no, what are you doing? Are you guys really going to leave me to die like this? You can't do this to me, you can't."

I wondered what Angelique had even done here. If this was a seance, shouldn't she banish the spirit from the body now? Isn't that what you were supposed to do, close the connection? Or shut whatever spiritual doorway you opened? She was just going to leave her in the corpse? And if she really was dying, and not dead yet . . .

Fuck.

We just turned and ran.

7

I don't think we were prepared for the scene outside Rose Hall. The fires had spread, and everything felt like a roaring wave of heat. Fire trucks scattered across the university, with hoses spraying water everywhere. It was complete chaos! And there, off in the distance, you could see the tail end of a plane sticking up from the center of town. Like a massive whale's tail, reaching up towards the sky. The plumes of smoke from the fires congested the air, and made the day feel darker and close to night. And we coughed the minute we got outside, bent down onto our knees, hacking.

Petal and Debbie were sitting down on a bench nearby. A cop knelt on the ground next to them, jotting down some notes on a yellow notebook, not even seeing us. They passed a clear white plastic mask back and forth. it distorted their faces as they inhaled deeply, then exhaled. It tubed up to an oxygen tank right next to them, and the more we coughed, the more I realized that I was going to need that tank as well. Already, our lungs felt worn out and broken from all the smoke in the air around us. It felt like breathing in dragon's fire. And each time I tried to stand, I almost collapsed once again. Cris came over, and she helped me walk the rest of the way to the park bench, both of us stopping every few moments to rattle our lungs. How had it all spread so fast? It felt unnatural and terrifying at the same time.

It really was the end of the world.

We hadn't even realized that Angelique went missing until it was too late. Cris said she didn't know what happened. one moment they were there together, and then she turned and waved to Petal and Debbie, and then Angelique was gone. Poof, just like that. We stumbled over to the rest of our Orphan gang, and collapsed on the ground next the bench. One of the emergency responders asked if we were okay through her N95 mask, and we just coughed and coughed and coughed in response.

"I need some more tanks over here!"

And then came a few shouts in the distance, and the sounds of running bodies.

The cop then turned and looked at us, his dark eyes peering over the kerchief he held over his face. "Can you answer any questions yet?"

We shook our heads no, our lungs too burned up with dragon fire to speak.

"All right, once we get you guys better, we're going to have to have a talk. Mostly about what you saw in Rose Hall, and if you know of anyone caught in the fires . . ."

We must've looked pretty shocked when he said Rose Hall.

"You were in Rose Hall, correct? Didn't I just see you guys run out of there?"

Hesitatingly, we nodded yes.

"Hmmm. Poor things, you saw the dead body, didn't you."

I didn't nod at all, but Cris nodded yes. Maybe a little too enthusiastically.

"Oh that is just horrible. I know how an experience like that can be very traumatic for someone your age. I think I was just out of the academy and my first week on the force when I saw my first corpse, in the flesh . . . horrible thing. All right, then."

And he tapped his cheek with his pencil.

"I'll make my questions short, okay? Time is of the essence here, and we've got missing students we can't account for. Oh god, I fear the worst, especially after the accident downtown. I am so emotionally wrung out right now . . ."

He paused, wiped his forehead with the kerchief that had over his mouth, and then started to cough violently. Once done, he placed it back over his mouth, and took a few deep breaths. We waited patiently for him to speak again, our nerves on edge after all we'd been through, our lungs still rattling, even as we sucked down oxygen from a tank. It's pretty amazing that we were only outside in the smoke for a matter of moments, and already we were feeling like shit.

"Okay, sorry. Okay. Look, we don't have much time, so I'm going to ask you some questions and you nod your heads yes or no, okay? And if you can speak without coughing, feel free to speak, too."

We nodded our heads yes.

"Good. Now, how long ago did you find the body of Grace Vincent?"

Grace Vincent?

"You said you found her body, correct? In Rose Hall? That's where the ER was going, as well as the cops . . ."

Cris removed the oxygen mask and handed it to me, and I breathed in deeply. She spoke hesitatingly, trying not to cough while she spat the words out, and failing miserably.

"No. Not. Not our teacher, Grace. A student. Sara Fisher."

"Another attack? Was she dead?"

Cris nodded her head yes, but I reluctantly shook my head no. I wasn't so sure, I was terrified that she was dying, or maybe we'd left her and she died while we were gone? I don't know. She had seemed dead when we got there, but . . . was she? My brain hurt, a headache rustling about inside my thoughts. I wish I could've just agreed with her, and been part of a We once again, and no longer a solitary I. But I couldn't. I just, I just couldn't.

"Okay, that's all I need to know. Can either of you show me where you found her?"

Cris looked at me with worried eyes. "Yes," I said through the mask, "I can."

He then looked over at the emergency responders. "Did you guys hear that? Bring a stretcher, and whatever else you can, someone might be in need of our help," and then he turned back to me, "All right, I'm going to need you to lead the way, if you're up to it. Are you?"

I took the mask off, stood up for a moment. The world tilted a little around me, and I tried not to breathe in, tried not to breathe too deeply. It wasn't going to work, was it? The responder handed me a spare N95 mask and said, "Here, take this."

I nodded, strapped it on, and breathed. No coughing, at least not right away. I still felt a little lightheaded and dizzy, but I could do it. And Sarah definitely needed help, if we weren't already too late. The air tasted like smoke and burning hair, even through the plastic of the mask. It made me feel nauseated, and I couldn't wait to get this done and over with already, and go someplace (anyplace!) that wasn't on fire.

I remembered the plane, in the center of town, and realized that everything was on fire. At least, in Dark Rivers, and maybe in a few of the nearby towns, too. Later, we would finally be able to breathe once we were all in the hospital together. We didn't want to go, but the cops insisted, and the nurses on hand insisted, and said that much smoke inhalation required observation. No ifs ands or buts about it.

Though it took a while to find a hospital with any room, after what had happened downtown, and with the number of students murdered on campus. We actually had to go the next few cities over, riding in the ambulances as they wailed at high speed down the back streets. Holding each other's hands in silence.

You may notice that I'm glossing over how we found Sara again. Maybe I don't want to talk about that. Maybe it's all a bit too much. Whoever killed her had come back and removed her right hand and slit her throat. We could've saved her, couldn't we? We could have stayed behind with her, and called out to the others, to bring them inside. We were barely nineteen or twenty, some of us just out of high school, and we were just kids. We didn't know what we were doing at all.

:episode 2:
The Sound of the Devil

1

How you guys doing?

Okay, I guess.

Yeah, me too. Though still hurts to talk sometimes.

My lungs make funny noises.

Did they tell you when we can leave yet?

I dunno. Where would we even go?

Right, right. No homes now. Are your parents missing, too?

Yes, for two weeks now.

Mine are three and a half.

No wonder they didn't bring us back home before. I just thought mine hated me.

The uni is going to be shut down for a while now.

A long while. It's going to take a lot to repair everything.

I don't even want to think about what's going on downtown.

I guess we're not the only survivors of the Dark Rivers Massacre.

How do you mean?

That's what they're calling it, the Dark Rivers Massacre, on the news and all of that. I guess most of the other students left behind were hunted down and killed, but not all of them.

Fuck me.

Just like Sara Fisher, you know, missing their right hands and everything.

I heard one of them barely survived, they say she was gutted, but was saved at the very last minute. One of our teachers, I think? The others were more lucky. She's in the ICU now—they say it's touch and go.

Fucking hell. What about Angelique? Anyone see her?

Nope. She's not in the hospital either.

How do you know?

Well, you don't see her here, do you?

She could be in another room, or in one of the other hospitals?

I doubt it.

You doubt everything.

Yeah? So? She's probably dead, like the others.

Why do you think that?

She up and vanished right after you two saw the body, right?

Correct.

All right, all right. And then when you went back, with that cop, Sara's corpse was mutilated, right?

Yeah. Right hand removed and everything.

What if whoever did that to her, did it to Angelique, too? Like that's why Angelique disappeared at the end there, because she was murdered.

Wouldn't we have heard about it?

I dunno. Would we?

I've been checking the news and stuff online. They keep listing all the dead, and I don't see her name there.

Not yet. They add new names daily, don't they?

Yeah, I guess so?

That's because they don't know just how bad it all is. It was so much chaos that day, remember?

Yeah, I remember, duh. I was kind of there? You didn't even see Sara's body. That shit is going to haunt me forever.

We shouldn't have left her there.

She was dead.

No, no I tell you—she wasn't dead. She was dying and we just left her there.

I don't believe you, you saw her, right there, when we came in. She was dead, dead! And Angelique summoned her spirit to talk with us, and that's all that it was.

I want to believe you, I do. But I know what I saw.

You both, hush. There is no use talking about this now, right? Dead is dead. There is no going back, no changing anything. What if she'd gone home, what if we all had gone home, what if there were no serial killers or any of that stuff, what if, what if what if. It's all bullshit, and it's all out of our control now, cause it's the past.

But I . . .

What, you got a time machine?

No.

Okay, then. So, Angelique, she's probably in the past now, too, and there is no going back and getting her, no matter how sad that makes me feel.

I can't believe that. I just can't.

Why not?

Because she could do shit, right? Look, you all saw it, you saw her push and then that plane fucking crashed. If she had powers like that? Well, a serial killer's not anything, then.

Killers. Plural, not possessive.

What? I didn't see that in any of the police reports?

During the seance Sara Fisher mentioned that there was more than one serial killer, and they each had a keyhole tattoo on the palm of their hands. She said something about them killing people with a pale shadow . . .

Oh, god damn, that's messed up.

That's creepy.

And her corpse said that?

Yeah.

Do we have pale shadows?

Maybe not, maybe that's why we survived.

Or maybe we survived because of Angelique.

See? She's got mad powers, of course she would protect us!

Or maybe she's the one leading them on, telling them who to kill and why.

Then why would she have Sara's ghost fill us in?

I dunno. But she did say we were part of her coven, right?

Yeah, what was that all about? She kept saying we had to get knotted up. What does that even mean?

A coven of devil-worshiping witches, you ding dong. It's like what everyone was saying, she was raised to believe she was the antichrist, right? And those killers are her soldiers in Satan's army. She's letting us know a little at a time, drip drip, to get us in on her side. It's all a god game, like in *The Magus*.

The what now?

Didn't you read that book in highschool?

I didn't.

Yeah, I did.

Of course you did, Cris, you went to a fancy ass private school, just like me.

So illuminate us, what is *The Magus*?

Huh. That's a lot to unpack. Did you ever see *The Wicker Man*?

Not the bees?

Well, not that one, but I guess that will do.

There's another one?

Yeah, Christopher Lee is in charge of a sex cult, and it rocks.

Oh, damn, I wish I'd seen that one.

So what does that have to do with this? You say she's going to burn us alive or something?

What? No. Maybe this is a bad example. I dunno. I think she might be inducting us into her Satanic coven, you know? But leading us on before she does it, guiding us through a secret ritual we didn't even know we we're a part of, making us a part of her army. And the serial killers are on her side, killing in her name. Or maybe she's even the one doing the killing. Maybe we'll be like the killers in the end, keyhole tattoos and all.

Creepy.

Yeah, creepy, and bullshit. Come on, Petal, you can't really believe that, can you?

I know I don't believe it . . .

Shh, you're just in love with her.

And you're not?

I don't know. I just know that now that we've been apart from her for a while I feel weird. Don't you feel it, too? Like something is off, like there is a splinter in my mind that I can't get out, digging under my thoughts.

Yeah. I feel it too.

But I don't think you're right about that, it just sounds too crazy and convoluted.

Well, I guess we'll find out eventually, right? If she's the killer or the killed.

Hopefully not the hard way.

Agreed.

Yeah, hopefully.

2

It had been over a week, and they still would not let us go. We had no idea where we would go exactly, we just knew that we were all cooped up and we needed to get out for a bit. Walking around the halls in here could only do so much to stimulate the mind. After a while, the walls all looked the same, and the paths we were allowed to go on felt shorter and shorter and shorter. We couldn't even go outside, they told us our lungs were still recovering, and if we pushed it too far, would be right back to where we were a week ago. Unable to even sit up without hacking or coughing.

That felt like a lie, though, and a stupid one at that. We felt better, and had to get out or we were going to go crazy. All we could talk about was what happened, and all we could think about was Angelique, and were she had gone, and if she had anything to do with the serial killers. It was the kind of talk that made us paranoid and anxious, the dingy walls of the hospital closing in on us. The mind even started to play tricks, and even though I hadn't seen it, Debbie swore two of the orderlies had keyhole tattoos on the palms of their hands.

Petal didn't believe it though, and it made sense. How could she have seen them? They all wore gloves, right? But Debbie insisted, the gloves were mostly transparent, and the ink on their palms were thick black ink, shining through like shadows at noon.

And then Cris started seeing Angelique everywhere, to the point of where we were really annoyed with her talking about it all the time. In the reflections of mirrors standing behind her, in the cafeteria, sitting at a lone table in the far shadowy corners of the room, the back of her head running through a crowd toward the elevator. On and on and on it went, and no one else seemed to see her at all. It was just Cris, and she saw her *constantly*. At least four or five times a day while we wandered the halls of our antiseptic prison.

Eventually she stopped talking about it, because she knew it was really starting to annoy us. But we could see it in her eyes, that haunted look of yearning that she got whenever she saw Angelique. And we tried to see her, too. But every time it came to pass, there was nothing there at all. Just a whisper of jasmine in the air, and the emptiness of an unfulfilled promise. That promise of Angelique.

We all kept looking up the lists of the dead and the missing, and Angelique's name never came up, so it kept us in this odd state of hope, and not wanting to hope. Knowing that hoping for her to return, and then finding her dead body washed up somewhere would be a blow to us, one that we might not ever recover from. No matter how hard we tried. So in order to keep our minds away from Angelique we started to branch out as much as we could, checking on the other survivors from our campus.

One was in the ICU, Lucy Diamond, and we couldn't see her at all. Guess she had it the worst of the survivors, and we all agreed we were going to have to talk to her later, whenever she could have visitors. If anyone could give us a clue on what was going on, it would definitely be her. We kept walking past the area, but were shooed away by various nurses and doctors. Cris got a peek and saw the crystal gleam of oxygen tents, and we had to wonder just what happened to her. Had she been burned up? Was she even conscious, or was she in a coma? We couldn't get any information out of anyone, no matter how hard we pried, and it was really frustrating. We couldn't leave it alone. You're probably wondering about the other survivors, right?

Yeah, they knew less than what we knew, and were just as scared as we were. We formed a new loose group of friends, expanding our *we* out and collecting them, and bringing them all into our little clique. We had to gather them up through several different floors of the hospital, following the lime green and orange lines on the floor like breadcrumbs in the forest. We talked about meeting times during the days we could hang out together. We asked about Angelique, and some of them had seen her around, too. Even though no one could verify it, either way. Like a ghost, Angelique haunted the corridors. And Simon, he said that he noticed some of the orderlies with keyhole tattoos on the palms of their hands, too. He just thought they were weird, had no idea what it meant. We didn't have the heart to tell him what we knew. He was Sara Fisher's ex-boyfriend. They had just broken up a week before she . . .

Well. Anyway.

We then compared symptoms and how well we were progressing. Some of the others had been attacked, knife wounds, hook wounds, axe wounds, and the like. Petal joked that these were weapons out of a slasher film, and we all laughed. A horrible nervous sound, the laughter of the damaged and the damned. You may think it's insane that we laughed, no, no, I get it. I think it's insane, too. But we did, we laughed. What else could we do? We had to, else we would have just cracked from everything. It was all too much.

And so we changed our name for our little group, from the Orphans to the Final Girls. A kind of ironic name now, right? Since we now had two boys in our little soiree. They didn't seem to mind, though. Simon even thought it was awesome, and suggested we got T-shirts made up that said Final Girls on the front, and the year of the Dark Rivers Massacre on the back. How funny is that? I guess not very funny when you really think about it. We tried not to think about it.

Just like we tried really hard not to think about Sara Fisher.

And yet.

I would go to sleep and wake up in the middle of the night with that image running through my mind, her begging us to call an ambulance, to get her help, of any sort. I wish I'd known her better before all of this, we all did. Somehow not really knowing her, and being the last people to see her alive? That made it all the worse. Now she was forgotten, a whisper, her dying moments the only lasting image of who she had been. A life summed up into the after image of a corpse, burned into our retinas. That was so wrong, and there was nothing we could do about it.

We weren't going to make that same mistake twice.

And so, on one of the last few nights, before the hospital really went to shit and we had to get out of there, we decided to stay up all night and just talk. Like a slumber party, our beds all pushed together in a loose circle, the dim lights that lined the walls like electric candles in the night. It made me ache for a simpler time, back before all of this happened, when I was a teenager and college was just a promise on the distant horizon.

3

Let's see if I can remember their names, all these years on. It's been decades, and a lot of what happened is kind of fuzzy and lost in my head. They say trauma does that to you, right? Ah well. The number of Final Girls had blossomed out from four to about twelve, though the exact number eludes me. That feels right, twelve, though it might've been just eight, I don't know. When I close my eyes and picture that scene in my head, I remember the room really well. Well enough I could sketch out a map for you, you know?

I don't think that hospital exists anymore. They tore it down, probably five years ago. I know, I went back to try and check it out. Maybe jog the mind a bit, and revisit some of the better memories I had from such an awful time. Now the place is an empty parking lot, cracked, with the fingers of weeds pushing up through the concrete. It's weird to think that this place only exists in my head now, scattered throughout my memories, like a ghost. Ironic that I was haunted by a house, and not the other way around, don't you think?

Anyway, even though I can map out the entire landscape of our room and the floors we wandered, I still can't picture everyone that night so clearly in my head. A jumble of bodies and faces, crammed together in that small space. But I'm going to try my best here, so we have it recorded for posterity. I owe the dead that much.

There was Simon, of course, and yes, it's that Simon you probably heard about on the news. Poor Simon, so misunderstood. At that point he was still well spoken, stylishly dressed, with a classic crew cut and black glasses. Not the rambling, unhinged boy who threatened the interviewer on NPR, trying to show you all something you refused to even see. Angelique had cast him out at that point, and he was spinning, unmoored, and untethered.

That's for later, we'll get to that, I promise. You probably want to know all about what happened that night when the world finally *saw us* and knew what we were all about. Just be patient, it's not something I can rush toward, you need to see it all in total, else it's not going to make any sense. Hell. It might not even make any sense after that.

Where was I?

Oh, right, trying to remember all the folks we had with us at that point. Other orphans left behind at the university, each of our parents missing and gone, all staying in that same creepy ass hospital. There were other things that tied us all together, things we discovered that night, as we stayed up until the crack of dawn talking, and trying to figure out exactly what was going on. One of the weirdest things? We all shared the same birthday, right down to the exact second. We each had a grandparent named Hazel, which was weird since that wasn't a very common name. Don't worry, we're not all related, the grandma named Hazel was different for each of us. Different pictures, different last names, all the rest of it. Just a really weird coincidence, is all. Stacked on top of all the other weird coincidences, it was really strange and uncanny. And there were a lot of them. Like the dream of the blue house, what Simon called the House of Sky and Shadow . . .

Anyway, let's see here. There was Simon, like I said, Abigail with two pig tails, Abigail with pixie-cut hair, and also Tobias (never Toby), and Niisha, and Yvette, Adam A and Adam B, and Tade. I'm sorry if their last names escape me, it's been a long while now, and it was hard for me to keep track of everyone even back then. I guess it's just the way my memory works, in pictures rather than in words and sounds. I could probably describe everyone, right down to the last detail, including what pajamas they wore, and what colors they painted their nails. But ask me to remember names, numbers and dates? Well, that all gets jumbled up inside of my head and it takes me a while to peel it all back.

But oddly enough, I do recall conversations really easily, but I have to play back the scene visually in my head, like watching a movie. I need to see the people talking, what they looked like, and then my brain fills in the audio. I know, it's really weird, right? But it's just how my mind has always been. Like, in high school, when I had to memorize something for a test, I had to memorize what the sheet of paper looked like, and then read it in my head. Or when I'm reading a book, and I set it aside, I won't remember the last page I read by the number. I'll remember what it looked like, and then see the number on the bottom in my memories. Though, sometimes the number will get all blurry, and then I have to flip through the book and look for the page in my head.

And it's weird, when we became knotted up and turned into a We, I felt my memory changing to match it. It became more communal. Like I was recording all of our thoughts, linked up together. I see that look, and I know what you're thinking, and to be honest I'm not sure what was going on with us back then. Memory is a funny thing, isn't it? And when it's all of us remembering together, it becomes . . .

Well, it's hard to trust who remembered what, and let's just leave it at that.

For that night, we still weren't quite knotted up just yet, though we would all feel closer and connected after the conversation. I guess it's always like that, isn't it? If you spend all night talking with someone, you grew into each other. Like roots of a tree, all tangled up and feeding off each other, the tendrils of self mixing up, until you're unsure of who thought what, and which idea was originally your own.

Adam A and B were sitting on the floor near the windows, on opposite sides. Even though they had different parents, they still looked alike in that weird way people with the same first names sort of look alike. We original Lost Girls/Final Girls/Orphans sat on our respective beds, with Debbie sitting cross legged and looking run down and haggard. I knew she was staying up all night and trying not to sleep. She told me later on, that her dream of the blue house was a bad one. The house was always on fire, and she heard screaming inside, but she couldn't go and save them. She had to just watch it burn.

Niisha, Yvette, and Tade were scattered in a semi-circle on the floor, with a deck of cards between them, in case we got too bored and wanted to play a game. We didn't get bored, so they sat there wrapped in plastic, unopened and inert.

The two Abigails framed the doors leading into our room, mirroring the two Adams on the other side by the windows. Unlike the Adams, they didn't even remotely look alike. Facial structure, hair color, eye color, skin color, every last detail on them was almost an exact complete opposite. The weirdest part was how Abigail with pixie-cut hair reminded me of Angelique. To the point of where I wanted to ask if she was her sister or cousin, but decided against it.

It's odd, but we didn't discuss about Angelique at all that night. You would think we would've talked about her, maybe wondered what happened to her, especially given all that was going to happen later on. And yet, we didn't even mention her once. It made it feel like she was a ghost, haunting this conversation, hiding behind every word.

The conversation started awkward. We made some jokes about how this felt like one of our classes, without a professor to lecture at us. Debbie said she was ticked off that she missed her philosophy class today, and then got sad when she realized the teacher was one of the dead.

"How did he die?"

"Hush, don't you see that she's upset?"

"We're all upset, it didn't mean it didn't happen, and we can't talk about it."

Tade tapped the deck of playing cards. "It was the fire," he said, "He was trying to make sure no one was inside one of the dorms. I'm not sure which one, I just. Well, I just saw what I saw on the news. He was in this hospital when he passed. It was odd—they thought he was going to survive."

"But he didn't."

"No, I guess not. But that's happening a lot lately."

We all turned and looked at him.

"What do you mean? You can't just say that."

"Okay, okay, okay. I was eavesdropping on the orderlies, don't tell anyone, all right? I don't want them to be pissed at me."

"Well, tell us. Come on."

"It's a hospital, right? So people die here all the time, and that's just how it goes. But these deaths . . . they're odd. One of the orderlies said they ended up calling the police, but the police can't do anything about it. At least, not just yet. It's not like it was back at the university, right? These are all heart attacks, or people near death dying in their sleep. And yet, there's something strange about them, right? Markings on their bodies, symbols painted on their doors. Tarot cards left behind, under the pillows. But nothing that pointed to foul play exactly, and getting a family member to agree to an autopsy on a hunch . . . well. That probably wasn't going to happen."

We had chills and goosebumps.

"Do you think it's the serial killers?"

"The what now?"

"The ones on campus, stalking us. Do you think they followed us here?"

He paused, and it looked like he didn't enjoy being the center of attention. Unlike Angelique, or Simon. They seemed to feed on it.

"Serial killers, plural?"

We nodded and filled him in a little on what we knew, but not how we came across the information. We didn't want to revisit the scene of Sara's death so soon.

"Shit, that's nuts."

"And I swear, I've seen one of the orderlies with a keyhole tattoo on the palm of his one of his hands."

"Are you sure?"

"Mmhmmm."

Adam A spoke up this time. "I saw one of the other patients with one, too."

"Are you sure?"

He nodded.

"I'm sure I'm sure. I thought it was really weird, he was shuffling about, an elderly gentleman, about the age of my grandpa, you know? And he had this weird curly mustache, and tattoos all over his neck and arms. But the palm of his hands stuck out in my mind, those keyhole tattoos. The ink was so black and thick, it looked like a void, or a starless night."

"Creepy."

"I've seen the guy, too, I know exactly who you're talking about," this time it was Niisha who spoke, her long black hair concealing her face. "He saw me staring at his keyhole tattoo, and started to laugh. He asked me if I knew that I had a pale shadow, but . . . I don't know. I didn't stick around to find out what he meant by that. I just had to run away. Everything he said was freaking me out."

"I saw him a few times," said Adam B, "He really sticks out, so how could I miss him? The odd thing is, I've never seen him in a hospital bed, or in a room. He's always just out walking around, especially around ICU, where they keep Lucy Diamond."

We all held our breath. "What's he doing there? No one is allowed in there."

"Maybe he's family?"

We weren't sure if even family would be allowed in the ICU.

"Anyway, he saw me staring at him and he held up his palms and said, *what do you see in the dark between my bones? Do you see the abyss? Or do you see yourself, a mirror made of emptiness, waiting to embrace the shadows beyond?"*

More chills.

"We should go check on her."

And the minute Petal said this, we all knew that it was one-hundred percent true. That's how Petal always was, back then, before we lost ourselves inside of Angelique. She knew how to step forward, do the tough things, and see everything for what they really were, and not the lies we told to comfort ourselves. Anyone else here would've just felt bad for Lucy Diamond, or worry about her or call the orderlies to warn them about what was going to happen.

But she saw the truth of it all and spoke. It was obvious Lucy was in trouble, and we had to go down and see her right now. The air felt ripe with terrible promises, and we all knew that someone was going to die before dawn. We were just wrong about the details.

4

It was kind of fun, in retrospect, sneaking around the hospital like that. We were a large group, and clumsy, and it was hilarious that we didn't think we would get caught. We tried hiding in shadows, acting like this was some great heist, that we were going to get our friend out and save her from the killer at large. How crazy this all seems, looking back. What were we even thinking? I mean, come on. How we were going to move the oxygen tent? How would a large number of us sneak into the ICU? Sure, there were less people around over all, but the orderlies were still there, and security guards prowled the halls with flashlights and tasers.

And yet, somehow, we got lucky.

For example, we were able to hear the stumbling footsteps of the security guard echo in the halls long before he reached us, so we could hide and hush ourselves, and try not to laugh at the absurdity of it all. And it was all so very, very absurd. Or we would see an orderly far away, in the long edges of the wing, and come up with some excuse or another why we were all out at once, in the middle of the night, when we shouldn't be.

And you know what happened? Nothing. He seemed to believe us. Or rather, not even care. In fact, the few people who did see us seemed to be hypnotized. I know, that sounds stupid. I get it. But they had this zombie look in their eyes, you know? Kind of a dead stare that was off in the distance, not exactly seeing you, or paying attention to what you were saying. It reminded me of the thousand-yard stare you'd see in shell shocked soldiers at war. I remember this picture on the cover of a magazine we had in one of our classes, I can't remember which one. Maybe it was one of the ethics classes? Something like that.

That particular class was about the horrors of war, of cults, and of societal group think and peer pressure. The magazine was *Time* magazine, I think? And the image haunted me. The look on the soldier's face was dulled down, a dead glassy stare. That's how every guard or doctor or orderly we met that night looked, that same shell-shocked gaze that looked through you, like you were a ghost.

In retrospect, this makes sense. All the emergencies happening at once, the hospitals filling up with the damaged and the dead. The murders, the plane crash, it must've felt like a war zone in here. They've must've been traumatized by the sight of it, overwhelmed by the size of it. PTSD. That's what it was that saved us.

Getting into the ICU was oddly just as easy as crawling around the hospital after lights out. No security guards wandering around that area, and even odder still, no nurses or doctors or orderlies. It was just us, walking room by room, past the extremely sick and dying. I get chills now remembering their faces, off in the shadows behind the doors. They looked terrified, the ones who were awake and with it, the fear of death and pain etched so plainly onto their features. Were they afraid of their illnesses, their accidents, their maladies? Or was it something else . . .

Something, or someone else, one who stalked these lone hours with a curly mustache and keyhole tattoo.

"What if there is more than one serial killer here, walking the halls?" Adam B whispered as we crawled closer and closer to Lucy Diamond's room. "You did say serial killers earlier, didn't you?"

"We did, and . . . let's not think about that right now. One we can probably handle . . . more than one . . ."

"Yeah," Adam A said, "I know what you mean. Let's hope it's just the one we all saw."

"Do you think it's a cult?"

"How do you mean?"

"Like one with a charismatic leader, someone telling them to hunt us down. Maybe they hypnotized their followers, or drugged them with LSD or DMT or something. To make them see pale shadows."

"That's not how LSD works."

"Shh, guys, we don't want him to find us, do we?"

And no, no we didn't. So we cut out the chit chat as we looked at each of the doors, trying to figure out which one hid Lucy Diamond. It took us longer than I wanted, but eventually we got there. The door was marked with the bloody scrawl of a circle, with an upside down triangle in the center, slashed with a crooked line. It was still fresh and crimson, not quite dried brown just yet.

"Does that mean she's dead and we're too late?"

No one wanted to answer Niisha's question—the possibilities were endlessly horrific. Would she be dead beyond that door, her corpse waiting for us in the oxygen tent, posed and displayed like a delicate doll? Or did the killer take her out with a lit match, the oxygen creating a fireball that consumed her completely, and we would just find a pile of ash in the shape of her body?

We stood in front of that door for what seemed like an eternity. No one wanted to pull the handle and see what lay beyond. Breathless, frozen in time. This was like that quantum experiment with the cat. As long as we did not open the door, the possibility of her still being alive was there, hanging in the air like a promise. The minute we opened it, though? There was no going back. Lucy would be dead and we couldn't do a damn thing about it.

I wasn't sure I could take seeing another dead body, not after what happened to Sara Fisher. I remembered her intestines hanging out, the way she begged us to help her, and I wanted to rip a hole in time and walk through it, going back to stay by her side. Maybe I would try to drag her out to an ambulance, yes. Or maybe I would go even further back in time, to the day before her murder, and warn her to go home, and if that wasn't possible, stay the night at a hotel. Be anywhere else but here, where death waited for you with open arms.

Sara's death lacked definition, and it left a hole inside of me. A hole that kept me from opening the door at this point, and instead staring at the bloody symbol. I remembered closing my eyes, and I tried to picture myself anywhere else. My body in the lake, the waves rushing around me, as Petal pushed open the door and pulled us all inside.

5

You ever have a moment when your real, waking world, felt like a dream? In a way that's probably hard to pinpoint, exactly, and yet that's what it felt like? You know the feeling. If you were to really sit back and remember, you could probably recall many times in your life exactly like that. When something not just odd happened, but something unreal and strange and illogical. When someone spoke to you in dream logic, or you see a dead tree with a riot of gray balloons caught in every tree branch. Maybe it's a shape of a dog, moving slowly toward you in a fog, or maybe it's an elderly man on a street corner singing a sad love song to the moon. We've all had moments like these. Be honest with yourself, you have too.

This was one of those moments. I tell you that now, so you'll understand, that I'm not embellishing any of the details. This all happened exactly as I'm telling it to you, and we all remembered it happening this exact same way. Believe me, if it seems unreal to you, it seemed unreal to us then, too. And this was only the start. After we'd met Angelique, our lives begin to overflow with moments like these, moments stolen from a dream and placed in front of us in reality.

We scuttled in around the body, a large group of curious kids. We were so young back then, but we felt like we were so much older. It's weird looking back and realizing that, but it's true. I guess, in a way we were older than a lot of our peers, there is no denying that. What with everything we'd been through up until this point. You can't experience that much chaos without it aging you, and breaking a little something inside of you. I'm not trying to excuse what we do later on, don't get me wrong. But I guess, I'm just trying to give context to our state of mind at the time.

A bunch of scared, traumatized kids. And there we were, around the body of a fellow classmate. One we'd assumed to be dead, but instead alive and breathing and still in a coma. She lay prone and twitching, tied up on her bed. She was under a plastic tent that wheezed and exhaled and was coated with condensation. Her eyes were shut, and they darted about in REM sleep. I don't know why they strapped her arms and legs down, but I'm sure there was a reason. The hospital gown was ripped in several places, and there were gouges all over her body, where the skin had been pried back with fingernails. As if she was trying to pull the burned skin off of her body piece by piece, leaving only raw muscle and bone behind.

Had she done this to herself while she was asleep? I get chills now just thinking about the whole scenario. On the chest of her blue hospital gown someone had taped a tarot card right over her heart. It was one I'd never seen before, none of us had. Though Cris claimed she saw it in her dreams, every night, around the same time she saw the House and Sky. She said in her dream it was both a card and not a card at the same time. Both real and cardboard, in the way things could only exist in dreams. In that liminal state between signifier and sign. Hah, there I go again, using my discarded philosophy major in the strangest possible situation. I guess I got to make sense of it all, somehow.

The card was a drowned woman. She looked much like that old painting of Ophelia, you know the one. It's hung up in countless dorms all across America. I think I even had one in my dorm for a while, though I wasn't the one who'd put it up on the wall. It had already been there before I arrived, and I didn't have the heart to take it down. Anyway, it looked like drowned Ophelia, and instead of a number it had a circle with a triangle in the middle and a slash through it. Just like the symbol smeared on her wall in blood. In her hand was a rose, and in the other hand was a cup, the water rushing around her serene dead body. At the bottom of the card it said *The Seer*.

What any of that meant was a mystery to us at that time, we just knew she was here and alive, and somehow that made everything okay. Maybe we weren't being hunted after all. Maybe something else was going on. After all, didn't they say that the people who died all had previous heart conditions? I don't think anyone at our uni had something like that, we were way too young. We were probably safe, and just freaking ourselves after everything that happened, right?

Haha, wrong.

Anyway, we had a sense of relief in that moment, and joy at seeing Lucy Diamond still alive and breathing, even though she was covered in burns and still close to death. Close to death wasn't the same as dead.

"She's saying something . . ."

"What do you mean?"

"Listen, listen. She's saying something . . ."

Lucy Diamond's lips moved and words tumbled off of her tongue. A soft murmur of a whisper, like waves at night. We all leaned in, concentrating on her lips and her words. "What's she saying?"

"I dunno. Can you hear her, Niisha?"

Niisha smiled, her eyes all pupil. "Yes. You can't?"

We all collectively shook our heads no.

"Okay, then. I'll translate."

And she leaned her head against Lucy's ear. It spooked us to see her like that, still and motionless, almost dead, yet her lips moving and her eyes twitching in REM sleep. There was something unnatural about all of this, but we couldn't place our fingers on exactly *what* that was, we just knew it was . . . wrong.

"She says . . . wait. Hold on. Wait. She's talking really fast, hold on. Okay. She says *do you hear the sound of the devil? It's everywhere, in the buildings and in our bones. Hear it in the trees? Something's coming, the daughter of the Wormwood star. Do you see her? She rides the darkness like a knife. Beware the key without a keyhole, and the boy without bones. Her name is a heart encircled by a serpent.* And then she goes back to the start and repeats everything over and over and over again."

I get chills even now, remembering what she said back then. I can see it, you've got goosebumps too, don't you? You can't deny it. I can see it puckering on the edges of your arms. There is something to that, isn't there. Something . . .

Yeah. Things to come.

Anyway, then Cris said, "I wonder what it means?"

And Petal scoffed and said, "Nothing, it's just dream talk. Come on, we see she's okay, and not in trouble. We need to get out of here."

"But is she okay? Look at the bloody symbol on the door, look at her. What's happening to her?"

"What do you want to do, carry her out of here? Look at all the burns all over her body. We would kill her if we moved her."

Her body there, so frail and burnt in that hollow overhead light. It washed out the darkness, like a spotlight on her oxygen tent, a halo around her body. We saw those claw marks where she pried up pieces of burnt skin while asleep once again, and realized no, there was no way we were getting her out of here.

"We can't leave her here to die! That killer, or even killers, will come for her, I know it."

"What if she doesn't have a pale shadow?"

"What are you even talking about . . ."

But we didn't have the time to go into that and explain the seance in painful detail. We just had to figure out what we were going to do. Would we be willing to leave someone here to die again, like what happened to Sara Fisher? No, no, I didn't want to think about her again. This wasn't the same at all, was it? She was in a hospital here, she was safer than anywhere else in her condition. Even with a serial killer about . . .

"I'll stay here," Tade said, crossing his arms. "And keep an eye on her, protect her."

The two Abigails nodded their heads and said, "We'll stay behind, too. Safety in numbers."

That would be the last we saw of any of them. When we left the room, I swore I saw a pale shadow around Tade and the Abigails, and I thought, didn't they say they dreamt of the house on fire last night? The same as Debbie. I wondered if Debbie had a pale shadow, too. I don't know why I saw them now, why I hadn't seen those weird auras before.

I should've taken it as a warning. Instead, I took it as a relief, knowing that I could see who was going to live and who was going to die, and I would be a survivor. Yes, that makes me sound like a sociopath, I should have cared more about my friends and if they would die . . . I really should have. Sometimes you have to numb yourself in order to survive.

6

Sleep came for us, once we got back to our room on the eighth floor. I don't know if we were exhausted and wiped out from everything that had been happening so far or what, but we struggled to stay awake the minute we crossed the threshold of our door. Dizzy, the smell of candlewax in the room, fuzzy headed with the edges of dreams in our peripheral vision. Did we light candles before we left? No, wait. Did we? We couldn't remember, but looking back I know the truth of it now. That should've been a warning. The candles smelled odd, too. Like burning fat or soap. And they seemed strangely shaped in the shadows, like leafless trees or hands with the fingers splayed out. And they flickered with an eerie, white light.

So still those sleeping bodies on the floor, as I struggled to climb up into my bed. So close to death already.

I did not want to sleep, though. I felt something horrible and twisted in the air, and in my mind I kept hearing the sound of fingers snapping. Was that from the edges of a dream? Was it only in my head? Where did that sound come from? Every time I nodded off or closed my eyes, I heard it again: *snap, snap, snap.*

Shook my head, stopped dropping off again for a moment. I realized with dawning horror that the candles were actual human hands. Not just shaped like them, no. I could see the bone beneath the finger candles burning. The scent was putrid and strong, and I felt like I recognized a ring on one of the fingers. Yes, that was Sara Fisher's ring. That was Sara Fisher's hand. I wanted to scream but everything was in slow motion and my mouth was all honey. Had we all been drugged?

But how? And when?

There were so many hands strewn around the room, placed on almost every surface. A circle of them stretched out in the center of the floor. It felt hot in here, I was sweaty and the dizziness grew in intensity, the room spinning. Again, I heard it again: *snap, snap, snap.*

I shook the slumber from my head as the shadows crawled into our room. Somewhere a clock tick tick ticked the seconds away, a metronome of death.

And we all watched as the shadows rose up, four in all, over the bodies of those sleeping on the floor, the pale shadows shimmering in that eerie light. They each wore a simple white mask, without any decorations. Two eye holes letting two eyes look out. Bloodshot, one with a scar over the left eye. Long shaving razors in their hands, blades out, snick and slick with blood. I heard a noise, a low throbbing hum, a deep bass song without words. Was this the sound of the devil? I did not know.

Even in this moment of horror I started drifting off to sleep. *Snap snap snap* I startled awake to see blades cutting across necks. Debbie was the first to die, her eyes wide in fright as blood pooled out of her neck and slid down her body in a thick viscous puddle. A scream was caught in my throat as Adam A and Adam B both fell to the blade. And then, all of a sudden, the sound of the devil got louder and louder, and then the *snap snap snap* seemed to go to the beat of that throbbing hum. I felt myself drift into deeper shadows, the darker edges of dreaming. And then two eyes bright and full of fire exploded in my vision. *Angelique!*

"Wake the hell up, loser! Don't you dare fucking die before I get there. I'm almost at the hospital now, come on, wake up! Fight back!"

And then a woosh and rush of clarity in the forefront of my brain. Eyes wide open, but my body still sluggish and weak. The orderlies, yes, that's who they were, orderlies with masks and black gloves on. But I knew if we would pry those gloves off, we would find that keyhole tattoo right on the palms of their hands.

I saw some of the others now rising up, sluggish zombies half awake and half asleep, Petal and Cris and Simon. We stumbled together, knocked into our killers, grabbed at their ankles and fought back. I felt the knife bite my arms and worried it was too deep, that this was going to be the end of me. I screamed and bit down on one guys leg, and felt the skin pull back in my teeth. That taste of blood was sweet and tinted with fear. He screamed and fell and I grabbed at him, all bloodied and broken, biting at him, feeling the razor slash on my shoulders and then my face as I bit down on his throat and felt it, felt that Adam's apple right there, and just chomped down, his screams deafening my ears as I closed my jaw, and felt it squish, pop and tear, as his screams turned into a raspy gurgle and then silence.

Even that low throbbing hum stopped.

I need to . . . I need to breathe for a moment. I'm sorry. Sometimes this stuff gets to me in ways I don't even realize until I'm talking about it, and then I'm reliving everything we went through again, and it's hard. I guess this would be my first real kill, and the memory of it hits me like a truck. Look at this, look at my hands they're shaking now and I'm crying. Yes, I know it was self-defense, but you weren't there, you don't get it. We'd gone feral just trying to survive. I don't know if it was everything leading up to now, or being helpless as we watched our friends get murdered right in front of us, and not being able to do anything. Not until it was too late. I can still taste the blood, and I remember exactly how it felt, his skin in my mouth. I just. I just need a moment to breathe.

Yikes. Even the smell of those candles, the foul smell of burning fat, I remember it so clearly. The whole room was filled with smoke, and I don't know if we knocked some down in our struggle, or what? But our lungs were still in recovery, and so now it was hard to breathe again, and we were dizzy from blood loss and the trauma of every-thing we'd just seen. I think I looked over, all dizzy and tried to see if we could see her, Angelique, in this room with us? But no.

Instead all I saw was my coven—yes, that's what we were, my coven. I saw us raw and bloodied, our mouths weapons against the recent dead. I think Cris spat something out and it looked like muscle or maybe an eye and I tried not to gag. She was crying, I think we all were at that point. "Was Angelique here, did you guys see her? I thought I saw her."

"I don't know. I don't think so, but I felt her, I saw her eyes on the shores of dreaming . . ."

"That finger snap, was that her?"

"What are we . . ."

"What are we going to do? I don't know. I think I'm losing a lot of blood. I think they cut me too deep."

"Me too. I wonder if this was a coordinated attack? Are the nurses dead . . . doctors dead . . ."

"Who will stitch us up?"

Petal looked directly at me and said, "Stay with us, come on, I see you nodding off, you need to stay awake right now, we all do. Going to sleep might be the end of it, and I need you to keep on living, come on."

But I couldn't resist anymore. I don't think any of us could. The candle smoke filled us up with slumber, the blood loss, the exertion, all the stress from everything we'd witnessed the last few months, it was all just so much, so overwhelming. And there wasn't a snapping sound anymore jolting us awake, it was just the distant shores of dreaming . . .

Along the shore the cloudwaves break . . .

:episode 3:
Daughter of the
Wormwood Star

1

Guys, where are we?

I have no damned clue, but this is definitely not the hospital.

Do any of you remember how we got here? I don't like this.

I don't have my phone. It seems to be missing . . .

Me neither. Do you think they took our phones?

They? Who's they?

I dunno. Maybe it just got lost in the shuffle, right? Left behind on accident.

I sure hope so.

When did you wake up?

Little bit ago. You guys?

Uh, dunno. A bit, I think.

I think I woke for a little while on the way out here, we were on a bus.

A bus?

Yeah. Old school bus, I think. One of the smaller ones.

Where are we though . . .

This is definitely not a hospital.

Yeah, no shit, Sherlock. What gave that away?

Come on, be nice. We're all a bit . . .

Yeah out of it. But where are we?

Looks like a cabin.

Yeah, I can see that. We're all in sleeping bags, too.

Mine's really tight, I think the zipper is stuck.

You look like a worm squirming about, trying to get free.

Yeah! Just like a maggot.

Shut it, that's not funny. Maggots are nasty.

Nasty. Yeah. Shit. What did we do?

I. I.

That happened.

Yeah.

That did, it happened.

Yeah.

It was self-defense, you saw what they did . . .

Shit. I hate shivering like this, I'm so cold, you guys cold?

Freezing my ass off. I think we have to light a fire for heat . . .

How did we get here?

Like Petal said, a bus, duh.

Yeah, but who. Right? Who drove us in that bus. Petal?

I didn't see the driver, I was moving in and out of consciousness, I was in pain. She was cleaning my wounds and it hurt, whatever she was putting on it. Burned like a motherfucker, and she said that I had to sit still, to stop moving about.

Goddamn.

Yeah.

She was ripping out stitches in my stomach, stitches that weren't there before . . .

Guess you got cut in the gut.

Yeah. And she was pushing on it, and this black ooze came out, and it smelled so nasty! Like worse than garbage vomit. Like shit. Like worse than shit.

Oh damn.

Uh huh. I passed out again from the pain.

Who was doing it?

I think she was one of the nurses from the hospital?

You think?

Yeah.

What was she doing there? On the bus with us? You think she follows Angelique, too?

Follows Angelique. Is that what we're doing?

Yes, yes we are! Hail Satan!

Oh, come on, Cris, get off it. She's not the antichrist.

But we are following her, aren't we?

She's fucking magnetic, that's what she is.

And she came into our heads. You saw it! She came right in and snapped us out of it and saved our damned lives. You saw it!

We killed for her.

No, it was in self-defense.

We did, we killed for her.

Show your work, math nerd, explain the logic here.

We wouldn't be hunted if it wasn't for her. She put us there, in that situation, with those killers, and she knew what was going to happen. That was why she up and disappeared! All part of her big plan to have us kill for her.

And why, pray tell, would she want that? No one wants that.

It's an induction ceremony into her cult.

Cult.

I thought it was a coven . . .

You don't kill for a coven, you kill for a cult.

Well, I don't care, I'm *in,* and there is no getting out for me. If that's not cool with you guys, whatever. But now you know where I stand, no matter what, and it's with Angelique.

She just has this way with us . . .

Magnetic, I'm telling you.

A cult. A killer cult. We're no worse than those losers with the keyholes on their hands.

Oh god oh damn I can still taste his skin on my teeth, that gush of blood when it popped . . .

You all right Simon?

No, no I'm not all right, I don't think I will ever be all right.

This isn't a cult, we didn't kill for her, it was in self-defense. No one is the antichrist, okay? She saved our lives, even if she didn't snap us out of it, she got us out of there. If we were still in the hospital, I'm pretty sure the other killers would've found us passed out and finished the job before we woke back up again.

Maybe we're all dead.

Oh shut it, that's not even funny.

I'm a ghoooooost, you're a ghoooooost, we're all ghooooooosts!

Okay, all right, yeah, that's a little bit funny.

It's goddamned hilarious, and you know it.

Right, right. So, that still doesn't answer the question, though. Where are we?

The windows are painted black, so I can't really tell.

Looks like shadows of trees beyond that window, though.

A forest?

Yeah, that would be my guess.

I'm just glad this isn't a log cabin.

Does it matter what kind of cabin it is? A cabin in the woods is a bad deal. Nothing ever good happens in them.

Oh, come on, those are just movies. My family used to go up to our cabin all the time. Every summer, like clockwork, we'd drive about an hour or two out to our country home and spend a few months in the middle of nowhere. Dad said it was relaxing, but I thought it was boring as shit.

This your cabin?

Hah. Yeah, no. This is nothing like my cabin.

So it could be a murder cabin.

No, it's not a murder cabin.

But it could be.

We don't know if it's Angelique that brought us here, or one of the killers.

Wouldn't they have just murdered us already, though? Why drag us all the way out here?

I dunno. Why decorate our room with the severed hands of our dead classmates?

Oh shit, that was real, wasn't it.

Lit up like candles.

I think I'm going throw up.

Oh please, don't.

Stop gagging Simon, come on.

I can't help it, this whole thing, it's just giving me this rotten feeling inside.

Yeah, me too.

Bunch of babies. We survived! We should be dead, doesn't that make you feel energized?

No, it makes me feel sad.

I don't even know what to do with you people. Sure, we're all frankensteined up and stitched back together from the edge of the abyss, and sure we're in some weird cabin in the middle of the woods, yeah. And of course we have no clue what's going on, I'll grant you that!

But?

But feel that heart beating under your ribs? Ba-boom, ba-boom! That's life pumping through your body. Feel that zing in your waking mind? That's life, too, because we came kissing close to death and stepped on through to the other side. Fucking hell! No one else gets to say that. No one else has ever experienced anything like that before. It's revitalizing!

What are you even talking about. My arms are numb. My mouth tastes like candlewax and a campfire. Every time I inhale, I feel like I'm going to die. And now I get this weight in my heart because I fucking killed someone. I did it, and you did it too! We killed those people like fucking zombies. That changes you.

Yes, yes it does. It woke me the fuck up. There is a fire inside of me now, and it is going to consume me completely, and yes that's what I want. I want to be eaten by these flames! I've never felt this alive before in my life, and you cannot take that from me. Stop being so sad and embrace this feeling!

Shut up.

Ow. Don't throw paper balls at me, come on, what's wrong with you.

What's wrong with me? What's wrong with you. What's wrong with all of you. We should be goddamned terrified right now after everything that's happened to us. We don't know what's going on or where we are, and we've already dodged death several times. There are only so many more times we can do that before the grim reaper catches up to us, and that's it. We're done.

I know, I get that, I do. But because of that, I'm going to ride this wave, you hear? I'm going to let it fill me up all electric and *shine*. And on the moment that grim reaper catches up to me, my death will burn a hole in the world. Just you watch.

You do that. I'm just going to keep my head down and try to live another day.

Simon, you okay? You're looking really green.

No, no I'm not. I'm not okay at all.

Okay, just lay down, try and get some rest. We should all do that, really. We're still pretty cut up, and we need to heal.

Go ahead, there is no way I'm going back to just sit here and wait to die. I'm going to go out and explore.

You do that, Cris, just don't get yourself killed.

I make no promises.

2

After Cris left, we looked over each other's stitches and wounds, to see how bad it all got. It definitely could've been worse, but it still wasn't very good at all. I remembered the slit throats and somehow wondered if Debbie or either of the Adams had survived, or that was it for them and they died. How long did it take to die from that kind of wound? I had no idea, I wasn't a doctor. Still, it was sad they weren't here with us. Nor any of the others that had gone down to protect Sara Fisher. Where they dead, too? Did the doctors die, the nurses, everyone else? How many in the hospital were killers, and how many were victims?

And what were we? Were we victims, or killers?

I didn't want to think about that.

"You seem okay, I guess. I count fifteen stab wounds, all stitched up."

"Oh shit, no wonder I feel like I got hit by bus. Everything aches! Do any of them look infected?"

"No, no they don't. How about me?"

I looked over Petal while Simon paced the room for a bit, chewing on his cuticles, waiting for his turn to get looked over and made sure he was okay. "I don't like these windows all blacked out, I have no idea if it's day or night. I just hear the sound of wind through the trees and it freaks me out."

"You have about eight, so a little less than me."

"How they look? If they look too bad just don't tell me, I don't want to know..."

"You look fine, I promise."

Simon sat down next to us and said, "You hear the wind through the trees, right? It just sounds odd. You know what I mean? Almost musical in a way."

"Yeah, I hear it, too. What about you, Petal?"

Petal paused, put her shirt and pants back on after the inspection and closed her eyes. "It sounds like that . . ."

"Yeah."

"That sound of the devil we heard in the hospital."

"What does that mean?"

"I don't know."

"Does it mean they followed us here? The killers?"

"I don't know. Do you want to get checked or not?"

Simon sat down and blushed a bit. "Look, I know I'm not like a movie star or whatever . . ."

"Oh, shut up and take your shirt off already."

I couldn't help myself but whistle when he stripped down to his underwear. Simon blushed again, and we all laughed. He seemed to loosen up a little at that, we all did. Strange how shared laughter can do that, help us forget all the horrible shit that happened to us. It weighed us down so much, and it was good to have some relief, if only for a little bit.

"How's it look?"

Petal looked him over while I walked up to the windows and stared outside. I tried to see beyond the smears of black paint, the whorls and spirals like the fingerprints of the damned. Little bits of light crept in, and if I squinted really hard I could see the shape of mountains off in the distance, beyond the creeping walls of trees.

"Ouch, oh damn Simon, you got the worst of us."

"How many?"

"Twenty-two, they really did a number on you."

"Oh, shit."

"At least they don't look too deep, especially the one here on your side . . ."

"My side?"

"Yeah. If they would've gone in deeper, they probably would've gotten your kidneys or something, you're really lucky."

He turned a pale green color and I thought for a moment he was going to pass out, so I turned and looked out the window once again, to try and give him some privacy. He did look pretty cut up once he took his shirt off, it looked like he'd been clawed by some ancient demon, and not a crazy asshole with a curly mustache and a knife.

"Do any of them look infected?"

"No, no. I think you'll be okay, it's just going to hurt like hell."

"Thank you." And he pulled his shirt back on, so I turned around again.

"I wonder if the nurses are here, too. The ones Petal saw on the bus."

"I guess so, why wouldn't they be?"

"I dunno. Maybe we should've waited for them before we did this. They would know better than we do how bad it all is . . ."

"Really, you could've waited another moment without taking a look?"

"No, I guess you're right."

I sat down next to two of them again, our bodies in a loose triangle on the floor. The sleeping bags scattered around us like cast-off cicada shells, and I wondered if we had been transformed inside of them. I know I felt different, in ways I couldn't explain. Maybe tainted now, with the taste of death on my tongue. And horrified, and scared, and yet . . .

Also connected to everyone else who had survived, in a deep way that was close to dangerous.

"I think I saw mountains outside of the window."

"Mountains?"

"Yeah, just the shape of them behind the trees. Where do you think we are, that we're close to mountains?"

Petal stood up and went over to the window, and placed her hands against the cool of the glass. Did she see what I saw? Or where the shapes of mountains simply my imagination playing tricks on me? I had no clue anymore. Nothing seemed real, it all felt slippery and like a dream infecting on our waking moments.

"We're at the foot of the Alleghenies, I think. Near the Mason-Dixon line."

"You sure?"

"Yeah. When I came up north to go to Dark Rivers, my family passed through this very area. I remember it so well, it was early morning and the dawn light coated the world in deep blue shadows. There was a mist everywhere, and I had just woken up from a nightmare. I don't recall what the nightmare was, but I really wish I could. It just left me this panicked feeling in my heart, and I remember seeing the beauty of the mountains and it somehow made my fear even worse, in a way I can't even come close to explaining. It was as if the beauty of nature terrified me, how vast and overpowering it was, how small and tiny and brief my entire life was in its empty shadow."

"Was this sound there, the one beyond the waving of the trees? When you came last time . . ."

"I don't know, Simon, that was three years ago . . . I wish . . . wait."

"What?"

"Oh shit. It was in my dream, I remember that dream now, and I really wish I hadn't."

"What was in the dream?"

"I. I don't want to talk about it."

"But the sound of the devil was there."

"Yes, I think so. I remember that part so clearly."

"Was it a dream of the blue house? The house of sky and shadow?"

And Petal laughed and laughed. It was a horrible, unhinged sound.

"Well, was it?"

"No, no it wasn't. Oh, oh god, I am so glad it wasn't. How much worse it would've been if it was . . ."

And before Petal could reveal more of her dream, the door to our room banged open violently with a loud crash. Bright light from the hallway cut a halo around a lone female shadow. We had no idea who this was, and I must admit at first we thought it was Cris. But it didn't take long to realize no, that wasn't her at all. This was some strange stranger, slightly heavier than Cris, with a short bob of hair and burn scars on her face. Dust motes danced around her body, and she smiled and looked down at the three of us, placed her hands on her hips, and said in a raspy voice, "Come on you guys, time to get moving. Angelique's got something she needs to say." Later on, we would come to know her as nurse Juliana, one of the survivors from the hospital, and the one that patched us up on the bus ride out.

Angelique. She wants to talk to us. Angelique. We remembered her eyes, then, her eyes in our dreams, in our waking moments, her eyes like tides dragging us along, dragging us under, dragging us beneath the deep. A terrifying, exhilarating feeling. Some people might fight that current, but we never did. The fear sang to us, and we listened, lost in her eyes and the call beneath the waves.

We're coming, Angelique. We're coming.

3

Nurse Juliana led us through the ruins of an old Girl Scout campground. Lodges just like ours were scattered through deep pine woods, with narrow dirt roads spiraling about and overgrown. The lodges were in various states of disrepair, and filled with the voices of people talking and laughing. I felt a connection to these voices, a tether from their minds to ours, like a bright red thread. Connected, all knotted up, just like Angelique wanted all along.

Golden rays of sun scattered through the branches, with gnats fluttering about as we walked along that spiral dirt road. Everything moved in slow motion, like the world was in a molasses dream, and I wondered briefly if we were even awake. Were we in gentle comas back in the hospital like Lucy Diamond? Dreaming our existence to life after being attacked and left near dead by a group of violent serial killers? Had one of them stolen my hand and used it as some fucked up candle? The sound of the devil was still there, humming distantly underneath everything else. It crept into our heads, muddled up our thoughts. Hazy, everything sluggish. That was the sound of a dream, not reality. It had to be. We weren't here at all, but still in the hospital, asleep. We had to be.

I flexed my numb fingers. They were real, if somewhat fuzzy and distant. Did that mean anything? I can't remember if I could feel things in my dreams or not. The sensations were lost the minute on waking, and maybe that will happen here at any moment now . . .

Petal leaned over and pinched me, as if reading my mind. (Had she read my mind at this point? I don't know, this is where things start to get hazy. We were knotted up yes, but I think the mind reading and stuff came later. Yes. I'm sure it did.)

"See, you're not dreaming. None of us are."

"I feel so foggy headed . . ."

"You'll get used to it eventually," Nurse Juliana said.

"Get used to it?"

"Yes, the sound of the devil has that effect."

It was a beautiful, sad, sound if you listened closely. Like a touch of sweet melancholia, tinged with fuzzy opiate edges, and a touch . . .

Well, a touch . . .

I felt wet and my stomach tingled and what is this . . .

"Shit."

"Hah, yeah, shit. You'll get used to it, too, trust me. It has a strong influence now, but eventually it will be nothing more than a faint buzzing sound in your thoughts. Though it will probably get worse once we get closer . . ."

"Closer to what?"

"To the source."

And Petal snorted. "To the devil, you mean? There is no such thing as the devil."

"No, not exactly, but maybe. You'll see, Angelique is going to explain all of this. Trust me."

Simon piped up, excitement in his voice. "Is that where we're going now? The source?"

"No, hah, we're going to go see Angelique, duh. Come on, enough questions, you're still new to this whole thing. You need to save your energy, or else you'll fall for its influence."

"And what will happen . . ."

"Crazy shit. Trust me, you don't want that to happen, so just keep your head screwed on until we get you guys under control."

We walked for a bit more in silence. I tried to think of, well, of anything. Just random thoughts, just little stories in my head, or maybe trying to puzzle out exactly what was going on. We were all so in the dark at this point, none of it was making any sense, and yet, somehow did make sense. The fuzziness seemed to turn up the more I thought, and then I felt my stomach tingle some more, and my legs grow weak. Images floated through my head . . .

I could fuck them all, we could just rip each other's clothes off and go at it, right here, mess up that dirt, get pine needles in our hair, and oh shit, we could bite each other and rip into each other, really rip into that skin with our teeth, just like you did in the hospital, you can still taste the flesh on your lips so sweet and feel the Adam's apple crush beneath your teeth pop pop pop.

"Hey! Hey!"

Snap, snap, snap, fingers in my mind and fingers in front of my face and I snapped out of it.

"Yeah, like that. You need to concentrate on our surroundings, understand? If you get too up in your head, it can get inside of you. Right? Look at the trees, listen to the birds, pick up and focus on tiny details of the path. Just keep your thoughts on the here and now and in front of us."

"Okay, I will."

And we all nodded.

"I'm serious. You look pale, but you'll be fine as long as you ground yourself. We don't want to end up like her last coven . . ."

"Last coven?"

Juliana stopped and closed her eyes and rubbed the bridge of her nose for a second. "No, I'm sorry, I think I said that wrong, you'll have to excuse me. It's hard for me to concentrate too, sometimes, even after I got used to that damned influence. We're all the same coven, always been the same coven, stretching back for long while, from the moment she was born and brought into this world. You guys just weren't an active part of it just yet, and there are many more of us out there. She's gathering us slowly, pulling us together, bringing us here."

Petal didn't seem to care about any of that. "So what happened? Before."

"They gave into their inner bacchae, that's what. They tore the dogs apart first, then the men, then their children, and then each other."

"Shouldn't we be anywhere else but here?"

"I'll let Angelique tell you what's going on."

Petal stopped, crossed her arms and looked dour and a bit pissed off. "I want to get out of this, whatever this is, understand? I can't do this anymore. I appreciate you sewing me up and getting us out of that hospital, but ever since Angelique came to our university shit has been disastrous, and I can't take any more of this . . ."

"Sure, you can leave if you want, but that won't change anything."

"What do you mean."

It's so weird, I remember this part so clearly. The sun beams, the gnats and the dust motes, the smell of pine covering up some weird rotten scent that hung in the air everywhere. Like moldy old cedar and corpses. And Juliana walking right up to Petal, putting her nose against hers, eyes to eyes, hands on either side of Petal's head. An intense moment, with the promise of violence right there, below the surface.

And then she kissed her, gently on the mouth.

"Because we are connected, blood to bone, the moment we are born. Connected to her, understand? Before her we did not exist, and after her we may not exist, and those killers know this. They are killing us as a way to get directly to her. Death by a thousand cuts, each one of us a part of her, slowly slicing away until they take her down."

"And what if she dies, do we cease to exist?"

"Maybe. But I certainly hope not."

And I remember Petal wiping tears from her face and sniffling. I'd never seen Petal cry before, and it was an oddly vulnerable moment that shook me to my core. And let me just say right now, I don't know how much of what Juliana said was true, but we sure as hell believed it in that moment. It felt so true, in a way things in dreams feel true, even if they could never ever be true.

Sure, we would find out later on that if Angelique died we would all keep on living, yes. But we would be changed. Oh god, would we ever be changed. She left her burning fingerprints on the contours of our hearts, forever marked by the Daughter of the Wormwood Star.

"Come on, let's keep going. Her lodge isn't too much further along now, and then after that I can introduce you around to everyone. It'll be fun, like camp."

And even though Nurse Juliana had turned around and started walking away from us, I could hear a wry smile in her voice, knowing that she was trying to lighten the atmosphere after all of that intense emotion on display a second ago.

4

Cris waited for us in the master lodge, at the center heart spiral of the summer camp ruins. This building seemed far older than the rest, the wood raw and barely cut. It gave the whole place a very open-air feel, like somehow we were still in part of the forest. This lodge was only one giant, long room, with a stage at the far north end. Upturned tables and discarded chairs were scattered everywhere, and overhead birds flitted amongst the rafters, frightened of our stomping heavy feet.

Cris ran over to us the minute we came in, and gave us giant hugs that squeezed our scars. Painful, but still somehow comforting. "Come on you guys, Angelique has so much to tell us! She was waiting until you got here before she did anything, and I've been going nuts just sitting here all by myself. Completely nuts!"

Angelique was on the stage, sitting cross-legged, reading a book as if nothing weird was going on. Two burning lamps next to her, letting out a sickly sweet-smelling smoke, like incense but not quite. To either side stood two super tall women, taller than anyone we'd ever seen in our collective lives. I would say probably six foot four, or six foot five, watching us walk in, scattering dust and releasing the raw scent of wood rot and mold. They both wore dirty red skirts, ripped at the edges, and red shirts with that same symbol we saw outside of Lucy's room at the hospital. I wanted to know what that symbol *meant*, but I knew now wasn't the time to ask.

Anyway, these two women turned to face us with arms across their chests, their eyes blindfolded with a dirty red rag. I saw their eyes veiled thinly behind those rags, so I could tell it was made of some light cloth that was mostly see-through. I wondered then if it tinted the world red for them, and if so, why? They also had scars and stitches all over their bodies, and I knew those wounds. I felt them all over my own body. Had they been in the hospital with us? Maybe on some different floor? Or in another hospital in Dark Rivers? I had no clue.

And their wounds looked raw and crooked in a way that suggested a metal hook. What the hell did they survive? And what did they do to survive it?

Angelique pushed her cane against the ground, leveraging her body as she stood slowly, her legs shaking a bit, her hair falling over her glittering red eyes. Tidal wave dream eyes summoning us again. She set the book on the table, and then walked toward us. Her cane kept the rhythm of her pace, a percussion accompanying her movements like a metronome. The two giant women followed behind her, and at the moment of a stumble, they were quick to place their arms around her, to try and help her walk. Angelique wasn't having any of it, and she angrily shrugged them off and kept moving forward, hair over her face, obscuring her features, yet letting her eyes shine on through.

"I see you three losers finally woke the fuck up. What took you so long?"

Petal's lip quivered, briefly. "Why did you abandon us?"

"I honestly thought they were just after me and not you guys. I thought if I left, went to round up some more members of our coven, that they would follow *me* and leave you all alone. When I realized I was wrong . . . it was almost too late."

"Not for Debbie, it was already too late for her."

"Yeah. Shit. Yeah." She perched on her cane for a moment, statue still. "You're all knotted up now, I can tell, just look at you. You're ready to help me out, to figure out this whole puzzle of my existence, and exactly what I am in this world. And you're all connected to me, can you sense it? From before you were born. You might not remember it, but we were there, all twisted up together in a void beyond life. And because of that, once we unpuzzle my existence, we'll get right to the bottom of your existence, too. The why of the killers, hunting us, and the mystery of our purpose in this world. For unlike those day-to-day jobbers sleepwalking around and feeding the zombie machines of life, we were born with a *purpose*. We just have no clue what that fucking purpose is . . . yet."

I know, you're probably seeing all these red flags popping up during her speech, and you're wondering how someone so intelligent and well-educated as myself would fall so hard for it. I'm right, aren't I? You don't have to say anything. I can't speak for the others, at this point their thoughts were only dim echoes in my head, like the distant voices of wave drowned ghosts. But I can say that this spoke to my own fears, those reasons why I quit being a philosophy major after my second semester. All those feelings of being confronted with a lonely and uncaring universe, of knowing you're not the center story of everything, of the horrifying truth revealing itself to you— *nothing matters, you don't matter, life is pointless suffering and when you die you don't exist.* Just remembering that moment in class when we were discussing Sartre and Camus and Simone De Beauvoir, and remembering that feeling, that anxiety of the weight of nothingness pressing down on me, knowing that we came from nothing, will amount to nothing, will return to nothing, even now I'm getting a panic attack. Feel my pulse, right there, feel it? Racing. My eyes, look into my eyes, see my pupils? How dilated they are? I can barely breathe right now, just from thinking about it.

So Angelique stood there, and told us with such assured confidence that not only did we have a purpose but also that we existed before we were born, will exist after death, and if we follow her, we would discover our purpose. That was a balm to our terrified, existential hearts. And in a way, she was right, kind of. Sort of. I don't know, I'm getting ahead of myself here, and if I tell it out of order it's not going to make any sense.

And of course Petal was the one who stepped forward, a mouthpiece for our own internal monologues. "What do you mean purpose?"

"Do you hear it in the air? Can't you feel it? The sound of the devil is strong, isn't it? It comes from beneath the earth, and even though it contorts us and tries to control us, it's also *pulling* us toward it, much in the same way I pulled you toward me. That is the sound of destiny, of our purpose, of what we were meant to do in this world. Why did Lucifer make me? Why did he set me here on this rotting Earth in the first place? There must be a reason, and I can feel it in my heart and my bones, the voice of a million ghosts pulling us there. To our purpose."

She paused for a moment, and looked up toward the treetops and smiled.

"And this world is cruel to those special ones like us, cruel and uncaring. And I was so lonely and lost in it, unable to find any place to fit in. My one and only family, murdered. The killers leaving twelve-year-old me behind and homeless. That was the darkest moment of my life, when I thought for sure that there was no such thing as the devil, and that my foster family lied to me. And that all the abuse and trauma I had experienced was for nothing, nothing at all. I tried suicide so many times, I lost count. It made me fearless, to see the end of my life at my own hands and survive. As if kissing emptiness made everything else seem petty and worthless and nothing to be afraid of at all.

"I lived on the street, begging, using my *pull* and my *push* to scrape by, influencing those boring work-a-day suits to shell out some cash for the grubby little urchin child, hitchhiking about all brave and empty on the inside. I killed a few times just to survive. I liked it, and afterwards I felt a burning inside to murder some more, just so I could experience that joy it gave me over and over again. That was around the time when the sound of the devil found me, and whispered to me, and told me to come and find it. And it said that I had to gather my lost souls together, just like how my foster family showed me, and build a coven in my name, and find the truth of my existence.

"I was giddy with the promise of a new dawn. I used my *pull* to find you guys, I pulled and I pulled, until the threads started to unravel before my eyes, showing the places where knots could be. And now, well, here we are. You feel it, too, don't you? The call of the sound beneath the mountains, restless and hungry and ready to give us purpose."

I looked over and saw Simon and Cris crying, and Petal slowly backing away. She wasn't leaving yet, but she was eyeing the two giant women with a nervous glance. Cris cried out, "Hail Satan!" and then Simon repeated her, and the two of them hugged Angelique close. I saw her crying as well, her eyes closed.

"Hail Satan, and the Daughter of the Wormwood Star!"

5

Later that afternoon, we all met in in the master lodge again, Angelique calling us all together with a thought broadcast. At first, I'd thought I'd imagined the whole thing, and who knows maybe we did. Maybe this was all a group psychosis? Or maybe a rumor that spread from person to person, until we all believed it to be true? I don't know. All I know is that we all got the message, in Angelique's voice, whispering amongst our thoughts. The phrases like static or feedback on a cheap amp, grainy and punctuated by a sharp hiss. Her eyes again, in our thoughts, sharp and flickering like candle-flames, telling us *to come, come to the master lodge, come, we need to speak.*

And so, even though all of us orphans in lodge 8 were exhausted and broken down and still healing, we struggled forward and walked the spiral paths again. I worried that we would get lost, but Cris seemed to know the way oh so intimately. Like she'd walked this path a million times before, and later on she would confide in me that she had, in her dreams every night, walked this same path. over and over again, broken down, cobblestone, overgrown. Ever since she was a little child, yes, and in the center of her dream was the house of sky and shadow. That large, towering blue farmhouse, and not the lodge that was there in real life.

In a way, we were all jealous of her dreams. Maybe it meant she was closer with Angelique? I don't know. All I know is that when I dreamt of the house of sky and shadow, it was in the center of a busy town, nestled between skyscrapers like an alien object. So still, so strange, so completely out of place amongst the endless stream of cars and buildings, yet still so peaceful.

I once asked Petal about her own dreams of the house, to see if it matched either of ours, and she just shrugged and said she did not like to talk about it. I worried, then, that the house was fire in her dreams, like it was in Debbie's dreams. And that maybe it meant that she would be the next one to die? But I didn't tell her that. I didn't want her to confirm my suspicion, that idea terrified me to my very core. How horrible it would be to know you were going to die soon, and in such a violent way.

Simon told me the house in his dreams was a dollhouse inside his childhood home. The funny thing was, he was convinced that his mom had actually had the dollhouse, and that it wasn't just a dream. He swore up and down that he remembered playing with it when he was younger, and finding the dusty bones of dead mice scattered on the various floors. I don't know if I believed him then, but I do believe him now. I don't know what's changed, or why I know he wasn't lying way back then. I just know in my heart of hearts that he had a very intimate relationship with the house of sky and shadow, one that none of us would ever understand.

She waited for us now, sitting on that stage once more, this time staring off into space, that book on her lap, with the spine pointing up. The book was a leatherbound notebook, the kind that you get at bookstores, with a small pen nestled up next to it. I wondered briefly what was written inside, and later on we would all get a peek, and what we saw confused and bewildered us. But that's neither here nor there right now. We'll get to that later, I promise.

"Come on in, losers, pull up a chair and sit down."

We nodded, turned the chairs over and started sitting down. At first, I thought it would just be us Final Girls, as we were still calling ourselves, Simon included. But no, all the other members of our new loosely knit coven started filtering in, too. One at a time, sometimes in groups of three or four, meandering in with a lost glazed look in their eyes. And I wondered what traumas they'd survived to get here. Had they been through the hell that we'd been through? How many friends or family members did they lose to the serial killers?

A brief thought about my family, and I realized they were still missing, presumed dead, and I felt a heavy knot in my throat, like a stone of anxiety, and I almost choked on it. Had the serial killers targeted our families as well, and they just hadn't found the bodies yet? I got a creeping sensation all along my skin and around my bones. My mom and dad and little sister dead in our home, the bodies hidden in the walls.

"All right, everyone here? Good. Before I get into today's lesson, I want to inform you guys about the latest expedition to find the sound of the devil. I got word from Rosemary the other day, and that they're about ready to go into the Jawbone Door. They're taking their time, *obviously*. Especially after what happened to the last crew that went down there exploring. If they make it back safe and sound, we'll send another party down there to explore a little further. If that one's good? Then we'll all go down there together, and hopefully get answers."

A hand raised in the back, and I got this weird feeling like we were in kindergarten or something, and had to stifle an awkward laugh.

"Yeah, what's up, Jane?"

"Why don't we just go down there? All of us right now."

Angelique paused, and had this horrible look on her face. It was a mix of sorrow and terror, and it sent chills down my spine. I wanted to know what she'd seen to make her look like that, but I also didn't want to know at the same time.

"Listen, don't listen to me, hush, and listen. One, two, three. Do you hear, do you feel it? What do you feel. Be honest now."

And Jane closed her eyes, and held her breath. We all turned and looked at her, as the sound of the devil rose up from the darkness, and my heart quickened, my pulse a racing fire, sweat trickling down my face, as those images started to crawl back into my mind. One of me crawling up to Jane, slowly, slowly, stalking her while she was still sightless and vulnerable, and taking my teeth, and running them along her delicate spine, biting down, and just pulling. Pulling with jaw and fist. Pulling and tearing and using my animal strength to rip that spine out from . . .

No. Concentrate on the leaves falling through the holes in the roof, the soft sounds of birds along the ceiling.

Jane turned pale and started to shiver, and under her breath she muttered *no no no no. I won't do that, I won't, I can't, but I want . . . I want . . .*

And I wondered what horrible things the sound pushed into her mind. Did she want to brutalize me, as I wanted to brutalize her? One of the giant women walked up to Jane and slapped her hard across the face. The sound ricocheted through the lodge, snapping us all out of our bacchanal trance, and brought us back to ourselves, all real and sharp in the dark.

Jane touched the sore edges of her cheek and looked around in shock. "I almost . . . I almost . . ."

Angelique nodded.

"We all did, it's not just you. That's the sound of the devil, and if you think it's strong here, wait until you get closer to the Jawbone Door. The first few groups that went down there didn't come back at all. The last one? They came back in pieces."

"Pieces?"

Angelique paused, closed her eyes and shook her head.

"We found their dismembered bodies strung from the trees like tinsel all around the campground. Their faces skinned off and nailed to the doors of the lodges. All except for the leader of their group, Sofia. She never returned to us, but I fear she's like the others. I never did find out what happened . . . I . . ."

She inhaled, held it in. Waited for a few moments, and then exhaled once more.

"So we worked on better ways to resist the images it pushed into our head, ways that would keep us safe, even when we got close to the source of the sound. Rosemary's group of six are down there right now, exploring. So far, so good it seems. I only hope that these new techniques will keep them safe, and we'll finally get answers."

There was a stark silence after she said this, as we all sat around, unable to figure out what to say next, uncomfortable and weighed down with trauma. In the distance, an old clock ticked away the seconds, and it felt weighted, and heavy, like a metronome to our hearts. First the serial killers, and now the sound of the devil. Death was everywhere, violent and gruesome.

And our minds wandered. Oh no. And as we thought, the sound of the devil started to move along to the rhythm of the clock. Tick, tick, tick, a low rumbling thrumming drone, discordant as it was beautiful, and there were tears in the corner of my eyes. So beautiful. As the images crawled back in. So beautiful. What our insides looked like outside. So beautiful. Red jewels and intestines unspooled like spirals in the dust. You could play for days with the guts of a friend. So beautiful . . .

A clap, loud and thunderous, knocking these images out of our heads.

"Gosh, you guys, I'm sorry, that was my fault, I wasn't even thinking, you don't even know how to snap yet! All right, I guess that's going to be our first lesson. I'm assuming Juliana already showed you how to ground yourselves, right? To concentrate on the here and now.

That's a good start, but sometimes the mind will wander, and that's when the sound digs in deep and gets you good. But snapping seems to work really well, and so we're going to start with that, all right? After that, maybe tomorrow I'll teach you how to *push* and how to *pull*, and if we're lucky, how to *knock*. But none of that means anything if you get caught in the devil's undertow and it pulls you down into the deep. We're not going to end up like the others, no sirree."

And she placed the cane on the stage again, and stood up all wobbly and unsteady. Her eyes twitched a little, and then she smiled a very wry smirk. "All right, you losers, you ready to learn some magic tricks? Come on, come closer, you're going to want to see this."

And then she snapped her fingers, loudly, and drew all eyes toward her.

6

Angelique taught us how to *snap*. She told us to snap our fingers, right in front of our eyes, and as we did this, we had to study and memorize our hands. The fingernails, the cuticles, the scars, the razor blade stitches. Any moles, the bump of the knuckles, the twisted veins. The way our fingers felt, the crisp movement of finger on thumb, and that hollow chime when they struck together like a match on a matchbook. Think about how you move the muscles, she said, think about how they feel, what parts of your brains itch when calling it out.

Again, now, again, yes, once more, and again.

Then she wanted us to think about snapping, but keep our fingers still. Trace those movements in the mind, feel how it should feel, imagine a shadow of your hand, the way it felt, the chime of skin against skin. *You see this, losers? This is how you break a curse,* she said, *how you cancel out a nasty hex. It won't work all the time, some chains can't break so easily. But if you can do it, and do it well, it becomes a powerful tool.*

Her voice was so strange, so larger than the room we were in. I know, that probably doesn't make sense, maybe I'm not explaining it right. There was a gravity and an echo to it, and it floated around and mixed with the droning sound of the devil.

Let's do it again, and again, and again. All night if we have to.

No one groaned or complained when she said this. It somehow made us feel better, to know that magic was so simple. All you had to do was *snap* and something happened. There was a change in the air with each snap, a sort of taut wire feeling that grew tighter and tighter each moment. I noticed, as the hours went on, a change happening to my mind, to my body. I grew weary and exhausted, even when I was just sitting there, thinking of snapping. It wore me down completely, and I felt something *moving* under my skin. Squirming was an even better word for that sensation, as if my muscles were alive and slithering under my skin. This was not a good feeling.

Some of us started to dry heave. We opened our eyes, the shadow snap still ringing in our thoughts, as we looked around the room. Connected, all knotted up, our thoughts twisted about. And we could see the squirming under our skin, like we had worms wrapped around our bones, moving. More dry heaving. A taste of rotten pennies on the tongue. Like crowfeather and offal.

"Take a breather now. Come on. Just take a small breather for a second. I know this isn't easy, all right? I do. But we need to do it, you guys mean too much for me to let you die like all the others. You're connected to me, feel that? You feel it now? How we're all knotted up? You're a part of me and I'm a part of you. See this?"

And Angelique held up her arms, as long shapes squirmed under her skin, wriggling against the bone. "This is us, who we are, becoming our true selves. The real us beneath the bones, the things we were before the world was hatched in a fiery sea of emptiness. These shells are nothing to us, cocoons waiting for the transformation to finish, and set us free."

Her voice returned to her normal voice now, chained to her body and no longer floating around us in echoes.

"This is what it means to be a witch. But the why of it, why we are the way we are? Different from those outside, the ones that hunt us, the normal boring workaday people, different from those who sleepwalk every hour of their lives. What makes us so special? The answers are down below the surface, in the caves where my foster parents found me."

And Cris shouted out, *Hail Satan!* And more and more voices chimed in, until we were all saying it. Yes, even me, the last holdout. I wasn't sure I believed it, not just yet, even with all the weird stuff going on. And yet, I said it like I believed it. And then someone else shouted out, *Hail Angelique! Hail the Daughter of the Wormwood star!* And we were moving back and forth, openly crying and weeping, overcome with emotion, the weird things still squirming under our skin, as Angelique sat down on the edge of the stage and smiled, the cane across her lap. She tilted her head back, and closed her eyes, still smiling, and I remember how beautiful she was just then.

Frail, and yet containing this immense inner gravity, like a star gone nova. The scar on her forehead pulsed with each chant, every time someone said her name, and she was crying now, too.

And then, the air changed. A scent of sparklers in the dark, and we all stopped talking, turned to see what happened, as the doors opened and a woman stumbled in. Outside wind whipped the trees, tossing branches and dead leaves like they were nothing. Thunder roared in the distance, as lightning tinted the forest in bright flashes of color. It surrounded this strange stranger with a halo of flashing light, the thunder rattling our bones.

"Run, Angelique," she said, "There is nothing but death beyond the Jawbone Door, you need to run now and never look back!"

And Angelique stood straight up, without wobbling or misstep, her eyes intense fire, her lips pursed together. "Rosemary? What happened? How did you get back here so quickly? And where is everyone else?"

Rosemary flickered, like a candle flame. "We're still down there," she said, "You have to forget about us, forget about the door! Let us die, and leave here, and never look back!"

Was she dead? A nervous laughter rippled through the room, tainted by the edges of fear. Rosemary flickered again, and her spirit floated towards us, moving in and out of reality. A chill followed her, in a wave of frost and winter wind. Dizziness, and a disorientation, just by her mere presence. As if our minds couldn't comprehend what we saw, no matter how hard we tried to square that circle.

"How did you untether yourself? Are you dead?"

"Don't go after us! We're dead already, you have to get away from here."

"No." Angelique's voice was a stone thrown into a pond of still water, it rippled in echoes around us. "I will not leave you girls behind, there's been too much death already."

"You must leave us! They want you down there, they want to control the sound of the devil, and they say you're the key to all of it. You haven't seen what I've seen, there is something here, something . . ."

And she wavered like heat from a flame, flickered and then cried out, a slash across her face, and blood across a razor, and she was gone. Silence followed, and then some more nervous laughter, and the brief chatter of confused conversation. Angelique tilted her had back, and motioned for all of us to quiet, now, be quiet. She held her cane up, her hair draped over her face, her two eyes staring out at across the sea of bodies.

"Shit, shit, shit. We can't just sit here and do nothing, can we? Hell no! Are you losers ready to go down there with me and get your hands dirty? So we can save Rosemary and her crew?"

Cris stood up in the back, tears streaming down her face. "I would die for you! Let us go now, and save Rosemary and the rest! Let us find the secret beyond the Jawbone Door! Please! Let us die for you!" And then she trembled and fell to the ground, shivering on the loose floorboards of the master lodge. "I love you, I love you, I love you," her voice barely a whisper, "I love you, let me die for you, I love you."

I saw Petal in the back of the room, her eyes terrified, like she wanted to run far away from here and never look back. I didn't have to read her mind to understand that fear, I knew it and saw it inside myself. We were so caught up with the group earlier, shouting her name in devotion, and even though I didn't believe in the devil, I believed in Angelique in that moment, in a way that terrified me to the core of my body. I don't know if she'd *pushed* us with her mind, or whatever, or if it was some kind of mass psychosis, I don't know, I wish I did, I do. But in that moment, I saw my shadow, I saw what I would do for Angelique in my heart, and it terrified me.

We all started to fall like dominoes then, one at a time, to the ground, shivering, muscle spasms, shaking our bodies, and whispering, "I love you, I would die for you, I would kill for you, we love you, let us die for you, let us kill for you, we love you. Hail Angelique! Hail the Daughter of the Wormwood Star!"

Fuck. I wish I could say I didn't get caught up in all of that, but that would be a lie. I wept, I screamed in adulation, I tore at my clothes and I felt lost in that moment. I had no idea who I was anymore, all I knew was that I was here, this was my destiny. I was a vessel for Angelique, and it felt right, and I tingled all over, and even though I was terrified in the deep-down core of my heart, I knew that I had to do this. I had to follow Angelique down below the Jawbone Door. Even though something was coming for us, something horrific, something that terrified Rosemary to the very core of her being.

We were going to do it. I really wanted to die for her, and look, if I'm a hundred percent honest with myself, I still feel like that now. Not all the time, mind you, but there are moments where I am overwhelmed with my love for Angelique once more, like a brief shadow over the sun, and I'm like *oh yes, there you are. I feel you again.* And it's like going home after being gone for so long.

:episode 4:
The Path of Silence

1

Guys, I don't think this is such a fantastic idea.

Oh, come on, Petal, it's going to be okay. Don't you trust Angelique?

No, look, no I don't, look at the facts, all right? By some sick twist of luck, we survived all of this, while all these people we know died. Fucking died. And it all started when she came to Dark Rivers . . .

You have to come with us, we need you.

Shut it, Cris, you drank that Kool-Aid. Look at you, look at all of you! Don't you see what you've become? This isn't right. We're all going to die down there.

You don't know that.

But I do, I can sense it, can't you? This awful sensation, like a millipede wrapped around my spine, tugging at it with all those little legs. I feel like I'm going to throw up.

Of course we feel that, but it's just nerves.

Yeah, just nerves! Like wedding day jitters.

You have got to be kidding me.

It's normal to be worried, but this is what our lives have been leading us toward.

The House of Sky and Shadow.

That sensation, ever since we were born, that we weren't like everyone else.

That we're special.

This is why!

Don't you wonder why those serial killers are going after us?

Don't you wonder why we have pale shadows, and no one else does?

Pale shadows, what are you talking about? I don't see anything like that.

You will.

We promise, you will.

I can't, I can't do this. Let me stay here, I think Angelique will be okay if I stay here. She even said so.

She did, I guess, yes.

But we need you, Angelique needs you.

No, no you don't. She doesn't even need you guys, you can just stay here.

And let Rosemary and the rest of them die?

You saw her! You did! They killed her, right there, in front of us. What do you think that razor slash was? That was them killing her.

You don't know that! Angelique wouldn't have us go down there so early if she knew she was dead!

This is what happened to the other parties, isn't it?

No, it was the sound of the devil! It made them attack each other!

Did it, though? You guys just assumed that was the case, but maybe something or someone was waiting for us down there the whole time. Why do you guys trust Angelique so much? You barely know her.

Because we love her.

I saw you earlier, all of you, but especially you, Cris. That was fucking terrifying, how quickly you guys leapt to murder and suicide in the name of Angelique.

You didn't feel it?

Feel what?

She didn't feel it. Maybe she should stay here, if she couldn't feel it. I think Angelique would be okay with that, then.

We can't believe you didn't feel it.

Did you even dream of the House of Sky and Shadow? Are you even one of us? Or are you a cuckoo, planting your egg in our nest.

Can we even read your mind? I know I can't. All I hear is silence.

Yes, she is, she is silent like a grave.

What are you even saying, do you even hear yourself? This isn't right! You have to know it's not right! Can't you feel it? Can't you see what's wrong with all of this?

Come on Petal, stop dry heaving. This kind of drama is unbecoming of you.

What, what are you even saying . . .

I'm saying you probably shouldn't be here when we get back.

No, wait, where am I supposed to go? We're in the middle of nowhere, and I have no cellphone, and I can't even drive . . .

That's not our problem, is it?

Guys, guys, come on, leave Petal alone, okay? She's just a bit confused.

What are you saying, Simon, hmm? Are you feeling doubt about Angelique, too?

Holy shit, what is wrong with you?

Maybe Simon should wait here as well. Does anyone else want to wait here?

Yeah, all right, I'll be here too. Just in case they need any help, you know?

Jones? Why do you want to be here? I know you're all in on Angelique, I can feel your thoughts worming around in my head right now . . .

Hum. Okay, you're not going to believe me.

No, go ahead, tell us.

I think I've seen Sofia in the woods. Usually at night, sometimes she sneaks into camp and I think I see her stealing food? A few times I've seen her watch people sleep, and gently touch their faces. I mean, she's muddy, and her hair is a mess, and she's missing an eye and some fingers, but I know it's her. She's still wearing that quilted Amish-looking skirt she left with, but it's now all tattered and ripped up.

And you just told us this now?

Because I knew you wouldn't believe me, no one else has seen her.

And why are you so special?

I get night terrors in the middle of the night, horrible dreams, and when I wake up I'm frozen, all right? I'm completely paralyzed and I can't move at all. I can't even close my eyes, I have to keep them open, and there is this weight on my chest. I'd never had them before coming here, but I love Angelique so much I can't leave, so I suffer through them. And at the worst moment, when I think I can't even breathe, and I want to scream, but I can't scream, I see her moving through the moonlight.

Oh. Okay.

Will you three stay up with me tonight, then? After the others leave. See if we can capture Sofia, and get her to tell us what's going on?

Maybe we should tell Angelique this . . .

Go, go ahead and tell her. I don't think that will change much of anything, she has her mind set on you guys going down to save Rosemary and the others now, and I don't blame her.

Thank you for staying behind with me, Jones.

It's okay, Petal, just help me tonight and we'll call it even. Anyone else? Yes? You? Okay, looks like there'll be four in total sticking behind.

You guys have to promise me you'll keep your ears to the wind, and your eyes on the candle flame, in case we need to contact you, and get some help down beneath the Jawbone Door. I'm really worried about what's waiting for us out there, after Rosemary came to us.

Of course. And remember, stay close to Angelique. Keep her safe at all cost, and let us know whatever you find out. If there really are answers down there, or just our promised death waiting for us.

2

On rainy, rotten days I like to think back and wonder what would have happened if I'd gone with them, instead of staying behind. Would that have changed anything to come later? I don't know. It's impossible, figuring all that stuff out. Those years in prison where the worst of it. All that time, going over the crap that happened, all the possible different outcomes of every event. It becomes infinite pretty quickly, you know? More reasons I changed majors, I guess. All that infinity made me feel tiny, small, a pointless speck in the heart of an uncaring universe.

But I've come to make peace with all that. In a way, all those infinite possibilities are what did it, you know? That multi-worlds theory that used to give me the willies finally gave me closure. A sense of calm to know that out there, in some other version of my life, there is a branch of me that is happy and content. She's got her shit together, she avoided all of this nonsense, and is living her best life.

Just knowing that is good enough for me. That it's not all misery everywhere, and in some small way, a piece of me is happy. Even if it was only an echo, connected to me through the thin psychic veil between universes.

But hey, who am I even kidding here? Of course, unwinding this one single moment would not change anything. Not enough to make my life perfect, to give me what I'd dreamed of since I'd been small and curious in the world. Already, we'd been infected and changed, with the fingerprint of Angelique pressed firmly against our hearts, leaving a smudge of shadow and ash across our ventricles. Already our minds had knotted together, and at this point we were starting to think in synchronicity.

I still hear their voices in my thoughts. Even though they're all dead. I don't want to think about that right now. Where was I? Oh, yes. I'd stayed behind with Simon and Petal and a few of the others. They were strangers, and yet I knew them still, in the way you know something in waking that you've only seen in dreams. You've had it happen, I'm sure, we all have. It's where the ripples of déjà vu come from—you know it, you've experienced it. It's confusing, yes, but there it is, that feeling.

And here we were, staying up late, sitting in the near dark while the evening hours ticked on. Several candles were lit and puddling on the floor, and we sat there, waiting. Simon nodding off, Petal singing to herself, as Jones just watched intently, his eyes never leaving the door to his dorm.

"Do you think she's okay?"

"Who?"

"Angelique. Do you think she's okay? I can't sense her anymore, nor any of the others . . ."

Jones shook his head, leaned back and said, "It will be okay, Simon, I promise. I've been here since the very start, I'm her foster brother."

The sound of thrashing wind as a branch scratched the window. Once, twice, three times. "And you're okay with staying here with us?"

"Angelique's tough as shit, Petal knows it. I can tell by the look in her eyes."

Petal stopped singing for a moment, and then sighed a full body sigh. "Yeah. She scares me, after all I've seen her do."

And I laughed and said, "You don't even know the half of it. You didn't see Sara Fisher, or the wreckage of the plane. Fuck."

I hadn't thought about that in a hot second, and really wished I hadn't brought it up right then. The memory of her body, of leaving Sara behind, the plane crash, and the mother's corpse, and the baby, and all of it. Fear crawled up into my stomach once again, and this whole thing felt wrong once more. I said I would die for her, I chanted hail Angelique, hail the Daughter of the Wormwood Star, and I *believed* it, oh god fuck hell, I believed it. And at the thought of leaving her, leaving all this behind, and moving on . . .

More loneliness. A rough wild beast that clawed at my heart. That feeling of never being connected to people like how I was connected to Angelique. That I had purpose here, that the universe had meaning when I was with them, all of them. With them gone, far away from me, the silence was unbearable, could I really live like that? Survive like that? Was fucking suicide the only way out of this?

All my meandering thoughts meant that the sound could crawl into my mind, and once again plant the roots of rotten images in my skull. Though, this time it was different. I saw myself bloodied and holy. Slashes down my arms, along the edges of veins, opening them up like a gift to the infinite. Neck hung and bones broken. Suffocating in a plastic bag, lighting myself on fire and embracing the end of everything. Death, yes, that was a cure to silence. Death.

I carried the sound of the devil within me, like an atom bomb in my bones.

No. Wait. I tried to ground myself, but it was no good. Simon came over and snapped his fingers in front of my face, but my vision wavered and I felt my smile so big it hurt my lips, it hurt my cheek, it was pain, that smile was all pain.

And then, shit. No. Fight it.

I tried to close my eyes, to picture the *snap* in my skull. To push out those images like Angelique taught us. But this time was different, wasn't it? I practically begged the images to come into my mind. My eyes refused to close. My mind refused to snap. It wanted it, all of it, to get out of this, to finally be free. Angelique was wrong and rotten and . . .

I grabbed the candles, scooping them up in my arms and placed my face against their flames.

3

I screamed and kicked as the three of them pushed me back down.
I wanted the fire to kiss my eyes and suffocate my sight with pain.
I wanted to push the melted wax down my throat and choke on it,
spitting out the wicks and burning up from the inside out. How
beautiful it would be, and it would be
all for
Angelique
all for
Angelique
Fucking hell, no, there was no escape from her, not even now. I
remember weeping, crying, no longer fighting back. I curled up and
said *no no no*, even my death would be connected to her, wouldn't it?
It would. I was fetal then, and cried out in anguish, and pushed them
away. But they wouldn't let me do it, and they just held me there,
pushing my hands down, so I wouldn't hurt myself. And in my head
I heard a voice whispering . . .

*I know. It's terrifying, isn't it? Knowing her, being with her, being
without her. Even without the sound of the devil it gets hard, and I've
wanted to do this very same thing so many times. Trust me.*

I glanced at Jones, his voice in my head, shy eyes meeting. Intense.
I felt something stir in the dark edges of my heart, and somehow
knew that he wasn't lying to me.

*But for now, we need you here. I need you here. This world needs
you here.*

And I nodded, and closed my eyes, and heard the snapping in
my thoughts. I pictured my fingers, pictured their muscles moving,
and heard the chiming as it struck against my thumb. The snap was
loud, bright, and scattered away those suicide images from my head.
I could exhale, oh, god, it felt so good to exhale.

*There you go, just like that. Perfect. Okay. Now think of us holding
you, focus on how it feels, all right? Our touch, skin on skin, the warm
stink of bodies in this chill autumn air. Use our bodies to anchor yourself in reality.*

And I did. Oh god I did. I exhaled a few more times, and then laughed. "Okay, you guys can move away now, I'm good, I promise."

Simon looked at me, and then looked at Petal and Jones. A nervous glance back and forth, and then Jones said, "I think she'll be all right now, don't you?"

Petal shrugged and let go of my body. "That's up to her, isn't that? And she said she's good, so she's good."

Simon moved his hands back, shaking with the movement like he was either cold or terrified. "You promise?"

"I do."

"Oh, oh okay. Okay. I don't know. My mother promised, too, and she's . . ."

And then came that horrible guilty feeling when I saw how distressed he was, and knew that somehow I'd brought back a long-hidden memory he'd tried so hard to forget. "I'm sorry," I said, and I meant it. I leaned over, held him for a moment, and said it again and again and again. *I'm sorry, I'm sorry, I'm sorry.*

"No, I'm the one who's sorry. She killed herself so long ago, I really should be over it by now, shouldn't I? And yet. I don't know. I don't think I'll ever get over this. I was about four or five, and I remember waking up and then I got ready for my first day of kindergarten. I remember going in the living room, so excited for my big day, and hoping that she would have breakfast all ready for me and everything.

"But, no. No. She was on the couch, I remember that, and I remember the awful color of her face. And, and, and that she was covered in vomit. And she wasn't moving anymore. Pills, so many pills, like tiny white maggots spilled out from her lips and crawled through the vomit. Several empty bottles scattered on the floor, I don't even know what she took, I just don't know, I just, oh fuck me. She inhaled once, and then sputtered, and that was it. I didn't even know how to call the police, I just went over and poked her and tried to wake her up. And when she didn't I . . . oh fuck me. I sat in front of the tv and turned it on. And just watched cartoons until the school called to ask why I was so late. After that, I don't remember much, not even the funeral. I mean, I, I remember going, but I can't remember any details. What kind of son forgets his own mother's funeral?"

I wanted to say, *what kind of mom kills herself on her son's first day of school?* But, I held my tongue. I knew that it wouldn't help anything, and what he needed right now was to know I wasn't going to do the same thing. Fucking hell. To carry such trauma with you your whole life, I couldn't even imagine what that's like. Not even now, not even remembering this all these decades later. Could you? Could you imagine what it was like, and really truly feel the same way? Probably not. Not unless you went through something similar.

And so instead, I held him close, and said, "I won't do it again. I promise, I won't."

And I meant it, too. Even though I knew that it would be the only way out now, we were all too knotted up to leave any other way. It was suicide or murder, and that was it. No other choice in the matter. Whenever I remember it, it always left such a sour milk taste in my mouth, and I want to go back in time and just find a way to help that little girl out, you know? That younger version of me, barely twenty, a lamb in the woods moving toward a world filled with wolves. But I can't. I just can't.

Fuck time travel. Just fuck it all to hell and back.

4

I hadn't even realized I'd been asleep until that sound woke us up. You know how that is, right? When you're in that hazy moment when you think you're awake, but no, you're actually out of it, and your body just didn't mention this fact to your brain just yet. And then something happens, and you're like, "oh yeah, that."

The sound? A window clumsily opening on the far end of the main lodge. The sun barely a sigh of red light, as a shadow crawled through the window. I reached over to Jones, who was asleep next to me, and grabbed his arm, and realized he was stiff, every muscle rigid with spasms. His mouth clenched tight, his eyes bugging out in terror. Oh shit, he was frozen again. Simon and Petal stirred awake and stared at the figure sliding through the window, none of us saying anything. We were, to be honest, in shock. Our trauma from the last night in the hospital descended on us in a blanket of terror.

We knew, deep in our heart of hearts that this wasn't the same. Even though our survival instincts were keyed up to the nines. That it was Sofia (look at her! Poor thing. She's been through so much), and not a bunch of serial killers with hooks and razor blades coming to finish the job. We were so groggy, so unsure of anything, and the sound of the devil hummed in a low drone just at the edges of our sleep. I wanted to be rid of that sound, wanted to get the hell away from here, and I understood Petal's need to flee, as I remembered my nightmares, influenced by the sound. I don't even want to think about those dreams now. The House of Sky and Shadow was filled with screams and blood, and I was in the attic crown of the house, splattered in viscera, and my smile . . .

Oh fuck me, my smile.

I wish I hadn't remembered this now, I hadn't thought of those dreams in so long.

Simon coughed, and Petal shot him a look. We stared nervously ahead, hoping that the sound wouldn't spook Sofia and frighten her away. Yes, that's a silly thing to think in retrospect, but at the time she felt like some wild feral animal, living in the woods beyond the campground. The shadow stopped, looked at all of us, and smiled in the new dawn light. I got chills even thinking about it now. That was the same smile I wore in my dream. Exactly the same. The way the teeth looked in her mouth (all wrong, all wrong!), the way her mouth twisted at the edges, full of secrets and madness. Her eyes glimmered under her hair, reflecting the loose light of the room in an eerie way.

"Hello."

We were not expecting that. I thought she might bark, or howl, or run around in a circle? Later, Simon told me he thought she would leap up and attack us in a feral rage. None of us, not even Petal, could have predicted the nonchalant, almost blasé and mundane way she said it. *Hello.* Like she was seeing old friends after a long hiatus. *Hello.* It was absurd, and yet, truly fitting.

"Hi?" Petal said, moving toward her, through the shadows.

"Is Jones okay? He doesn't look okay."

I glanced over at his rigid body and snapped my fingers in front of his face, at the same time *snapping* in the way Angelique showed us. Part of my brain tingled at this, and it felt warm and fuzzy. Jones still didn't move, damnit. I was out of ideas.

"He told us he gets like this and it passes . . ."

Sofia finished moving through the window, almost tumbling out and falling onto the hardwood floor. She landed on her hands, pushing herself upward, lupine, a wolf in the savage dark. That was when we saw her completely, the light glancing off of her ragged clothes, and the trophies she had strung across her neck and wrists. Twine lined with finger bones and eyes and knotted bits of hair and teeth and nails. Later, she would show us the bodies they came from. So many serial killers, *dead.* By her hands. Out in the middle of the forest.

"I didn't know he had night terrors. Is that why you never said hello when I came to visit you, Jonesy? I just thought I might've freaked you out a little," and she laughed, "Hell, I freak myself out a little. Especially that one time I caught myself in the body mirror over in the eastern lodge? Shit. I looked like that one feral wolf girl, you know? Messed up stuff."

"Feral wolf girl?"

"Yeah, the one in France, and they had tried to raise her or something, teach her to speak and act all civilized, all that *Pygmalion* crap."

As she moved forward, Jones began to lighten up and relax a little. His arm muscles first, then his eyes, his jaw, then his shoulders, then his hands. His fist finally unclenched, and revealed bloody half-moons from his fingernails digging in deep. He exhaled and leaned forward, shaking his head. "I will never get used to that, fuck, never ever get used to that."

"You all right now, though?"

And he nodded. "Why are you here now?"

"What you mean to ask is, why don't I just return for good, and live in the camp with everyone else, right?"

"Yeah."

"Because they're here, they've been here waiting at the Jawbone Door, waiting for us to go down there and try and find it. They know who we are, they know why were here, and they were sending spies, fucking spies! I had to stay out there and protect you, all of you, from the Brotherhood of Key and Serpent. Especially Angelique."

We had so many questions, the words tumbling out of our mouths and tripping over our tongues. *What brotherhood? Protect us? Who are they? Why are they waiting down there? How did you protect us?*

Though, I think we all knew the answer to that one. We could see it dangling around her neck like windchimes. "Oh, hush, hush, you little excited children. Hush, hush," and her one good eye flashed green, and I felt a twinge in my heart, like a butterfly flapping its wings, "Sofia is here now, and everything will be all right. They waited for us outside the Jawbone Door, they wanted us to let them in. They said there was something inside, something that spoke to them, something that was theirs alone and no one else's. They talked about a void in the heart of everything, and how we were anomalies. Things that should not be, broken tears in the universe. That was why we have pale shadows, they said, we were Children of the Void."

"So they just said all this to you?"

"Yes. And we said fuck off. The sound of the devil was so strong and bright, it burned us and we had no choice but to listen. Even when we *snapped*, it still came in and we had to do the bidding. I think that brotherhood could sense that we were going to turn full feral right in front of them, and they had this dead-eyed way of look-ing at us, like they saw us as nothingness. Not even an object, just blank empty *nothingness*. Our very existence offended them. Out came the razor blades, the hooks, and the leader, a guy who didn't move from the edge of a tree stump, leaned back and tipped his hat like he was the perfect fucking gentleman and said, *be a good girl scout and let us inside, or else we're . . .*

"He didn't even get to finish that last sentence before we went nuts. We just opened up and let the sound inside of us, and let me tell you how freeing it is, to just surrender to it. It does something to you, yes, I can still feel it inside of me now, floating around in my blood and tainting my thoughts in crimson. It's this raw, peeled part of you that wants to destroy. And it is so good at destroying, yes it is. Let me ask you guys a question . . ."

We all paused and sat for a moment, unsure how we should respond. Water dripped from the leaky roof in the distance, tip, tip, tip, splash. Finally Petal said, "Okay? What's the question?"

"You ever think that this sound of the devil is a good thing?"

Nobody said anything.

"I'm serious, I am. Did you ever let it inside of you, unbidden, have it ride your bones and control every aspect of your being? Oh you did, I can see it in your eyes, no use lying to me. And what happened when you did? Oh, it scared you, I bet it did, and what you did next probably disturbed you and made you sick to your stomach, no doubt. But . . . and this is key, okay? It helped you survive, didn't it?"

We all nervously nodded our heads yes, one right after the other.

"Yeah, of course it did. You would all be dead if it wasn't for the sound of the devil, or the voice of god, or whatever the hell it is. I like to call it my deeper self, you know? It brings out some hidden, shadow version of *you*. And as horrible as that part of you can be? Well, when it comes right down to it, it helps you survive."

"I just wished I could've seen the source of the sound, and know what's doing all this to us. But, no, that wasn't meant to be, not for us, anyway. The minute the sound took us over and started riding us, the world turned into a blur of neon fire and blood and sinew. I still remember that taste, that awful taste of raw viscera in my mouth, and these whirlwind sensations of emotion and pain and sorrow. Two days later, I woke up alone in the woods, my body bruised and bleeding, my left eye gone and a few fingers bitten off. I don't know who did what, I just knew I barely survived, and that those assholes weren't alone in the world, and that their friends were coming soon enough to finish me off.

"I didn't even have time to mourn anyone. It all just sat in my chest like a stone, pressing down on my lungs, a trapped scream, waiting to come out and rip the world apart. I vowed then to keep all of you safe, to patrol the campgrounds every chance I could, hunting those that hunted us."

And then she beamed in a goofy, childish manner. "I've killed close to fifteen of them by hand, all with the help of that *sound*, and the power it gives me. You fear it, but oh, oho, ho, it should fear you, and what you bring to the table when you fully embrace it."

Jones coughed and then stood up, wobbly on his legs. I wondered if being frozen placed a strain on his muscles, but decided that now was not the time to ask. I just leapt up, put one arm around his shoulders, and helped him walk over toward Sofia.

"I can't believe you're okay. I mean, I saw you so many times since then, but I was sure it was a hallucination caused by my sleep paralysis. I just had to know for certain, and here you are, and you're okay. You're okay."

"I wouldn't go that far, hah. I don't necessarily feel okay, but I guess none of us do," she looked us over quickly, and then chuckled. "So. Do you motherfuckers want to see my nest?"

And she beamed a proud child smile at us again, her one eye wild and excited to show us her home away from home.

5

She spider-crawled ahead of us, bounding under stray sunbeams, scattering dust motes and dead leaves. If you squinted just right, you could see where her ad hoc path led, the way the trees were cut, the tall grass pushed down, the underbrush cleared away just enough. It led up this small hill, the incline gradual enough that it wasn't noticeable until it was too late. We all held hands as we walked behind her. Silly, I know, but at that time we needed that. That connection between us, flesh against flesh. We could feel our heartbeats through our palms, gently syncing up together. Even our breathing was in sync at that moment, our thoughts a clatter in our minds.

Jones pointed ahead. There at the crown of the hill. Some of the edges were cut away into cliffs by a stream. The new day sun just along the edges, a halo obscuring our sight. *Do you see it? I see it. Oh I see it, too.* Our thoughts drifting and conversing with each other.

Their thoughts had these echoes and distortion, like hearing someone talk on a really old wax record. Or maybe a loudspeaker system, like they used to have at our school and the voices sounded like they were underwater, or at the far end of a hall. That's how their thoughts sounded in my head. I wish I could show you what I mean, but we're not knotted up like that. Oh. I'm so glad we're not. Do you know what it's like, to be that connected to another person?

And the pain when the connection is severed.

They linger, you know. Up here. They linger and they stick around. I can hear them now, the voices of the dead Final Girls, our last group of survivors, the lovers of Angelique, the daughter of the Dawn Light and the Wormwood Star. Excuse me, just for a moment. I knew it was going to be hard, but I had no idea it was going to be this hard. Just, give me a moment, and then we'll be okay, okay?

Okay. All right.

Anyway, I listened to them, and looked ahead at the crown of light at the top of the hill. Our path was a serpent, a spiral up to the nest that waited for us above. Her nest. Holy shit, her fucking nest. A nest makes it sound so comfy and cozy, and maybe for her it was? But to us, no, no it wasn't. We pictured a bird's next, filled with robin eggs and wicker. This was not like that at all. Oh fuck. You ever heard of the wasp that kills spiders, and builds its nest out of their corpses?

I think you know where I'm going with this. Let's just say, whatever you're picturing in your head right now is nowhere near as brutal (or beautiful) as the sight that lay before us. Body parts crammed into tree branches and tied together with loose vine and stolen bits of rope. Sunlight, red and bright, moving through intestines strewn about. An archway of gristly bones, with the meat half chewed off. Walls made of torsos tied between tree trunks, with a roof of skulls. How many bodies did she have here? It was hard to tell. The sheer number of limbs and torsos were mind boggling. I counted at least thirty, forty corpses, way more than the fifteen she'd said earlier. And there were flies everywhere, like a cloud of decay. The sunlight tinted the color of viscera as it shone through the intestines like stained glass. This was a cathedral of pain. She had killed our killers, one by one by one. Cut them up. And then arranged their bodies, here, in a makeshift rotting house. We could smell it from all the way back there, where we stood, that rot, mixed in with lavender and whatever else she used to try and suffocate the horrible scent, to no avail.

"Don't vomit," she said. She must've seen how green we were. "It will lead them to us. Did Angelique teach you how to *sleep*? It's kind of like pushing, and pulling, but for your senses. If you can, just put your nose to sleep, and keep on going."

Simon leaned over and started retching. "I don't think I can go on."

"Oh, come on, suck it up! I see the shape you guys are in, you can handle a little more death, can't you?"

You going to be okay?

No, no, no. I can't do it.

And so I spoke up. "Simon didn't see everything we saw, nor Petal. If they don't want to go up, maybe it's for the best, and they can stay behind?"

And she looked at me and Jones. "Do you really feel that way?" She sounded so sad, like a child who was told that she wasn't going to go to Disneyland that day after all.

Jones spat on the ground. "Hah, no, I'll come up and take a look. How about you?"

"Um," and they all turned and looked at me. I wanted to see, but I also wanted to stay here. I couldn't put my senses to sleep, and if the smell was worse up there . . . I don't know if I could take it. I was numb to death now, and that left me aching for my older self, the one who hadn't experienced all that *trauma*, and that would feel fear and disgust at the sight of a corpse. How did we get here? How do we get back? I had no idea. I still don't think I'm *back*, even now, even with my kids and my husband all these years later. A part of me died the night we met Angelique on the roof of our dorm. And yet, from that death, something new emerged.

Some part of me is still there in the past, terrified, living out those moments day to day. I guess that's why I called you. Maybe getting this all out there into the open will chase these ghosts away? And then I could just get on with my life and get some sleep and be a normal human being once again. Living that suburban mom family dream. And yes, that is really what I want, I can see that look in your eye. After all I've been through, isn't that what I deserve? Isn't it? Why must I still live on that knife edge of anxiety all these years later. I've suffered enough, we all have. Their ghosts need to be put to rest.

Hell, my ghost needs to be put to rest.

"I'll come up, too. Will you guys be okay here by yourself?"

Petal gave me a dirty look. "No, there is no way in hell you're just leaving me behind again, not after what happened last time. If I'd been there, I'd . . ." and she choked for a moment. "Fuck. Sara Fisher might still be alive if I'd gone with you guys."

I honestly felt that wouldn't be the case, but I didn't say that to her. She'd seen it in my memories, I'd shared it with her during our slumber party nights in the hospital, so she knew. She absolutely knew exactly what happened. But that's how Petal was, she thought she could fight against the numb mediocrity of shock and do the right thing, even if the right thing was a million miles away from any rational thought.

We all turned and looked at Simon. "Shit. Okay. I'll come up, too. But I don't know how to *sleep* or whatever you call it, so if I vomit, I'm sorry. I really am. But I can't just stay here by myself to get murdered, that's unacceptable."

Sofia beamed her childish smile yet again, and bounced on the balls of her feet, swaying back and forth. The trees around her swayed with the breeze, imitating her, and sending dead leaves fluttering around her body. "Oh, this makes me very very happy! You guys, wait until you see it, I'm so proud of what I've done to this place, it's like something out of Swiss Family Robinson. It's so, so, so cool."

And then she ran ahead of us again. "Come on, lazy bones! I have so much to show you."

And as we struggled to follow, I had to hold a finger under my nose. Better to smell the stink and dirt of my own skin from days without a shower, than to smell all that rot. I heard Simon gagging again behind us, but trying, yes poor guy, trying to keep up and not fall behind. Petal had wrapped a kerchief around her face as a make-shift gasmask of sorts, and I wondered if it really filtered out that awful smell or not. Did she have a spare one? I beamed that thought at her, but she didn't seem to notice it, nor care if she did. I only got silence in response, and chuckled a bit to myself. Silence. How very like Petal that was. Silence. Ha.

I grabbed a stick off the ground, used it as a makeshift staff, and followed closely behind. I don't know why I did that in retrospect, it just somehow felt like the right thing to do. Just one of those ideas I couldn't set aside, and had to act on it. I had so many more of those after meeting Angelique, like she woke up some sleeping part of me. Some part of me that had been waiting an entire lifetime before finally meeting her, and uncurling awake inside the cage of my heart. Later, I would see it as a cancer, slowly devouring me piece by piece and leaving only a skeleton of my former self behind.

But at that time, yes, at that time? It felt freeing and powerful, like a stronger, more confident part of myself. The kind that carried a staff, and killed a serial killer with my bare teeth. I remembered the feel of his wind pipe under my tongue and smiled. Maybe Sofia was right. Maybe embracing the sound of the devil was a good thing, a way of truly experiencing reality.

Oh god. What a fool I'd been back then, to so eagerly run towards my own self destruction. I really thought it was freeing, that I hadn't been embracing annihilation, but instead power and freedom from nothingness. But it was a facade. Nothingness was under it all, I just couldn't see that yet.

Fucking nothingness everywhere. And Angelique really led us to believe that somehow, she was the one who would free us from this empty feeling. That together, we could make something out of the void of our lives. It was all hollow, a promise that hid the truth with pleasing shadows. A puppet show on the skin of nothingness, tricking us into seeing something that wasn't even there to begin with.

6

The tour of her nest was probably one of the more surreal things I'd experienced after meeting Angelique, and that said a lot. It was like visiting a housewarming for your best friend's new place, except grim and foul and reeking of rot. The disconnect between her attitude, our blasé expressions, and the actual nature of her nest was dizzying. Even in retrospect I couldn't believe this had actually happened to me at some point in my life. It was all just a rough dream, it had to be, something ragged around the edges where reality poked through.

And yet. I know it wasn't a dream. I have the scars to prove it. Dreams don't scar you, at least not like that.

And this whole time the sound of the devil buzzed gently in the background like a splinter in my mind's eye. Stronger, louder than it was anywhere else I'd ever visited. It was as if the sound knew Sofia, and was friends with her, so it felt comfortable buzzing about. It was hard to think, I was constantly snapping myself out of it, using the tools Angelique had shown us as best as I could. But it was so hard, and I felt those images just on the outside of my thoughts, wandering around, trying to get inside and set me free.

Should I embrace it? I remember looking at Sofia, watching her move about, showing us everything. Here's where she curled up with a good book she'd stolen from the girl scout library. She called it her book nook. here's where she made tea and dinner. She had stolen tea bags, a cast iron tea kettle and several cast iron pans, and a small fire pit filled with the ashes of dead branches. Was she thinking about our deaths right now? Images of murder and cannibalism floating through her mind? Or did embracing the sound help her control it somehow?

Fighting it was giving me a headache. Brutal. Probably the worst migraine I'd ever experienced in my life. The others looked the same, eyes pinched, faces green, fingers against their temples, fighting back the murderous urges. She showed us her *thinking spot,* an outcropping of rock against the sharp edge of the hill and a clearing of trees. *I can see the whole world stretched out below, and where they are, where they coming from, and what they're doing now. They're at the jawbone door again, I can tell. I watched them head down there, and the sound of the devil tells me what's going on right now. Can you hear it chattering to you? Just listen. Listen.*

And I wanted to listen, I did. But I was terrified of what would happen if I let it inside of me. I didn't want to kill Petal, or Jones, or Simon, and I knew, I just knew that it would do that. It would take me over and we would be a whirlwind of fury and then nothing. Death. Our bodies used to line more of her nest.

"Just listen," she said, "Trust me, trust me, just listen. Angelique was wrong about the sound, she just didn't even know it . . ."

And then she paused. And the sound paused. It was all of a sudden, a violent silence descending on everything. For a moment there was no sound at all, not even the buzzing of the flies, nor the crunching of the leaves. Just pure quiet and nothing more, the world holding its breath, waiting. Absolutely terrifying. I thought I would be happy to be rid of the sound of the devil . . . and yet . . .

"This isn't right," she said calmly. "Do you hear that?"

"I don't hear anything."

"Exactly. Nothing."

Simon leaned over and vomited and said, "Oh shit fuck shit, I'm sorry, I need to get out of here. I can taste the void on my tongue, and it tastes of ashen shadows."

"No, stay for a moment. Just stay."

"I can't, this is too much, I really can't . . ."

Petal stooped beneath an intestine, strung under the edges of the roof, pushing it over her head, as goopy blood dripped down, and walked over to Simon. She placed her arm on his shoulders, and brought him in, pressing his body against hers. She gently patted his back, and he sobbed on her shoulder. "It's okay, I promise, it's okay," and then she turned toward Sofia, their eyes meeting, "We should follow the path of silence."

Sofia thought about this for a moment, and then smiled and nodded. "You're absa-fucking-lutely right about that!"

"What? What do you mean . . ."

"The silence cuts a path through the air—can't you feel it? Someone moved the sound of the devil, and I bet if we follow that silence, we can find it. The true burning heart source of it, whatever that may be."

I wasn't sure I wanted to find it, but I knew I couldn't be left alone again. As terrifying as this silence was, being cut off from the others was even worse. I'd never experienced loneliness like that before, and there was no way I was going to ever experience that again. It was a depression darker than suicide, more harrowing than existential despair.

"Okay," I said, swallowing my fear as best as I could. "Okay."

"All right, this humble tour of my nest will have to wait for another time, we have work to do. Let's get going."

Her smile was wider, almost beaming once again, and I got this nauseated sensation that shit was going to get way worse than I'd ever seen it before. Everything inside of me screamed no, turn around, don't do this, just get out of here already! And yet, I ignored that sensation, and followed Sofia as she led us out of her nest, and followed that eerie quiet back down the hill.

"Can any of you sense Angelique?"

Jones shook his head no, "I lost my connection the minute the silence hit us. Fuck. I hope that's not a bad sign."

"Wha, what do you mean?" Poor nervous Simon. It was only going to get worse for him, wasn't it? His very concept of reality slipped underneath him like sand.

"It's probably nothing, never mind. Angelique is a tough cookie, if anyone can survive this stuff, it's going to be her."

"Yeah, she's been doing that since she was twelve and they killed her foster family."

"Antichrists are made of tough stuff."

Petal laughed. It was a bright, unsettling sound. "I don't believe in the devil."

Sofia turned and looked at her. "Maybe it's not the devil like you're thinking about it, maybe it's something else."

And then Sofia held up a finger and said, "Wait, shh, do you hear that?"

Even Petal stopped talking. Up ahead the silence grew louder, like a beating heart of nothingness. It vibrated against our bones, like the bass on a stereo turned way too loud, the emptiness rattling our skeletons. The pits of our stomachs dropped, and I screamed, and my scream was eaten by the silence.

"Down there, look," and we saw a shadow walk through the girl scout camp not too far beneath us. I couldn't tell who they were, but they carried a very small body, about the size of a puppy. Maybe it was a dog, I don't know. It was hard to tell from so far back, we just felt the emptiness against us, pressing our spines in a heavy weight.

And they turned, looked at us, her face revealed in the startling afternoon light. Another witch wind blustered through the trees, the branches like waving arms, celebrating the shadows beneath them, and scattering leaves like rose petals in whirlwinds around their bodies. I knew that face. Oh. I knew her so well. I'd seen her every night in my dreams for so long. The keeper of the House of Sky and Shadow. I never knew her name, but I knew her the minute I saw her. And every part of me tingled in fear, the hairs all over my body standing on end. You weren't supposed to see the things of dreams in real life. That was not how the world worked. That was wrong, so wrong, just all different shadows of wrong.

"Rosemary!" Jones cried out, "Rosemary! Is Angelique okay?"

She had tears on her face. The thing in Rosemary's arms moved about, hiding under swaddling clothes. The eyes were small black stones, glistening. The mouth opened, mewed, sucked on a finger, and I swore I could see the bones under translucent skin, even from all the way up here. I wanted to scream. What was that?

"No, she's not okay! We need to get supplies so nurse Juliana can fix her up, and we need to do it fast. I don't know how much more time she's got."

We didn't need to hear anything else. We all ran down the side of the hill as quickly as possible, almost tripping a few times and tumbling down. Petal stayed behind at the top of the hill, looking down at us. She didn't move, she just stared, and I had no idea if it was in fear or anger or frustration or what. The look on her face seemed to be either blind terror or blind fury, but maybe it was both at the same time? I don't know. Her hands balled up into fists so tight I swore I saw blood dripping down her knuckles. Her jaw clenched, and she bit on her lower lip, her eyes bugged out in rage, and I saw the temples throbbing, and a big vein just pulsating on her forehead.

"Petal!" we called out, "Come on, we're going to need your help!"

She just shook her head no, and said nothing to us. I think I understood where she was coming from, just then. It was all too much, wasn't it? Too much to believe, too much to understand, everything was exploding around us, and nothing made sense at all. And the rare moments you weren't swept up in all of this *stuff*, you could see it for what it was, a cult. The cult of Angelique. None of us would use that word, of course, but that's exactly what it was, and there was no other rational explanation for it. And Petal did not want to be part of a cult.

So she just stood there, and watched us go away.

:episode 5:
The Needle Stitches
Between Her Teeth

1

Where do you think Petal went?

I don't want to think about that, so just . . . shut up.

Yeah, traitorous bitch, I hope we never see her again.

Never ever, that's for sure. I knew she was going to turn tail and run.

You did, did you? How'd you know that.

Oh, come on, she wanted to stay behind, remember? And convinced Simon and the rest of them to stay with her. She's the reason we're all in this mess, because she's a coward.

How's Simon?

I don't know. Last I checked he was still sleepwalking everywhere, and not waking up.

Fuck. We shouldn't have left him behind.

No, no we shouldn't. Petal fucked everything up.

At least we got Sofia back, I guess?

Yes, it's good she's out there protecting us . . . you know those assholes are going to come back, and we can't leave just yet.

How's Angelique?

Recovering.

Shit. Shit, shit, shit. Who's on watch with Sofia tonight?

Lucas and Jones.

Oh, I guess that's all right, then. They'll keep her in check, in case the sound of the devil wakes up and she goes berserk again.

Yeah. I mean, good thing she's protecting us, right?

Until that sound makes her think we're the enemy.

Uh huh. Speaking of . . . what the fuck is up with that.

Shhh. We need to make sure she stays asleep, okay?

I don't know what's worse, when she's awake or when she's asleep . . . this silence just freaks me out.

I know, but at least it doesn't send us into murder rages.

Hah. True, true. But what is she? Is she a premie-baby? That's what she looks like. How can she be alive without one of those warmers, or whatever.

No, not a premie, that's wrong, she looks like . . . she likes like a giant fetus. Like an early-stage fetus, just bigger. Look at those black eyes, the translucent skin...

Oh god, stop it, you're giving me shivers just thinking about it.

And what was she doing down there, under the mountains? Behind the Jawbone Door?

I don't know, okay? I don't fucking know. Angelique said it was her twin sister . . .

How was that even possible? She's in her twenties! Are you telling me that thing is in her twenties?

Oh god, I think I'm going to be sick.

God's not here, ha. Only the silence of his absence.

Fuck, it's just an expression! I can't even look at her.

Why not?

You can? I mean, come on. Look at her! Tell me it doesn't hurt you to see her like that.

It doesn't?

You have no empathy.

Come on, that's not empathy.

What is it then?

I don't know, but I know it's not empathy, fucking hell. Empathy would be you wanting to care for her, and that's what I want to do. I want to make sure nothing ever hurts her, just look at her. So cute and innocent, and so raw and vulnerable to the world.

I . . . I just feel pain in my chest when I look at her, and this feeling like I'm falling, you know? Tumbling through this endless void. Don't you get that feeling when you look in her eyes? Ugh. It makes me want to . . .

What.

I don't know. I don't want to talk about it. Maybe it's some residue from the sound of the devil, even though she's asleep.

If it is, it's just you then.

No, it's not just her, I feel it, too.

Anyone else? No. Good. Maybe it's just you guys and it will pass.

I hope so, I hate feeling like this, it's horrible. Look, I'm going out for a walk, anyone else want to come? No. Okay. I'll visit Angelique, and be back in a bit.

Kay. Right.

Right.

What did you guys see beyond the Jawbone Door?

We didn't even get to go inside . . .

What happened down there?

Rosemary, that's what.

What do you mean?

Don't you remember her? From your dreams.

No?

The keeper of the House of Sky and Shadow.

Oh shit. Was that her?

Yup.

She's scary.

Yeah, she's pretty damned scary in real life, too.

Wow. Fuck. So what happened?

Rosemary happened.

What do you mean?

She claims it's the sound of the devil, but I don't know. I just don't know.

All the rest of them were dead when we came down there and she was covered in all this, I don't know, viscera. Her mouth was awful. I can't explain it. And she was sitting there, right in front of the Jawbone Door, surrounded by the bodies. Some of them were serial killers, and some of them were ours, you know? And she was sitting there so calmly, and in her arms was Angelique's sister, and she was asleep . . .

Asleep?

Yeah, and the silence was everywhere. She must've just fell asleep, right? So it couldn't have been the sound of the devil, it couldn't have been! Her sister *is* the sound.

What happened?

Fuck. Rosemary attacked us, that's what.

What.

She, she walked up to us, and. And. She handed Natasha, that's Angelique's sister, to Cris, and then she looked right at Angelique, right? She just looked right at her and growled and it was the most fucked up sound. That's when shit let loose.

Oh, you don't have to tell us anymore, it's okay, we can talk about it later . . .

Shit, look, I'm sorry I'm crying. It's rough, fuck. You would think I would be used to all of this by now! Aren't we supposed to be numbed to violence? After all we'd seen?

It's different when it's Angelique.

Ha. Yeah, I guess so. I fucking love her so much.

I know, I know. We all do.

Anyway, I need to say this, I have to tell you guys. Just keeping it in my head is the worst thing ever, I keep returning to it over and over again. And I just want to stop, I just need it to stop, so maybe telling you guys will get it to stop, fuck.

Go on, if you need to.

Anyway, anyway, anyway. She growled and then her eyes went white and she leapt, like a wolf or something. She tore into Angelique with her hands and teeth and bashed her head against a rock, over and over again. At first we were all in shock, cause, what the hell? Right? Why, why would Rosemary do this, she's the keeper of the House of Sky and Shadow! She's one of us! Why?

Okay, then what happened?

We tried to subdue her, even Cris. She set the baby on the ground like it was nothing and we all ran forward. I can't remember anything after that. Not until you guys woke us up, and Rosemary was there with you, and she was unscathed, holding Natasha tightly to her chest, so protective. I was going to say something then, but she gave us this chilling look, and placed a finger to her lips. You know? Like this. Shhhhh.

Fucking hell.

Maybe I shouldn't be telling you all this. Maybe it's going to get me killed.

I'm glad you did, she's dangerous . . .

Oh, yeah, but we all are, aren't we?

What?

Dangerous. We're all dangerous.

I guess so.

Shit's going to just get even more dangerous from here on out.

Why do you even say that . . .

Why is Natasha asleep now? What did Rosemary even do? Is she even the one in charge of her body . . .

What do you mean?

Maybe Natasha's not asleep after all. Maybe there is something else going on here, something we can't even see completely. Maybe she's the real antichrist, and she wants to kill her sister, Angelique?

Shit. Come on, get off it, that sounds like conspiracy theory stuff.

I still want to know what's under the earth, you know? What's behind the Jawbone Door. I feel like we're going to get answers if we go down there.

What are you saying.

I'm saying I think we should get a secret party together and go down, and see for ourselves.

No, shit. No. No way I'm going to do that. I don't want to know, I don't want to even see it.

Fine, suit yourself. What about you guys? No?

We're not going to split up again, fuck that. If we'd just left before like Rosemary said . . .

Oh.

Oh?

Oh.

Why did she want us to leave. She took care of the serial killers hunting us, hadn't she?

Yeah, I guess so?

Then why did she want Angelique to leave. And why did she attack Angelique when she came down there? Something else is going on

Oh.

We need to go down there, we need to see for ourselves.

Hell, Cris. You're in no shape to do this, none of us are. We've been so close to death so many times.

So? Fuck death! Fuck her right in the eyeballs! Fuck. It's all around us, look! Look! Don't you see it? Everything is slowly rotting since the day we were born. I'm not afraid of death anymore. I'm afraid of being alive now, and just sick of waiting for it all to get worse. We need to be proactive. We need to do this.

Okay, okay. But you gotta be careful. No mention of this again, not where Rosemary can hear us. Not even to Angelique.

Fine. I guess.

2

Sofia waited for us at the edges of the camp, leaning up against a tree. The moon reflected in her eyes, and she looked like a ghost. Just shadow and eyes, flickering. "Where do you three think you're going?"

We hemmed and hawed, and then said, "We're going to see the Jawbone Door, to maybe get some answers."

She seemed to think on this moment, and then walked out from under the tree and fully into the moonlight. She looked more haggard than even before, with new scars crisscrossing her cheekbones. "All right, then. I'm coming with you."

"But don't you need to be here," we asked, "To protect Angelique?"

"She can protect herself, she's well enough she can *push* now, and that will fuck anyone up. You know it, you've seen what terror that can be, I see it in your eyes. And Natasha is with her, if she wakes up that sound inside of her? Well, I would hate to be on the receiving end of that fury."

She wasn't listening to reason, and I felt like I had to say something. "But what if it's Rosemary who attacks her again?"

"What the fuck are you talking about?"

Cris spoke now, her eyes haunted. "Didn't you hear? Rosemary did that to her, she attacked her. They said it was the sound of the devil that made her go berserk and attack her, and Rosemary refuses to talk about it, won't even admit that's what happens. She just clams up, and then goes to take care of Natasha, nursing her . . ."

"She's acting like a wet nurse?"

"Yeah."

Sofia looked back, toward the light of our campground. "Damn, I can't believe I'm going to say this, I just can't. But, I need to go with you guys, even if that means leaving Angelique in harm's way. I have to know, I have to see what's down there for myself. Do you guys really think there will be answers? Really truly?"

We shrugged. "We hope so."

"What if there are only more questions?"

But none of us wanted to answer that. We just knew that we needed to go down there, and see for ourselves what was going on. At this point our minds were all twisted up and knotted together. I can't explain what that's like to you, because really, looking back? I'm not sure if I understand it all myself. My thoughts no longer felt like my own, there was this other mind inside of my mind, and it spoke in first-person plural. Somehow, it was my thoughts and wasn't at the same time.

I know how that sounds, I do. And I know that this is an absolutely terrible explanation. Let me go about this a different way. You know when you think, *I'm going to raise my right arm,* your arm starts to rise milliseconds before you thought that? Like, it moves before the signal from your brain reaches your arm muscles. How does your arm know how to move? Is it your mind signaling your arm, or is it your arm signaling your mind?

That's sort of what this other voice in my head was like. The one that was both my voice and not. The one that spoke in a chorus of words, and yet my thoughts were a part of that chorus and I honestly thought that I controlled it. That my part of the *we* was the one that mattered. Shit. I know, this isn't making much sense. Maybe this is better . . .

Our thoughts were an ocean, and my thoughts were the wind on the ocean. Was I a wave? Did I cause the waves? What were we at that point? I could remember all these memories that weren't mine, memories I never experienced before. They weren't in first person, I could see all these other people, the other minds inside of me. Part of that ocean, all these waves, and the memories of the waves, all mixing together.

And the worst part? I can't remember who was talking, what was a thought, any of that. In my memories, here and now, I have to struggle to remember if *I said this,* or if *she said this,* or if *we all said this, at the same time.* The last one seems impossible, and maybe it was, I don't know. But in my memories, this was all real and bright and true.

Terrifying. Thrilling. Beautiful. All of this wrapped up into my experience of this moment. When I look back, I feel both anxiety and joy, and I miss it so much. You don't understand just *how lonely* it is for me right now. Most days I'm perfectly fine, and then I'll be watching my little girl, and think *why can't I feel her thoughts, she used to be a part of me. We shared food and flesh and a heartbeat. Why is her mind closed off and locked inside her body?*

And the loneliness will hit, and I'll remember what that was like in the thick of it. I guess it's like withdrawal, but that's not quite right. A loneliness so crushing and physical. I want to scream and cry and try and knot up with the ones I love, to get back into that plural thinking, but they can't, they can't do it. My husband, my kids, they never dreamed of the House of Sky and Shadow.

I'm getting ahead of myself again, and you're probably lost, wondering just what the hell I'm talking about. Don't worry, we'll get there soon, yes, soon. We're almost to the Jawbone Door now, aren't we? Soon, soon. If I tell you this now it won't make any sense to you. I have to go slow, unwind this story in the right order. Consider it a thread in the labyrinth of my mind. I am your spider, unspooling in front of you.

The walk down to the door was a surprisingly uneventful one. We were on edge, worried that some of the killers had stayed behind, unseen and waiting to kill us the minute we stepped into the light. For an October evening the sky was lucidly clear, without a single cloud amongst the stars. And the moon was the bright pregnant sort of moon, plump and full and hanging over heads orange and watching. The forest was eerily silent. No animal sounds, no whisper of the tree branches in the wind. Only our footfalls crunching on dead leaves, and the odd nervous laugh between us. But we didn't speak, we didn't have to. Our thoughts ran around between us, speaking for us.

We were far away from the Great Silence of Natasha now, and yet we felt it there. Hanging damp in the air, like a suffocating blanket. It waited for us, patiently, to wake when we returned.

3

The size of the Jawbone Door was mind-boggling. Here, I thought it would be like a regular house-sized door on the side of the mountain. How silly was I to think that! It was nothing like a door at all. More like a giant, gaping cavernous mouth. Tall enough to fit a semitruck, wide enough to fit five of us arm in arm walking through. The darkness beyond was absolute, the kind of darkness that got under your skin and stained your bones with night. It filled my nightmares afterwards, and I would wake up in cold sweat, my heart racing, remembering that feeling of standing there, enveloped by all that black nothingness.

This was what it must have felt like before the birth of the universe. Before the Big Bang, before stars stretched out and lit the night sky. This utter and complete *emptiness*. Everything I feared was beyond the gaping maw, calling me toward it. I wanted to run. I think we all did, our thoughts knotted together and screaming to just turn around and never look back.

But Sofia wasn't knotted up inside our plural thoughts, so she just walked forward, and was enveloped in the darkness. I screamed, I think, maybe. Maybe I didn't actually scream, maybe I felt like screaming. Maybe it was someone else, maybe it was Cris screaming, I don't know. I remember it echoing around us, and then getting sucked into the silence beyond the Jawbone Door. That same silence of the sleeping Natasha, oppressive, all consuming. Like that darkness. And I think we were crying, but we couldn't remember why. Something about this void, this emptiness, as terrifying as it was . . .

It felt like home. Fuck me. To feel nostalgia for the shadows, what a strange thing. I feel it now, even remembering this moment, see? Goosebumps. You ever hear that song, "On the Nature of Daylight?" Whenever I hear it now, it reminds me of this moment exactly. I don't know why, I can't explain it, but that sorrow, that beauty. Goosebumps, and this yearning to return to the darkness, even though it terrified me deep down to the very bottom of my bones. I wanted to go into the emptiness, and welcome it with open arms.

Fuck. I'm crying, I'm sorry. This part. It just.

I need a moment. Please. Just a moment so I can remember how to breathe again.

All right. All right. I'm good now, all right. I think I need to call my daughter soon, to see how she's doing, to make sure everything's fine with her. It doesn't make much sense, I know that, but these memories make me fear for her life, even though this is all behind us now. Most of them are dead, the threat is gone, we did it. But when I think about that darkness and what lay beyond the jawbone door . . .

It's still there, waiting. We'll never be safe, will we? No. Because this threat isn't physical, it's existential. The very thing that made me change majors was right there, waiting for me. You can't run from emptiness—the void is everywhere. Trust me, it's behind your eyes right now, in your head, it's on the ground, in these walls, glancing at you from the mirror. It's under the skin, crammed beneath your fingernails. Real, true, brutal unforgiving emptiness.

There is no universal consciousness, I saw that in the Jawbone Door. My greatest fear was there, realized. The void was at the heart of everything. And it was home.

And from that darkness Sofia's head re-appeared, lit by that harsh moonlight. It seemed to float, shoulders and neck, her body still hidden in the shadows. "You guys coming or what?"

A gulp and we walked forward, as her head was eaten by shadows once again. And as we followed, we too were eaten by that inky night of the cavern. Strange how the darkness felt alive around us, pulsating, breathing. I wanted to run, but I could not. We held hands now, our own fear getting the best of us, and we clung together like anchors against a sea of living shadow.

Claustrophobic, as we moved further, breath tight in the lungs. Felt like a million hands pushing against us, and with each step, they pressed harder, and harder. This was what it must feel like to do deep sea diving. All the darkness. All the pressure of the living ocean, pushing down on us, undulating against us, breathing quick and difficult, the constriction of our lungs, all boa tight and throbbing.

Can you even see her?

No, no we can't.

Whose thoughts were those? My thoughts? Their thoughts? I . . . I couldn't tell anymore. The voices in my head less distinct, more like an echo of my own voice. Or was my voice an echo of theirs? I couldn't tell, I wanted to be able to tell who I was, who they were, to have separations of body and voice. And yet, at the same time, it was pleasing to be washed up in this hive mind. To not be alone anymore. To be connected.

My childhood had been so lonely.

I wish we'd brought a flashlight.

Or maybe matches? Why didn't we bring matches.

A lantern. I remember there being an old oil lamp in one of the cabins. Probably from the nineteen hundreds or something.

Twentieth-century tech, like record players and reel to reel films!

No, we don't want light here.

Who said that? Later on, Cris would say it was the darkness speaking, and in a way that felt so true it was terrifying, and none of us wanted to believe that. So we pretended that it was a dumb idea, and even though we knew better, made fun of her for it. I know, I know. We shouldn't have done that, but the idea was just too right, it was unsettling.

Our communal thoughts ended after that intrusion, and we walked in the dark, yearning for light, but not speaking about it. Not even thinking about it. Not even imagining the bright halo of a lamp in our mind's eye. Even though it might have comforted us, to even have that image. We ignored the temptation. Somehow, we knew collectively that it would make the darkness mad if it saw what we really wanted. That light. That solace. And not the deep terrifying void around us. Alive. Pushing us further into the mountain. We were deep beyond the Jawbone Door now.

Lucifer was the morning star, the sun at dawn. He was light, and this is light. The thing that shattered the darkness. Maybe Angelique and Natasha are both his daughters? Daughter of the Wormwood Star. What was the Wormwood Star? Another name for the morning star? No, it sounded primal, more alchemical of a name. Daughters of two stars?

And it felt odd to think these thoughts. I didn't believe in the devil, nor god, nor any of that nonsense. So why did I scream *hail Satan*? Why did I praise Angelique and the Daughter of the Wormwood Star? Something wormed itself against my skin, waking me up to something else, something in the darkness. That poem from earlier, the one we all remembered . . .

Why? Why did we remember that?

Come look upon me, rebel angel, the star of morning, and see what gifts I bring to your wasteland. Love me and fear me in great measure, for I am the cancer that eats the heart of this world.

Where did that come from? Why had we all felt such a connection to her, a love for her . . .

And why did her sister, Natasha, terrify us so?

Something more is going on here. And I knew, I knew that once I adjusted to the light, once I saw exactly what lay beyond the Jawbone Door, I would understand. It would all be made clear and true and everything would make sense. Who I was, who she was, who any of us where. Why we had pale shadows, and why the cult of serial killers stalked us.

How wrong I was, oh god, how wrong I was. All that lay behind was more questions and more questions and even more questions. It was that same terror I felt when we studied existentialism, that slippery feeling of reading Sartre, and how identity was a mask, created by actions. And the actual us, the core being of who we were, didn't really exist. It was just a void, covered by a mask, and another mask, and another mask.

And at this point, in this room, beneath the edges of the mountain, I could feel my masks . . . slipping off . . . sliding away.

4

Memories. All tangled together, knotted up as Angelique would say. Which of these was mine? Did it even matter anymore? We all we all we all were one were one were one. A song, rough, beating of the drum in a slow funeral march. I remember, I remember, I remember . . .

Walking through the funeral home, no bodies on the benches. Just emptiness. And a mother's hand in the dark. When we moved the world whispered. The dead was there, asleep in front of us. The casket was still, breathless. This was not my memory. Who was I? No mirrors to be found. Were we all remembering this memory at the same time? Echoes. The face in the casket gray like newspaper, gray like rainwater, still and motionless. If you look closely, you could see the needle stitches between the teeth, keeping the lips sewn shut. I want her to breathe. I don't want her to breathe. Mom's hand is gone, disappeared in the dark. Where did mom go? The corpse smiled, stitches popping out one by one. Was this a nightmare? No. A fly crawled out from behind the lips, and then another, and then another. The buzzing was loud, the world was quiet.

Mommy?

A memory of a child. Here, we are this child. Maybe this is my memory. Maybe this is all of our memories. Maybe we've all experienced death like this, a missing mother, an empty funeral home, and the buzzing of flies.

Another memory, teenagers, running in the sharp night air. October in the Lakehill Amusement Park. The crisp sound of leaves under our feet. Four of us? I think. This place has been closed for so long. And yet, other memories. Memories of the four of us as children. Same age as the coffin memory, running through these same paths. The Ferris wheel is alive and turning bright with neon lights. Laughter that mixed with screams of joy. The scent of onion rings and elephant ears. I feel lost and sad, in this memory within the memory. The four of us climb that rusted out old Ferris wheel, the sound of it creaking beneath our weight, as we reach the apex. The moon crowned the world below. And we sit in that carriage, rocking it back and forth, wishing for it to light back up again, one more time.

Was this my memory? No, it couldn't be. I kiss a boy, and I feel our lips all electric in the night. He holds our hand. Shared memory? Maybe. We remember and we remember the child laughing in the house of mirrors, chasing away the memories of a dead mom and an empty funeral home. This world is haunted by our memories. All of our memories. And we remember that kiss, after returning to the empty amusement park. The place of such childhood joy. His lips tasted like onion rings, and then, I realize with a throb in my heart that we're a boy in this memory too. And we're in love in a secret way that only few understand.

And another memory, this time it really was my memory, I think. It felt like mine. And yet, they all felt like mine now. Was there an end to us? A beginning? We were all connected there in the cave beneath the mountains. All of our minds rooting around, memories merging. What are we now, even? These memories? Imprints on wax? These fingers holding hands and terrified of what lay down below?

Oh. This was how we fought the darkness. By remembering. See? The hands aren't pushing down on us any longer. They're no longer scraping nails against our skin, nor whispering terrifying dreams in our ears. This was it, our memories, merging together, walls against the silence and its wicked influences. My memory, my memory, my memory, was it real? Was it really mine? Did it even matter any longer? It felt real. It felt like mine.

Falling from a top bunk in the middle of the night and my ear feels horrible. I think this was an ear ache and so I rushed into the bathroom and we look in the mirror. We see blood but we don't know what it is, or why we're bleeding. But the ear hurts so much and we wash it, and it feels wrong, somehow. Every touch was fire. Oh god. What have we done? The pain so great. We crawl back up, to the top bunk and almost fall out. Dizzy, all that pain, vertigo. Lay down and scream and beat the walls until dad comes out and turns on the light.

And the minute he sees us he screams and takes us to the hospital. My ear had been sliced in half and they have to sew it on. They hold me down. My dad, five nurses. No anesthetic, it's too close to the skull. Pin him down. The stitches hurt worse. I think. We think. Black out.

When we come to, our ear is Frankensteined onto our heads and it makes us happy. We always wanted to be a monster. And here we are, monstrous.

And now, childbirth? Pain, no. Too much blood, something's wrong. We're too young, where are we? Back of an ambulance, rushing through the woods toward civilization. How did we get out here? We were back at that haunted amusement park? Whose memory was this, it couldn't be mine, it couldn't, and yet, and yet, it felt so much a part of me. Each fiber of pain, connected back to that ear, to falling off the Ferris wheel after the kiss, being shoved into the air by jealous friends. That time a car stopped on the side of the road and the kid got out with a blackjack in hand and a fierce grin on his face. Remember what he said? Remember? *How do you like this Dukes of Hazzard shit we got going on right now. Going to fuck you up. Stay back, all of you, this is just between me and him and a few broken bones. This will teach you to stop looking at me like that, you hear? I don't like your stare. It's not right, staring at me like that. This will teach you all right, teach you to keep your eyes to yourself, pretty boy. Going to fuck up that pretty boy face something good. Smash in the cheekbones.*

All tied together, these memories, the pain bridging the moments between us. The baby? Stillborn. So small and tiny, like a pebble in the hands. It looked just like Natasha and there is a scream that rips the world apart. Are we screaming? Maybe. Maybe not. All that pain and it's hard not to scream.

This shared sorrow moves us. It melds us together. It strengthens our bonds against the terrifying dark. We are a wall. What was this? This thing surrounding us? It was alive. Emptiness alive. Sentient, trying to get inside of us. What did it want with us? It tried to lay secrets of destruction. But now we fought it. Fought it with our pain. With our sorrow. With our bright melancholy terror. This was more powerful than *snapping*. There was a music to it, soft and broken. A music box song, tinkle, tinkle. Another memory, a willow tree, outside of the house on a dead-end street. And the house all bright and blue, outlined by a halo of morning light.

The real deal. Yes. The House of Sky and Shadow. It was a real place. Memories don't lie, not these memories, we gasped as we moved further in the dark. The memory tickled some deep part of us, struggling to bob up on the surface of our thoughts. The house is out there, the house is real. It calls to us, and helps protect us. What does it want from us?

Everything. It wants everything. Was the house alive like this darkness? *Yes. But not at the same time. It was alive in the way a ghost was alive, or a memory without a person to remember it. Floating, free. It was a concept, a shadow of an idea.*

But it must be real, it must be. We all saw it here, in our shared memories. We all dreamed it every night.

It's on fire now. Remember, remember. It was always on fire.

And the darkness hid away from us, clung to the edges of the wall. Amber lights flickered up ahead like giant fireflies. Lamps the size of a fist, ten or eleven, dangling up ahead. We didn't know what it was until we got closer, and closer, and closer, and it was too late. The silence was replaced with a deep thrumming hum, a drone not unlike the sound of the devil, and yet still different. In tone, in texture, in the way it made us nauseated and vertigo sick.

Oh fuck. Fuck me. Fuck all of us. What was that up ahead? What what what . . .

This should not be. This could not be. We had to turn around. We could not turn around. The darkness waited, hungry behind us.

Oh fuck. Fuck me. Fuck.

5

Let me just say this: the darkness was terrified of the tree.

Our memories hadn't sent it back. The Tree of Flesh and Bone had. And oh, we understood the terror of the tree. Understood it so well. We felt it the minute we laid eyes on it. Knees weak and muscles trembling. I think, maybe, Jones vomited? I'm not sure. That doesn't sound like something Jones *would do*, and yet? I'm pretty sure he did.

The room was cathedral tall, and filled with an undulating, howling mass of flesh, poured into the shape of a tree. Taller than oak, sturdier. It looked cancerous. Or like cancer. My skin crawls just thinking about it even now, all these years later. How do I even describe something like that? I wish I could draw it for you. I wish I could just rip this image out of my mind, and hand it to you, forever to keep. A physical memory just for you, no longer inside of my head. I don't, I don't want it in my head any longer. I don't.

Maybe, maybe finding the right words would purge this image from my mind. As a journalist, don't you find that to be the truth? When I was in prison, and haunted by all this, I found that by writing it down, trapping it in words, it would leave me be. I would no longer be haunted by such things. I was never able to do it for the Tree of Flesh and Bone—it kept squirming out of my mind, unable to be pinned down in a coherent description, so it haunts me still. I dream about it while I'm awake, you know? I will be sitting here, thinking normal thoughts, and it will appear, just outside of my vision, waiting. Like something that crawled out of a nightmare.

Okay, here we go, let me try this yet again. This is the final act of magic, right? To get all of this shit out of my head once and for all, so I can just be a mother and that's it. Lead that happy fucking suburban life we were all promised as children. Don't I deserve that? Why must I suffer still.

Oh fuck me. I can still taste warm flesh on my lips, feel the sensation of skin under teeth ripping in chunks. It doesn't pull off easily, you know? You have to really bite down and give it your all. Shit.

Why am I remembering this now? Not yet, not yet, not yet. We were talking about the tree.

The light was all wrong. Yes, let's start with that. The light was all wrong, it was the wrong color, the wrong shape, and cast the wrong sort of shadows. The light made things look still that were moving, and made still objects move with a strange life of their own. Amber, flickering, strobe candle light casting. We were all made unreal. Our masks of self untethered, floated away. We were connected to this tree, all of us, and shared its shapeless memories. All except for Sofia. See her there? Unknotted. Unconnected. Something broke her away from us a long time ago. *Outsider.* Did she even love Angelique like we loved Angelique? Even the tree loved Angelique. Loved her and Natasha both. Loved all of us, like children born from the ooze of its memories.

Maybe that was just an excuse for what happened. I don't know. I wish. I wish I'd left a long time ago. I wish I'd never seen Angelique, never met her on that rooftop. But I also knew, oh shit, I know this even now, don't I? The tree revealed this to us, showed us the horrible truth. No matter what, no matter how our lives bent and twisted, we would have found our way to Angelique, to Natasha, to this tree. It was not destiny, per se. But instead, yes. Out truth. Our will. The self beneath the mask. Not a void, no, but instead this. This. This.

We were nothing but fruit from the Tree of Flesh and Bone.

A tree in the shape of bodies, moving, human, some skinned, some fleshy, muscles tight and ecstatic. All interconnected, like knots and burls and roots and limbs and branches. Weeping willow arms dangled down, and along the edges of the branches grew umbilical fruit. Fist-sized, lanterns in the dark, with the flickering glow coming from their bioluminescent hearts. Fetal. Fetus. Curled up in a membrane, a fruit womb, their tiny black stone eyes staring out into the shadows beyond their glow. An intelligence there, ancient. Those thoughts in our head, those memories, images, of a million lives and stars and ships on ancient seas and suns exploding, and seeds in the soil, what were these doing here, in our minds? What were these things in the wombfruit of the flesh tree?

Our flesh tree. Ours. A connection. A memory. *We fed on you, lips in the darkness, breathing like fish and feasting on your protean yolk.* No. Fuck. No, this was not my memory, it couldn't be. It had to be *their* memories, in the wombfruit of the tree. Not mine, not ours, just . . . theirs. It had to be.

They look like Natasha, don't they?

Cris, yes. I think that was her thought in my head? Maybe. It was still so hard to tell. All knotted up. Maybe it was my thought. I don't know.

Yes. Or maybe Natasha looks like them?

There were a few empty wombs on the branches, about ten or twenty from the looks of it, like husks. No light, dripping their juices like soft acid rain on the ground. Pitterpat, in the dim light of the cavernous dark. The tree shivered in recognition, seeing us, feeling us there. Memories shared again, and they were horrible. I think I forgot most of them. You know how the mind does that, right? It can't remember pain. It remembers being in pain, but the actual memory of the pain? The mind thankfully forgets. Here, all those memories the tree shared with us, I thankfully forgot. The tree, that tree, was evil. Maybe we were, too, if that was where we came from. I couldn't, no, I couldn't face that. It couldn't be right, it wasn't real. My mom and my dad were my mom and my dad, I wasn't like Natasha at all, I was me, and I was real. And yet, we were connected, no doubt. All of us. Except Sofia. We saw it, so bright and clear there. She never had a pale shadow, hers was always black or grey, but never the pale red ours were. Her thoughts? Never connected with ours.

I did not blame her for what she did next. None of us did. But we couldn't let it stand.

Knife in hand, she moved feral and fast, primal sounds spilling out of her mouth. Barbaric yawp, as she tore and ripped and pulled out tendons. The fruit screamed in pain as she cut them down, knocked them from their branches, and dug deep into the marrow of the tree. How could a tree bleed like that? Blood red and thick, human in the cavernous dark. At first we were all in shock, the pain in our heads a hammer, we felt so sharp and clear, it blurred all of our thoughts together. We felt what the tree felt, shivered and cried out. Would we die when the tree died?

It was Cris who *snapped* first. A snap so loud it shattered the pain away and returned us to clear, methodical thoughts, rushing in all at once. Everything tangled up, I'm not sure who was the first to think it? Maybe we all thought it at once? Or maybe the tree put this thought into our heads, I don't know. All I know is that we had to act, we must stop this from happening, Sofia was not one of us.

We must feed her to the tree.

As if on cue, a wound opened in the trunk, a sideways horizontal slit of skin peeling back in a smile at first, and then opening more and more. Now a gaping maw, pink and fleshy insides squirming beyond the lips of the wound. Hungry, feed me, feed the tree. All the fruit smashed on the floor, their lights dimmed out to darkness. Only the spare few wombs on the branches remained, scattering their umbilical lights across the cave. The shadows looked so wrong. Made us monstrous in their halo glow. And yes, we were monstrous then. Maybe it revealed the truth of ourselves to ourselves, and we were too blind with need to really see it.

The need to feed the tree.

Overpowering. How can I even justify what we did next? And yet, we did it. Fuck. We did it and there was no going back after this moment. I'm not sure why, but somehow this memory was one of the ones that hurt the most to remember. We'd killed before, yes, and we'll kill again, you know that already.

And so we moved in the dark, our pale shadows stretched and shivering. Our eyes felt different, somehow. I wonder how they looked, to see them as Sofia must have seen them. Glinting white opaque, without a trace of pupil or iris. How horrific we must have seen to her. Oh, and bless her brave soul, she stood without fear. She did not scream, did not quiver, she turned and looked at us and smiled. "Fuck you," she said, "How can you see this and not want to kill it?"

But we didn't speak. We only growled and moved and tore her apart with our bare hands, like a bunch of maenads worshiping Bacchus. We shoved the parts of her into the tree, our body covered with the slick of her gore. Cram, cram, cram, making sure it could all fit. She never screamed even once. A few times she laughed, and then moaned in pain. And then? Was silent after we removed her vocal cords.

I know. I'm shivering. I'm sorry. I just. Fuck. To revisit that, to remember it. So numb and fleeting. It's . . . I don't know. It's a bunch of images now, in my head, you know? I'm not explaining it right. I don't remember exactly what it was like in that moment, I can't remember my thoughts, our thoughts, any thoughts at all. I can't even remember the physical sensations? Right? I just remember these still images in my mind, of the horror of what we did.

Poor Sofia. She said *thank you* at one point. As if she was so sick of being alive in this world, and just wanted it to be over with already. Or maybe I'm not remembering that right. maybe she didn't say thank you at all, maybe she yelled at us, called us names? I don't know. I just know this memory, this fractured, broken-up memory. It's not from my point of view, if that makes sense. I remember this in third person, from outside of my body, floating. A camera that recorded, but did not participate. I guess that was a form of self-preservation. Else, I don't know. I would have to face the brutal reality of what we'd done.

The tree's mouth closed with a wet slurp, returning to a thick scar across the undulating trunk. Already, it started to bud along the branches, their lights like tiny stars. Constellations of new weird wombfruit. We stood around for a moment or two afterwards, unable to speak. The slow-moving realization of what we did, dawning on us, the horror. Skin crawled, unable to read each other's thoughts.

Jones spoke first, solemnly, "We have to go back now."

Cris nodded, followed up with, "Oh god, what if Anglique's not okay?"

A dawning realization of everything we'd done. We'd left her vulnerable. Natasha vulnerable. The whole camp. Sofia'd been protecting everyone, and now . . . now. Now we were covered in her blood and . . . and. Oh fucking hell. She'd wanted to see what was down here, what started it all, and she couldn't handle the truth of it. And we couldn't handle her reaction, and now we couldn't handle our own reaction. I think I dry heaved. I remember the bitter taste of bile on my throat. The ache and burning pain.

And then the realization that we would have to brave the darkness beyond. That there would be no tree to save us, once we were out of the safety of its light. Something inside of me broke and screamed and I wanted to be us again, a we again, I felt so alone inside of my head, and I had to face the reality of what we'd just done, and it spun around over and over again. I didn't want to leave. But we couldn't stay here. We had to go on. Through the darkness. Back to Angelique and hope against hope that she was okay.

"Can you feel her thoughts? Any of you? Do you know if she's okay? Any of you?"

And nobody said anything. The silence inside was too great to take.

6

The camp was on fire. There was no time to be numb, no time to worry about what the darkness took from us, the second time we walked through it. No, none of that mattered once we hit the light and saw the fires on the hill. Burning, blazing, the crisp autumn leaves kindling. The trees swaying, their branches alight with light. The camp. Was. On Fire.

Was Angelique okay? Was Natasha? Was everyone dead? In the panic of the moment, we knotted up again, even though our threads felt weaker than before. As if they'd frayed along the edges. I'm not sure if it was from the darkness, or from the tree, or from the murder of Sofia, I just don't know. But the connection of our minds was weaker now, spotty and staticky, like an old announcement system at an elementary school. *Can you feel them, are they alive?*

Yes, I think so. Though, I feel . . .

Danger. We feel danger.

Yes, we feel it, strong sense of danger . . .

Do you know who survived?

We don't, we can't . . .

Natasha is missing.

Dead?

Missing.

Dead.

Missing.

Angelique?

Terrified.

But alive?

We hope so. If not, these are ghost thoughts.

Can a ghost even think?

No. Maybe. I don't know.

That doesn't matter, that's not the point. The point is, she can think. So something is still there to save.

We rushed up that last half a mile, the blaze so hot, unbearably so. Closer and closer, it was an oven against our skin. I felt the soft hairs on my arm singeing, and the smell of it all was overwhelming. The harsh black smoke of burning leaves, that sticky sweet scent of wood burning, tainted with the crunch of building collapse and the chalk of concrete dust. For a moment we were in two places at once, all the fires we had seen in our lives. Our campus on fire, that crashed plane downtown in Dark Rivers, all of it mixing and combining.

I trembled as I ran. I wanted to turn around, to run away, and never stop running, not until I met the edge of the world and jumped off, into sweet oblivion. But I knew there was no edge of the world. Not behind us. There was only the Jawbone Door, waiting at the foot of the mountains, and the darkness that lay beyond. The darkness did not take much from us, just enough that it left a tiny hole inside. And knowing that it could take more, knowing what lay beyond the darkness, that kept us going.

I felt the frayed knots of our communal mind strengthening in the panic. So hot, fuck, how would we even get out of here? No, don't think about that yet. One thing at a time. The trees collapse, and there, look at all the scattered bodies. But they hadn't been killed by the fire, had they? No. Faceless corpses. Skulls like masks. But no, they were the opposite of masks, weren't they? The faces were peeled off, the skull the real thing beneath the surface. The bone nude in the dim blaze of the firelight. The skin was the mask. I felt my own face as we ran, felt the mask I wore and wanted to rip it off.

Was that what happened here? No. I saw tall burly men, one like a bear, pulling the bodies into the flames. Some of them were on fire themselves, and they didn't seem to care at all. If we looked at their palms, would we see keyhole tattoos? Of course we would, who else would it be? Those fucking cult of serial killers.

The Brotherhood of Key and Serpent.

Sofia had been keeping us safe, but the moment we fed her to the tree, we sealed our fate. It was as if they knew we'd be vulnerable and came, thunder with fire in their fists. Were they knotted up with us somehow? Connected with the same tissue of thoughts that connected us? Oh fuck. I didn't even want to ponder that.

Some of the bodies moved, crawled toward us, and we rushed now, faster, faster. Jones screamed, "Hey motherfuckers, stop it! What the hell is wrong with you assholes, what did we ever do to you?"

They didn't say anything, they were too busy at work to hear us. And one of the crawling, still alive bodies? That was Rosemary. Her face had cuts along the edges, but not fully removed yet. And over there, Juliana, see her? She was bruised but not even close to dead yet. Standing up now, weakly fighting off her attacker. The killers wore gasmasks. Was that why the smoke wasn't affecting them like it was affecting us? And oh fuck. I coughed. I'd just gotten over all this smoke inhalation shit, I really did not want to go through *that* all over again. Goddammit.

Can anyone see Angelique?

And we looked around at the bodies, and couldn't tell. Blur of haze and smoke wafted through, black fog turned us all into shadows. Was that her cane shattered over there? Near that tree? Or was that a tree branch?

There, look! There she is.

And oh fuck, even thinking about this now, I get goosebumps. See? Look at my arm, fucking goosebumps. It's not easy reliving all this for you, you know? It's strange—in a way I feel like I'm right back there with each memory I uncover. Some of them I haven't thought about in years, while others I returned to over and over again, the memories sharp enough to cut. In some ways I regress as I tell this to you, and it's just so weird, to feel like a young twenty-something once again. Those ages peel away, and I have to remind myself that I have grown-ass children now. That this heart requires medication to keep on pumping, and that I have to measure my meals in calories and sugar content. That I am not that person anymore, that the roots of me were there, but not the real me, fully grown.

Angelique was there, and she floated in the air. Elemental, the fire moving out of her way. Parting of the seas of light. Her eyes a reflection of the flames, crackle snap, her hair floating around her body, like she was drowning under water. None of the brotherhood seemed to notice her? Maybe it was the heat, obscuring, I don't know. I recognized one of the cult members from the hospital, the weird creepy one with the curly mustache, and I thought he was dead? Was he undead now? Zombie serial killer? What the hell, none of this felt real anymore, and none of it was making any sense.

The House of Sky and Shadow is always on fire.

So were we, it seemed.

And that curly mustached asshole ran up to Rosemary, but didn't start pulling her, no. He held her down with his foot on her chest and pulled out a scalpel, watch it glint in the light. He was going to finish the job.

NO!

We all screamed and ran up the hill, but the air was sludge and we coughed and time dilated, slowed to a crawl. It would take forever for us to get there. He pushed the blade against her face, started cutting again. When Angelique turned and looked at him with the dead eyes of the fire. "Return to the void," her voice a harsh whisper, her throat burnt raw from smoke.

And with a loud pop he turned inside out, and collapsed on top of Rosemary, who pushed him off, her movements filled with the ragged strength of adrenaline. I felt her cry out in our minds, *they took Natasha! They stole her from us while were busy putting out fires.* And her voice was so sad, so grief-stricken. An echo, the mother's corpse, protecting her daughter on the news that terrible day when this all started.

Angelique then turned and looked at Juliana, now against a tree, coughing, fighting off the killer in the gasmask. And once again, Angelique smiled and spoke, "Return to the void."

Pop. Another inside out corpse twitching on the ground.

Could she stop the fires, too? Was she that powerful?

No, the fires bowed before her, but did not stop. She turned her gaze onto the other shadows moving in the dark. Those burly bear men. And she coughed and pointed, and they fell as well. Was this the *push* she kept talking about? Or was this power something else, something far darker? I remembered the Tree of Flesh and Bone in that moment, another echo of a memory tied up and mixed together with this one. The fetal lights, the wombfruits angling down, swaying. Had Natasha been inside the fruit, just like that? Had Rosemary pulled her down, opened it up and pulled her free? Cleaning her off and feeding her with her own milk? Was that where Angelique came from as well?

And, and, and . . . were we the same as they? The ones murdered by Sofia under the earth?

Oh fuck. I hope not. Fuck, fuck, fuck. I really hope not.

Angelique whispered, "We must go find Natasha. Now. before they get too far away. They stole her from us, and she . . . she is part of our purpose. Can't you feel it? She is the why of our existence. Why Lucifer sent me here, sent us here, planted that tree in the ground. We are all connected, silver threads in the dark. We must find her and save her from the brotherhood . . ."

And then she collapsed and we ran forward, helping her up, helping Juliana up. We didn't have much time. Weak from smoke, weak from fire, weak from all our wounds and the terrors of the day. We had to get the fuck out of there and hope against hoped we didn't leave anyone to die.

:episode 6:
A Chorus in Our Bones

1

I am so fucking sick and tired and just done with truck stops.

Truck stops and campgrounds! Fuck them.

What, princess, you want a motel room?

Not one of the ones we can afford, no thank you.

Yeah, I hate truck stops, but I hate those murder motels even more.

That one, you know it had bedbugs. All those tiny brown dried-up blood spots on the edges of the sheets.

Either that, or fleas.

Fleas, ticks, bedbugs, ugh.

Fuck. I can't stand this anymore. We need to get something better.

Like what?

I don't know. Let's see if Angelique will let us get one of those campers.

Campers?

Yeah, over there? See? Those vanlife weirdos.

What are you going to do? Buy one from one of them? With what money!

No, no, no. We're going to use some of the tricks Angelique taught us.

What, you going to push them a little?

Naw, pull them a little. A push would just make things worse, you know? But if we pull them a bit, and then a bit more, reel them in like a fish on the line . . .

I see, make them see what we want to see.

Yeah, that it's in their best interest that they just give us the camper.

Ha. How many you think can fit in that thing? It's small.

I dunno. I mean, it's got those two, but I bet we could cram four of us in the back.

What, and one of us across the front seat?

Maybe. Can't see the front from here, don't know if that's possible?

So then, what, four in the back, two outside on the dirt?

Maybe we can pull straws or something, cycle it on and off.

Come on, get off it, we're not going to do that.

Why not?

We're just not! You think Angelique would be okay with that?

Hell yes, if it will get us closer to Natasha!

Yeah, I guess, I guess. Do you think Simon is right?

I dunno. He's so fucking weird now, after that last one . . .

Yeah. Really fucking weird, but that's good, right? If he's our oracle. Oracles are fucking weird.

I guess, yeah.

Oracle. What the fuck. A human GPS is what he is.

Still, do you believe him? Do you think he's actually got a connection to them and can see them? Natasha and all that.

I do.

Why?

Because Angelique does, and she knows more about this occult shit than we ever will.

Yeah. She was raised in it, right?

Right. Fuck. I don't pity her for that, you know? The powers are cool, but what her foster family did . . .

I don't even know if that's the right word for them.

What do you mean?

They're not her foster family, they're kidnappers. They just took her, and went off the grid and raised her in the shadows, until the brotherhood came and killed them.

Kidnappers. Like us?

No, like you, Rosemary. You're the one who took Natasha.

Good thing I did, I saw what happened with Sofia.

Shit. Don't remind me, you weren't there.

I saw, though. We all saw.

So you think what you did was okay?

Yeah, I do! We had a connection, in a way I don't think you guys would understand.

I bet Angelique's foster parents thought the exact same thing.

Maybe they were right.

What? Kidnapping her? Putting her through all that stuff in her childhood?

I dunno, she survived, right? They helped her live.

And they saw her for who she was, and taught her how to use her powers.

You really think she's the antichrist, Cris? Still? After what we all saw beneath the Jawbone Door?

Hell yes! Hail Satan! You're telling me that's all natural and organic and how babies are made?

It wasn't supernatural though, was it?

If not, well. What was it? I mean, there is definitely no natural explanation for that . . .

Guys, guys, guys. I don't like talking about this, that tree, it just . . .

It's where we came from, it's who we are. Angelique's caretakers knew that when they took her in, and gave her the tools to survive out there.

Like she's doing to us.

Yes.

Which is precisely why we need to get that camper van, she deserves the comfort of living the van life. We owe her at least that.

Fuck. Okay, yes, what if I agree with you and say you're right, can we stop talking about the tree?

Why? What's so wrong about . . .

It makes me feel weird, the whole thing. That's not where we came from, it can't be . . .

All right, all right.

So we're going to get us a camper van and get the hell out of this place.

Yup.

You realize that won't solve our campground problem, right?

Yeah, but we'll be camping in style now. Not on the dirt like a bunch of peasants.

And just because it's a *camper* van doesn't mean we have to limit ourselves to *camp* grounds, duh. You're being too literal, we can go anywhere in that thing, sleep anywhere in that thing. The world is our oyster! Parking lots! Seaside boardwalks! On the side of the fucking street!

Aren't there like, laws against that?

Fuck the laws. We've killed and we'll kill again, laws mean nothing to us.

Yes! Fuck the laws! Hail Satan!

Hail Satan, and hail Natasha! Daughter of the Wormwood star!

Maybe we're all children of the Wormwood star.

What does that even mean . . .

I don't know. But it feels right, you know?

Oh fuck me, it does, doesn't it?

Yeah, it does. I had this weird dream last night, there was this guy standing outside the House of Sky and Shadow, right?

Oh yeah, the man in the white suit!

You dreamt of him too?

Yeah.

What about the rest of you?

Me.

Me too!

What? No. You guys are weird.

Ah, I see, just the three of us. Well, he told me that we were all the Children of the Wormwood Star. And together, we were more powerful than anything else. Even Angelique.

Oh that's bullshit. Your dream is such bullshit.

It is not! It's true. Trust me, he's going to visit you too, I promise.

All right, enough with the casual evil, let's get down to business. How are we going to get us that camper van? We going to act as one, use our knot to choke them with a good spell?

Are we sure we want that one?

Sure, we're sure.

It's cute!

All right, then. What if the knot isn't enough? Should we get Angelique in on this?

No, she's been through enough, let her rest a little longer.

Yeah, let's surprise her!

Like it's her birthday.

Okay, okay. But what if the knot isn't enough? What if our powers just aren't there yet?

We killed before, we'll kill again.

Hail Satan!

Shit. Okay. I'm not going to say a damn thing that will change your minds, will I?

Nope. The knot has spoken!

All hail the knot!

All right, all right. let's get to work. It'll be dawn soon, and Angelique won't be asleep for much longer.

Agreed. Let's go and fuck this shit up.

2

We'd also stolen a cane from the truck stop, as well as some shitty road food. We still couldn't get anything that needed refrigeration, this camper van barely had some beds in the back, and a hotplate, and that was it. Nothing to keep anything from spoiling, so our options were limited. We laughed about it, but a few days later and all those bags of chips and jerky were making us sick and restless. We needed real food. Angelique never asked us about the camper van. When we showed it to her she smiled, and hugged us, and then said maybe we should shower? Just to get the blood and viscera of the old owners out of our hair and clothes.

Of course, the blood wasn't so easy to get out. Eventually we stopped at a thrift store and walked out with some newish clothes, leaving the blood-stained ones behind. The cashier didn't mind that we did this, and she seemed super happy to help us. Even though her smile felt a bit broken and maybe a little scared? I'm guessing Angelique or one of the other knots did a push or a pull and she went along with it. I hope we didn't get her fired. Maybe we did.

I remember that cashier now, yeah, I remember her. In my mind she resembled a mouse, with her gray cardigan sweater, her tiny mousy teeth sticking out over her lower lips. Her eyes a rough brown color, tinged with sadness. You ever meet someone so lost and lonely that you wanted to just take them in and care for them? To never let the world hurt them ever again? That's how I felt about that little mouse girl, sitting behind the counter, playing video games on her phone. Her eyes said so much. She needed rescuing. She was like us, I knew it, she could be knotted together and be one of us, and we could make sure she was never hurt ever again.

But the knot said no. No. She's not one of us. She was not born of the tree, see? Look at her shadow. It's so normal and boring. Look at her, really look at her, she would weigh us down, and our life would kill her. You know it. We would have to leave her corpse behind—you can see it just as much as we can. You know it's true.

I tried to argue. Mention all the deaths we've had so far. After all, what's one more?

No, they said. No more deaths. Not anymore.

Not when we're like this. For now we are death itself.

I tried to appeal to Angelique, but they took my tongue and twisted it. I don't know if it was a pull or a push or what. But it was something, and it was strong. I tried to snap it, but I couldn't, I couldn't get it to stop. No matter how strongly I snapped in my mind, I had to bend to their will. And I hated it. I just . . .

Hated it. I almost left them at that point, stayed behind to care for that poor girl in the thrift store. Maybe we could have had a great life together, in some small podunk town in the middle of nowhere. Living paycheck to paycheck, drinking cheap rum and Kool-Aid in the evenings, laughing, getting into fights, making up in the morning with a quick kiss and brief sex. How different would my life had been, if I'd just done that. So much simpler.

But I knew that wasn't for me. I had blood on my hands. I'd seen everything I'd seen. As much as I hated to admit it, the coven was my family, and I would stick with them. The loneliness I felt when I was away from them, if even for only a few moments, was far too painful to even contemplate. Even now, the loss of them sickens me, makes me feel pale and feverish. The only way I could combat that feeling was by having kids of my own, a family of my own. If I had known this at that time, I would've stayed behind and started a life with this strange mousy girl, started a new family with her to replace the rotten one I'd left behind. Adopt a few needy kids that needed homes. It would be a hard life, but it would be our life.

Fuck. That wasn't for me, not yet anyway. Not until we had finished and everything was done. Maybe we were just following the will of the Tree of Flesh and Bone? I don't know. Maybe Angelique was the one in charge of us, and we only thought we had these ideas ourselves. Angelique, manipulating us with her push and her pull. Making us act in ways we never would have before. Emboldened by the music of her thoughts.

It was more subtle and intoxicating than the sound of the devil, but just as dangerous. Maybe that's what Natasha would be like when she grew older, got to be about our age. No longer the silence or the sound, but instead a force of raw manipulation, her very thoughts worming their way into people's minds. In moments like that I wondered if we too could have powers as strong as Natasha or Angelique? If we'd learned these magic tricks at a younger age, learned to curb the sound of the devil inside of us, rattling in our bones. After all, we were born of the tree, weren't we? It had to be the case. It only made sense.

And yet. Just thinking about it now, being a womb dangling down from the tree, seeing the world in fetal hues. The tree feeding us sweet umbilical milk. My stomach turns, and I want to scream and cry all at the same time. We were monsters back then, so might as well embrace the monstrous. We had to. It was a necessary sacrifice. I wouldn't have this life now, would I? If I hadn't done this.

I see the way you look at me as I say this. But you weren't there, you didn't know, you couldn't feel that feeling inside of us. Restless, worming, made stronger by the knot, a feedback loop growling in our bones. We had to let it out, in order to move on. There was no future otherwise, was there? It had to end the way it ended. It had to. I could dream about mouse girl futures, and a million what ifs, but it doesn't change what was inside of each of us, and how agitated it got when severed from the knot.

If I didn't see this through, follow the thread to the very end, that worm inside would wake up, and I would violently, ruthlessly, murder that mouse girl. That's the thing. We acted like the sound of the devil was something outside of us, but that wasn't exactly true. It came from our bones and our blood, much like it did with Natasha. Somehow, we'd learned to let it sleep through the years.

And it wouldn't let that happiness last. It never could, not then. Not until we saw this shit through to the end. Fuck.

It hurt me to leave that mouse girl behind, back there with our bloodied clothes, all that evidence of murder. And I think *they* knew it, the other members of our knot. No longer final girls, now the only girls. No longer fleeing death, but death incarnate. And they began to regard me differently, knowing that weak heart called out to someone else, someone outside of our little clique. They started to distrust me, and I felt it, like a pinched nerve in the back of my neck.

I knew, if I was going to keep going (and I was) I was going to have to prove myself to them again. Make sure they understood that I wasn't like Petal. That I wouldn't betray them like that. I still loved

Angelique with every last breath and beat of my heart. I had to make sure the knot understood that, that I would die for her, for them, for all of us.

Otherwise, I knew, that they would turn on me in the end. And I could not have that. Not after everything we've been through together. *Please, please see me as I am. Please, please love me as I loved you. Nothing has changed.*

And yet . . .

In a way, everything had changed.

3

We made a stop at a campground near the edge of Nevada. We'd been on the road forever, and some of us were talking about Simon losing the scent. That maybe Natasha was too far gone. Some even whispered that she was dead, but we knew that wasn't true. We felt it, the roots of her reaching out to us in tendrils of thought. That song of the devil again, wide awake. Had they woken her? I don't know. But somehow, the music had matured. More complex now, no longer a relentless droning of dissonant chords, but instead a weaving of minor scales. There was a sadness mixed up with a suicidal sensation. Thankfully, it was still far away, and its influence was weak, and we could easily snap it away without much thought.

The campground was mostly dry and yellowed with dead grass, the trees blackened and withered up. The branches could be snapped right off, and I swear you could see the beetles moving underneath the bark. Like maggots under the skin of corpse, about ready to burst out. The air was dry, too, and I knew a stray bit of fire, or a spark from heat lightning, and this whole place would be set ablaze. So we weren't going to light a fire tonight, that was decided straightaway.

Angelique had us all sit around her in a circle, once we were able to get up and stretch for a bit. So long cramped up in that car, and even young muscles get sore and achy. The circle was rough, almost an oblong, but it didn't seem to matter. She stood at the center, as her legs wobbled a little bit, the cane keeping her upright. Her head tilted back, and that ragged sun outlined her features, sharp angles like a face on a roman coin. Her hair, pushed back, cascading down her shoulders. And I ached, and that ache ripple through the entire knot. That love now, full on, the heart calling out to her. *Fill us up, Angelique. Give us what we need from you.*

"Simon. Come forward."

And he walked to the center, nervous, his eyes glancing back and forth. We could feel it in the knot, a tension, pulled tight. Anxiety and fear mixed with that love. Angelique never hurt us. Never. And yet. The terror of what she could do ran through us all electrical and sharp, biting at our insides. He audibly gulped, his Adam's apple bobbing up and down. As she pushed the cane into the dirt, digging it in so it stood upright. A tower of steel and plastic, glinting in the bright afternoon light. She leaned in—you could see her balance shifting, her muscles struggling to keep her upright. She radiated a mix of both strength and weakness all at the same time. Strength of will, weakness of muscle. There was a power in that contradiction, a hidden force that could devour worlds.

She placed her hands on either side of his face, and jealousy roamed through us hungry and vapid. She leaned in some more, face to face, nose to nose, forehead to forehead. She kissed him, gentle, on the lips. We all felt it. Something inside stirred. A beast in the heart, serpent and wrapped around the ventricles. Teeth sharp, biting down. *My name is a heart, encircled by a serpent.*

"We are in the center of it all," she whispered, and we all heard it. All of it. "Isn't that so amazing? To be able to be here at the keystone of this world. Imagine, out of all the people born, you were born here, in this place, so close to the center of everything. And you lived a life that led you here, to this moment. This is the meeting place of a million ley lines. Consider it the spiritual highways of the universe, like a spiderweb radiating out from here, this center point. And we are not flies, no, we are spiders. And what do spiders do? They walk the web. They speak to the web. The web is their memory, their voice, their everything. It is like another limb to them, you get me? This is our web, right here. You get me, Simon? You get what I need you to do?"

And he was crying and he nodded and shook his head. I don't know if you understand how beautiful a moment like this could really be, it's hard to put it into words. When you see someone you know, someone you've come to care about great deal, experience such a raw, vulnerable emotion? And you're there to share it with them? There is nothing like it. It touches you, deep down, strengthens that connection. And here was Simon, raw and vulnerable at the center of the universe, in Nevada of all places. And we all felt it, and the knot strengthened again.

And yet . . . my edges were still frayed. The connections not as strong as they used to be, before mouse girl. I still had to figure out a way to prove myself, to gain their trust back again. Even being here, experiencing this profound moment of vulnerability was not enough.

It would have to be something more extreme. A bonding experience of my own, a raw bleeding of my own inner wounds.

"Good," and she kissed his forehead and smiled. "Talk to the web, Simon. Get us where we need go."

"Okay, I, okay. I . . ."

"Use your *pull*, just like how I showed you. But instead of using it on people, use it to pull on the webs, see? Pull, gently, exactly like this, and they will tell you so many things."

"All right, okay, all right . . ."

Simon's head tilted down, as Angelique's head tilted back up. His eyes closed, her eyes wide open. Both of them shadows outlined by that rusted Nevada sun. A hum and we felt something moving again, out of the corner of our eyes. A shadow, closer, darkness, there were clouds in our lungs and I felt like my reflection. Or maybe, I felt like an echo. I felt like something that wasn't me, but instead a copy of me, existing just out on the edges of reality. I was in freefall in this moment, my whole concept of self obliterated, replaced by this aching nothingness. Hollow, like the opposite of the ache of Angelique, which was all about wanting to be filled with something. This was the ache of the empty.

Fear followed. A drowning feeling. Gasp. You ever stay too long underwater, and it hurts to breathe? It felt like that. Lungs constricted, heart sluggish and pounding against the ribs, demanding to be let out. Overwhelming exhausting fear. All from this shadow, looming on the edges of our sight.

"I don't see anything at all, it's, it's just this nothingness, a black hole. Do you feel it? It calls to us . . ."

Angelique smiled and it was a terrible sight. We wanted to run, but we stayed. After all, love could be a terrible thing. "Yes," she said, "That is what we're looking for. We've been going the wrong way because you were too scared to embrace it, but now you need to embrace it. Where is it? Where is this nothingness? Show us the path, Simon. Lead us to Natasha."

"No! No, I can't do that. Don't you see? It's a trap. They want us there, they're going to kill all of us . . ."

"They cannot kill us."

"They have! They've already killed so many of us! This is all just a lure, to get us into one place!"

"Simon, Simon, open your eyes and look at me."

And he did, and we did, a chorus of eyes opening and looking at Angelique. The emptiness and fear slid away. She wasn't outlined by the sun, no. She was the Daughter of the Wormwood Star, the Light-bringer. She was *the* woman clothed in the sun.

"Do you know who Satan is?"

"What?"

"Do you know who Satan is."

"What are you talking about . . ."

"He is my father, he is your father, all of our fathers here. In the beginning there was the void, yes, a void of all things. But Satan showed up, a burning star on the horizon of nothing. He shattered that void with his light, and brought everything into existence. Do you understand? The void is nothing to fear, for we are Satan's children. Do you understand now? All of us here, connected and knotted up, the Children of the Wormwood Star. We are the ones who shatter voids. And they are the ones who fear us, which is why they seek to destroy us, because they have the void inside of them, eating away at their hearts like cancer."

"But, I don't want to die."

"Aw, come on Simon," and Angelique smiled so wide it threatened to crack her face in half. "Dying is nothing at all. Come on," she waved at everyone to come closer, "Tighten up this circle you losers, I've got something we need to talk about."

And then Angelique sat down, squat flat in the dry grass. A crow called out from the bones of a tree behind us, cawing loudly. Others joined in, and landed on trees, surrounding us in a loose circle of their own. She placed the cane on her lap, and then coughed into her hands. "All right, we're going to play a little game, okay? But this is a deadly serious game, and you guys all have to take it really seriously. I've taught you all how powerful it is to really picture something in your head, right? How it can alter reality. This game is like that. I like to say it's playing dead, but it's more than that. You all ready?"

And the knot thrummed in anticipation.

"Close your eyes now, I want you to picture your death. Not just any death, mind you, the worst possible death you could ever imagine. I want you to see this and be terrified. What I usually picture is a car crash, and being pinned underneath the terrible weight of all that crushing metal. Unable to move. Do you see it? Now picture all the senses, all the little details. The smell of raw gas, the metal puncturing your lungs, your legs pinned beneath your body in an impossible position. The glimmer of light on chrome and plastic."

She paused for a moment, giving us each time to pick a death and picture it. I don't want to tell you my own death here and now, though. That's a secret for me and for no one else. Just do what she asked, what we all did, and imagine your own death, too. Can you do that for me? Okay. Now after she let us experience our death, really visualize it in our minds, she continued.

"There. Do you feel your life slipping away? Watch it go, your breath a slow rattle as the shadows encircle your vision, constricting light with dark. Yes. Now, I want you to sit with this for a little bit. Really soak it in. Can you see it? Can you feel it?"

And she smiled.

"Good. Now that you're dead, anything is possible."

After that, Simon did not have any more problems finding the shadow, and taking us to Natasha.

4

Along the way we'd decided to stop at one of the last living malls in America. I don't even know where we were anymore, what state we were in, what city. The landscape was a flat blur of Midwest nothingness and howling winds that shook the car something fierce. I felt even more of the disconnect with the knot, the edges now unwoven, no longer just frayed and shaggy. I could sense their sinister thoughts, moving my way, seeing me as an outsider. So I was relieved when we parked the camper in the mall parking lot, that great concrete monstrosity. Only a few cars lay scattered, the place mostly devoid of life. I could imagine a better day for this place, back in the eighties or nineties, maybe? When malls were the lifeblood of our culture.

We got out of the camper, milled about, shaking the road from our bones. I hadn't showered in so long, and the grit in my hair and under my nails was palpable. It left me with this gross, grungy kind of feeling to it. That hair knotted up and almost in dreadlocks. I dared not look in a mirror, not even my reflection in the glass doors as we walked toward the mall. Some people milled inside, mostly teenagers and college students. People our age. And yet, we felt so much older than they were, it was crazy. We'd seen some shit, that was for certain. And it aged us. Fuck me, it aged us. I swear, by the end of that trip I had a streak of gray in my hair, like a wild stripe. I looked fucking forty years old, and I wasn't even twenty yet.

All for the love of Angelique. All of it. It was like she'd been siphoning the life from us as we followed her, and the more knotted up we became, the more she fed on us. But we didn't see it that way at the time. Hell, even now I struggle to make that comparison. It feels both right and wrong at the same time, you know? I don't want to believe it. And yet, the more I think about it, the more it seems true. That she was feeding on us.

But even if I thought it at that time, I dared not say it. Hell, I dared not even think it too loudly. My connection to the knot was frayed, yes, but it still carried the signal to my sisters. Our coven already saw me as an interloper, this would just seal the deal. So I kept this thought like a whisper in my head, a secret only I could hear. And only if I listened very, very closely. I still had to redeem myself to them, prove my love of Angelique.

And I did love her, I did. At that time I wanted her to feed on me. I wanted her to feed and then empty me out and fill me up. She could do that, yes, I knew it in my bones, she could fill me completely like a cup and I would never be empty again. She was an answer to the void inside of me, a question that had plagued forever. Togetherness, always. The void a loneliness, a lack, an emptiness of space eating away at my heart. She was the cure to the cancer that was entropy. I knew it. And sometimes the cure would kill you just a little, not much, just a little bit. And then in the end? Everything would be so much better.

If only you could have met her, and saw what we saw. You would understand, I swear, you would. You look at me now like I was crazy, but you never saw her in her prime. I think there was a small bit on the road where we tried to convince her to record some of this, to share her with the world. She refused, always. *These gifts are for you, and you alone. Not for the world. The world does not deserve it, they're not ready. They've already embraced the entropy, look at how they consume everything, seeking an end to themselves and all the world around them.*

And Cris would pipe up with, *They were not born of the tree! They would never love you like we love you. Sister, oh sister, Daughter of the Wormwood Star!*

Oh, but if she would've let us record it all for posterity? If she could have allowed us to put it all online for everyone to see? You would understand, you would. You would get why I had to do this, why I had to do what's next. I. I don't think you'll understand, not like this. Yes, I'm avoiding this next bit, I know it. It's so hard. This is one of my biggest regrets, and it still hurts me to this day when I think about it.

Okay. Sigh. Inhale, hold it in, count to three, exhale. Here we go. Fucking hell, how I'm dreading this moment. Some things are easier to revisit than others, you know? Okay.

We were planning on finding a way to skip out on a meal, maybe order food and then run off before paying. Jones got this wild idea to steal a credit card and just use that. Angelique nixed it, she said we could *push* and get it for free, no need to steal. But we'd have to be the ones to do it, she wasn't doing so hot, and the stress of a good *push* might just put her out for a week. And we didn't have a week, not with Natasha's life hanging in the balance and the trap waiting for us. Angelique didn't look too good, either, none of us did. She was frailer than usual, paler than usual, her lips chapped and her body spasming randomly here and there. Not a full-on seizure, mind, just minor muscle spasms, and her eyes were rolling back in her head. Sometimes she would almost fall, and the cane would hold her up just enough.

She definitely needed food. We all did. I caught a reflection of us in some buffet glass and it was a scary sight. We were all emaciated, starved and half mad. We had sores on our skin I hadn't noticed before. Probably lack of nutrition? And lack of sleep? I had no idea. We didn't look good at all. Maybe our next stop would be a truck stop and we could use the showers there, and maybe get a good hot meal. Jones could steal a credit card there, and we could use it to gas up and get going. I sent that thought across the frayed wires of my mind, but the knot seemed distant, and echoing. I wasn't sure if they heard me or not.

And as we were just about to order our food, with Jones, Cris, and a few others *pushing* as hard as they could, convincing the cashier that we'd already paid so she could make our order, I caught sight of *her* out of the corner of my eye. The mouse girl. Walking through the front doors of the mall, heading our way. It was impossible, it couldn't be her! We'd left her behind a half day's drive ago, how did she even get here, had she been following us this whole time? And if so, why?

At first I thought I was mistaken, but no. I never forget a face. They're burned in my mind like all of the houses I've ever lived in. I could revisit the contours of her features even now. The mouse girl, from the thrift shop, it was her. She was here. Impossible. I didn't want to believe it, but it was her. Her teeth, her eyes, her sweater. No mistaking it, it was her.

Shit. I can do this, I can do this, I can do this. This is just a memory, nothing more. I'm not that person anymore, right? Even though she pulls on me, that twenty-year-old I was long ago. She tugs on my thoughts, wanting to come out again. And I will admit, this whole interview has done it, it's given her a voice that I neglected for years. I only hope she goes back into the shadows when we're done. I can't live with her controlling my thoughts anymore, not with the life I have now. She's too dangerous to be around my family, I don't know what she would do. Okay, here we go. Okay.

Fuck.

5

She saw me see her, and without missing a beat, she waved. Why did she wave? We only had one moment together. Had we connected that deeply already, just by that mere interaction? Or was my desire for that imagined life with her so strong it *pulled* her toward me? Oh fuck. Oh I hope not, I really hope I hadn't cursed her to follow me. This would be her death, and I was the one who did it. I looked away, looked at Angelique, and felt joy and need shimmering inside of me. She said she *pulled* us toward her, yanking the knot into place. Was that what happened here, with mouse girl? Did she feel the same way about me that I felt about Angelique?

My stomach lurched and my mouth filled with the bitter taste of stomach acid. This was not good. I snuck a glance again, and she caught my eyes and smiled and waved even more, trying to get me to come over to her. I wanted to run away. I had to get away from here. If they saw this, oh no, if the knot caught any of this, I was doomed. There was no way out of it. We were both doomed. How could I have done this to her?

Shitshitshit. I ran to the bathroom like there was no time left in the world. They looked at me, all of them, the entire knot turning at the exact same time to stare at me. Eerie, yes. Completely uncanny. The look in their eyes was an intense haunting. I felt my cheeks burning and didn't know if the fire inside of me was real or imagined. I muttered, "Been backed up for hours, it's finally come unplugged . . ."

And hoped that this brazen lie was so nasty they wouldn't even question me on it. They watched me run, but did not follow. Did not even send an envoy to watch me. They only turned to face the cashier, and worked together, all at once, to *push* her. I felt it, even through my frayed endings, the combined strength of the *push*. It made me weak in the knees and I stumbled, almost fell, before I righted myself again. I didn't even turn around to see if mouse girl was following me or not. I, I didn't want her to. I wanted to be alone. If I went into the woman's room she could easily follow. If I went into the men's room . . . well. That would be stupid.

The handicap toilets? I knew I was going to hate myself for this later, and I only hoped against hope no one would need to use it while I was in there. *Please oh please oh fucking hell please.* I didn't even knock, didn't even checked to see if it was unlocked. I just yanked it open and flung myself inside. It was empty. Thank god. A light flickered on the minute I came in. The whole place was cramped and tiny, and covered in hand rails, with a wheelchair accessible toilet in the corner. I leaned over and retched, dry heaving, that bitter stomach acid taste strong in my mouth now. Like licking a sour battery. Shit. Is that how I tasted on the inside? Like a leaking battery?

A restless thing roamed around inside of me. I wanted to crawl out of this skin. I wanted to be a reflection again, a copy again, this moment was all too real. I couldn't escape. I couldn't cut out this heart and leave it behind. I was. I was. I was stuck and sobbing and dry heaved some more. *No more death, please no more death.* And yet, even then, I knew what was going to happen. No matter how much I *pushed* that thought into the knot, it would fall on deaf ears. Together they were stronger than little old me would ever be.

Were they even stronger than Natasha? Than Angelique?

A terrifying thought.

And then.

We know where you are. Whispers. *She is coming for you.*

No, no, no, she isn't, that's not her, that can't be her . . .

It is her. We called her to us, pulling, and pushing her toward you.

Why? Why would you do such a thing?

And then? A knocking on the bathroom door. Playful, like a dance of knuckles and wood.

"Hey, you in there? I'm worried about you. Are you in trouble? You looked like you were in trouble, and I found those bloodied rags . . . and now, look at you. Do you need help? My sister, she joined up with this cult or fellowship, and oh. It was horrible. I couldn't get her out, not before she, well. Before they ended up killing themselves, you know? And I see the same look in your eyes she had near the end, I recognized it the minute I saw you. I couldn't save her, but I feel like I can *save* you. Please, let me save you, for her sake. I can't let someone else die in the same way, I would just hate myself."

Kill her.

No, no, I can't do that.
Kill her now.
Why do you want me to do this?
Kill her kill her kill her
Nononononononono I won't, I can't do this . . .
Silence.

They cut me out of the knot completely, no longer just frayed edges, no. Snip, snip, snip. Silence in my head, silence around me in my world, so strong and horrible and deafening. Like a tomb, locked away in this tiny coffin of a toilet. I yearned for them again, I needed them, I wanted to have them here with me, to love me, to keep me safe. I couldn't do this alone, not anymore. I'd been alone for too long in my life, spent so many hours by myself and reaching out, reaching out to anyone, and missing them completely. Hand swiped right past them, no connection. Like a bubble I floated in a sea of shadows, and then . . . then . . . Angelique . . . the knot . . .

No, I couldn't go back to how it was before I met them. That loneliness was so crushing. I was. I was crushed. I was.

She trespassed on your heart. That is our heart. Ours.

"Please, let me help you. I need to save someone, anyone. Please."

I swallowed. It won't be me. No. She wasn't going to save me and I wasn't going to save her. I knew this was always going to be how it ended. I told you that before, hadn't I? How this would end. How it always ends. No matter which world I ended up in, this would always be it, the ending we deserved. It was impossible that it would be any other way. Fuck.

Kill. Her.

I opened the door, wiped the sick from my lips and the tears from my eyes.

"Oh, oh, you poor thing, oh, I had no idea."

And she ran in and hugged me close. It was just as wonderful as I always knew it would be. I had to calcify my heart. I had to. I had to harden it. Toughen this up. Don't, don't lean your head on her shoulder (I leaned my head on her shoulder), don't, don't touch her cheek with your hand (and yet, there it was, warm against my palm), and don't, don't listen to her heartbeat, echoing in the acoustics of her bones (lubdub, lubdub, lubdub, a strong heart for a strong mouse).

"Oh god, I'm so sorry."

"No, you don't have to be sorry. I'll get you out of here, and we can go somewhere together, and you will live. You will live, and I will live, and it will be . . ."

"Perfect."

"Yes, perfect, yes. Let me save you . . ."

"I'm sorry . . ."

Before she could say anything else, I pushed her back with my entire body weight, cramming her against the bathroom wall. She was so surprised, she had no idea what was happening. She couldn't even fight back, she was too confused. "But why, why are you doing this, I want to save you . . ."

Kill her kill her kill her

My hands around her neck now, tears streaming down my cheek. I howled and sobbed as I pushed my thumbs against her throat, digging them in, pushing that windpipe down. She gurgled in pain, her eyes wide with betrayal and fear. Her hands clawed weakly at me, as her lungs struggled to breathe. I may be all angles, skin and bone practically, but it was enough to hold her down. To keep at it. I wanted to let go, I wanted to let her go and then let myself go. This wasn't right. But I had to do it. I had to. The pulse so weak in her neck against my killing palms. And then for a moment, she gave into it. She stopped trying to fight death, and just relaxed her entire body. One last gurgle, the fear in her eyes giving away to an ecstatic spiritual gaze that still haunts me to this day. I was raised Catholic, and went to a Catholic school, and her look, yes. That look right there. You ever see any of the old paintings of saints? That look on their face, right before death, right there, that was the look on her face. That exact same look. I still get chills and it makes me want to scream.

In that moment I felt the sever of the knot and it freed me. How could that be? How could this loneliness be so freeing? And yet, there it was. I leaned back against the bathroom wall and stared at her corpse. Her face tilted up, her smile unmistakable. I had choked her to death, and she was the one who smiled. I smiled in return, and decided to stay in here for just a little bit longer. After all, they knew I was here, waiting for them. They could come and get me when they wanted to leave.

Their thoughts tickled around in my head, but now it was like a dim buzzing. The edges of the knot were being patched back together,

I felt it, a whispering vibration. After all this, after all they made me do . . .

I wasn't sure if I could go back to the knot again. Not like it was before. I had changed too much. Hell, they had changed too much, and I just hadn't noticed it until now. It had been running in the background all this time, growing stronger and stronger. But here it was, the horror we'd become. Did Angelique know about this? She couldn't read our thoughts, I remembered that. That wasn't how it worked for her. She had no idea what we were capable of, no idea what I'd just done.

Later on, when they opened the door and pulled me out, I realized that they didn't tell her what happened. They just said I disappeared and went missing. When she asked me later, I told her that I just felt terribly ill. Feverish, vomit sick. She had no idea about the dead body, and I wasn't going to tell her. I wanted to keep Angelique safe from what we'd become. If they turned on her, oh. If they went that far . . .

I would have to be the one to save her. To do what that mouse girl couldn't do for me.

6

Cris was the first to bring the sound of the devil out of her own bones. Angelique was in the front seat and driving, so she had no idea what was going on until it was too late. It started as a soft echo, like hearing a song being played next door, through a wall. Then it got louder, rougher, static coated like being on speaker phone in the middle of nowhere. We all recognized the sound immediately, and it set my teeth on edge. Everyone else clapped and smiled, and the knot was abuzz with excitement.

I heard their voices still dim and distant, just out of reach from my thoughts. I wanted to sever them completely, be my own person, but not yet. If I did that now, it would be dangerous. I had to spy on the knot. Had to keep an eye on them, keep Angelique safe. I don't think she understood what kind of danger she was in. They were keeping secrets from her. They worshiped her, yes. But people eat their gods all the time. That was a lesson I learned early on at Catholic school growing up. And I felt it, their greedy need for her. It was terrifying and beautiful all at the same time. I had to protect her. I had to.

The images danced for a bit in my head, placed there by the sound of the devil. Stronger than the knot, more powerful and all-consuming. I pushed them away. I did not want to see them anymore. It was difficult, like pushing a statue through wet cement, but I did it. And was rewarded with a horrible headache for my efforts. Worth it, though. So worth it.

Those images. All of us, together, killing and fucking each other. No one gave in, but everyone smiled, like it was the greatest show on earth. Our lips cracked, chapped and dehydrated, we needed to stop again, soon. For water, maybe some food. We were getting close to Natasha, and to the cult. Maybe about four or five more hours of on the road, and then that would be it.

How did you do it?

I felt that so staticky in my head. Bad radio transmission of a voice. The knot was talking inside their minds again, not wanting

Angelique to hear it. Not wanting Angelique to know what they were doing. When had they stopped loving her and started worshiping her in secret? Maybe it had been like that for a while now, and I was too caught up in the middle of it to even realize. It was strange being outside of a hivemind after being nestled up inside of it.

It was easier than I thought it would be. You have it inside you, too. You just need to sit quietly and listen closely. Listen to your bones, listen closely and drive out any other sound in your vicinity. Concentrate, concentrate. You hear it now? Yes. Now tug on it, like a loose thread, slowly unraveling your bones as you do it. There. See? See! You're doing it! You're all doing it!

A chorus of bone music. And it echoed along the frayed edges of the knot. Inside outside all around, it surrounded me from all sides. Nervous heart pounded, I snapped, over and over again. They tried to overpower my snaps, and it was hard to struggle, to stay present. The camper started to slow down, to pull over to the side of the road.

Don't fight us. Give into the horror.

But I wasn't going to stop snapping. I looked over, and saw Simon with a nosebleed now, his eyes pinched shut in concentration. I realized I hadn't heard his voice in the knot in so long. Probably from around the time we connected to the web, to find Natasha again. Simon the oracle. Simon the dreamer beneath dead stars. Did he see something in that moment that terrified him so? A future. Our future. Angelique's future.

I reached over and grabbed his hand, tight, and he smiled, but did not look up. Together we could have strength. The camper pulled over, near the edge of an interstate forest. A whisper of a parking brake pulled tight, and then Angelique turning around, looking at us. "What the hell is going on?"

Shhh, don't tell her a damned thing. Or else we will devour you while you sleep.

"Simon said it's Natasha, we're getting close, and his trance is somehow amplifying the sound of the devil."

Tell her that or you will both fucking die right now, we will kill you both, Angelique be damned. She will understand, in the end. She will. But it's not time yet. We haven't met the man in white yet, then she will understand. She will understand everything.

Simon nodded and wiped the blood from his nose. "Yeah, when I connected to her last she was awake again, and it just poured into me. I tried to stop it, but well. You see what happened. Fuck, I have such a horrible headache right now."

"Oh, well that's good news! Did they move, or they still in the same spot?"

Simon coughed. It looked like it hurt him so much to talk, and I understood. We just went through a lot. "They're still in the same spot. And there's something else . . ."

"What, what? Is she okay?"

The knot turned and looked at him at once, in a moment that seemed choreographed in its balletic perfection.

Don't you fucking dare

"Yes, she's just older now. I know it seems impossible, but she looks like she's about five or six in the last vision. And she looks just like you . . ."

"Of course she does! She's my sister."

"Right, right. I had to disconnect, it was too much, fighting the sound of the devil like that. And I ache now, I ache all over, like every single one of my muscles is on fire. I had no idea just sitting here and concentrating could be so exhausting."

Angelique nodded. "Yup, it is. It will sap you a little at a time, so rest now. Rest. You can borrow one of my spare canes if you need to."

"Thank you."

"Sure, you won't be any help to us if you wear yourself to nothingness before we even get there. We probably won't need to check again for a while anyway, I doubt they're moving now. Like you said, they laid a trap, so they're probably going to just stay put until we get there."

Simon groaned and leaned his head on my shoulder. I put an arm around him, protective, making sure they didn't get any ideas. "Go ahead," I whispered into his ear, "Take a nap. I'll keep watch over you."

"Thank you," he whispered into my chest, directly at my heart. "Thank you."

And then Cris piped up, and said in a cheery, unsettling voice, "I bet there's a motel at the next overpass. Isn't there always? We should go and spend the night there, just so we can all rest up and be ready to fight the next day."

Angelique thought about this for a moment. She drummed her fingers on the steering wheel, and then said, "All right, that's a good idea. Jones, you still have that credit card? They didn't cancel it yet, did they?"

"I have no clue? No phone and no internet to check."

"Whatever, I saw you losers push back at the food court. I'm sure you could do the same at the motel, and we'll all be good."

The knot nodded and smiled in perfect synchronicity, and it creeped me the fuck out. How did Angelique not see what was going on? Maybe she did and wanted this to happen. Maybe this was her entire plan. I don't know. But I worried now. I worried about what they had in store for us at the motel. They were up to something, and I had no idea what, and that terrified me. Maybe me and Simon could escape that night? Just get out of here while they slept in the motel? Shit. I had to keep these thoughts as whispers. They still might be able to hear me . . .

The sound of the devil is our weapon now.

A bright and beautiful weapon it is.

An atom bomb we hold in our bones.

Let's call them to us.

Yes! At the motel, tonight. Let's pull those serial killers our way.

We can take them out all at once.

Now we're laying our own trap.

Perfectperfectperfect

They will never see it coming.

Yes. Let's bring them to us.

Yes.

:episode 7:
Are You Okay?

1

It's so weird, but I can't remember my childhood.

You can't? What do you mean . . .

Do you remember the faces of your parents?

Of course I do.

But when you were a kid, right? Like a little kid. Do you remember their young faces?

I . . . I . . .

I don't know. What the hell . . .

Why are you asking this now? Shouldn't we be going to sleep, I mean. They're coming soon, aren't they? Probably before dawn, if our *pull* works as good as we think it should.

I can't sleep because I can't remember any of it.

Nothing.

Can you?

I don't know, I mean, I know I cried the first day of kindergarten, I missed my mom so much.

I did too.

You know it, but do you remember it?

What do you mean?

Is that an actual memory of yours? Or something your parents told you.

My parents . . . fuck. Where are my parents?

Or my parents. Are they still missing? I, I forgot all about them.

So much is going on.

Everything is going on, fucking hell.

Everything, everything, everything.

And no way to access the internet, still.

We should've hit the library in the last town, used the public computers . . .

Why did we get rid of our phones?

Where are our parents . . .

And do you have any memories? Any memories before, what, you were twelve?

Not even, I can't remember anything before sixteen.

Sixteen!

Yeah, can you?

I mean, of course I can.

Can you. Come on, be honest.

I am, I can remember! I can. I . . .

What, give us a memory.

I don't like this game.

It's not a fucking game, Cris, come on. Do any of you remember your childhood.

You, Simon?

I do. I can remember really far back, actually.

Liar.

I can, I remember the first time I got shocked, sticking my finger in a light socket on accident.

Your parents told you that!

No, I remember so clearly. It felt like my bones jumped inside of my body.

What about you, Clara?

I . . . I don't want to talk about it.

Why not?

Just, let's change the subject.

Jones. How about you?

Oh, I've never had any memories of my childhood, not even ones given to me by my parents.

Why do you think that is?

Because we were never children. Not in the normal sense of the word.

What the fuck are you talking about?

The tree of flesh and bone, you saw it.

I did.

That's why. Like Natasha we grew fast and faster. We just don't remember it because it was a blur of moments.

Fucking hell. You lie.

You know I'm right, think closely now, think about everything that's happened to us so far. It's right.

Then what about Simon?

Yeah. What about him?

Simon, can you hear this? Simon?

Simon, answer him.

Yes. A little. It's growing faint . . .

How about you Clara?

This is so stupid. Let's go to sleep, come on.

Are you still connected to us? Or are you a traitor, like Petal?

Guys, leave her alone. This isn't like us.

What isn't like us?

We're here for Angelique.

Yes, yes we are, of course. Angelique.

Then why does any of the other stuff matter?

Aren't you curious? What does any of it mean, the tree, who we are, who she is? Why are they hunting us? What do they want from us?

Not right now I don't. Right now I just want to get some fucking sleep before tomorrow comes.

Tomorrow is the least of our issues.

Yes, exactly. How are you guys going to spring your atom bomb trap if you're not fully rested?

Shut up, Clara.

Yeah, shut up!

Maybe we should cut her off.

You think she'll tell Angelique on us?

She won't believe her. She'll believe us.

And if she doesn't?

We can push her and she won't even know what hit her.

Angelique? She's the Daughter of the Wormwood Star!

The antichrist! Hail Satan!

Oh you idiots, haven't you been paying attention?

Hey now.

The tree, the lack of childhoods, we're the same as Natasha and Angelique!

No, no we're not, we're not . . .

We have the sound of the devil in our bones, correct?

Fuck. No.

Even Angelique told you, and you didn't even listen.

What are you talking about?

Earlier, when she said, *Do you know who Satan is?*

Yes, When she made us imagine our deaths.

What did she say after that?

He is her father, Natasha's father . . .

And all of our fathers.

Shit. Yes, she did say that, so what?

We don't need her.

But we love her.

Yes, but sometimes one grows out of love. The man in white told me that in my dream, and it's true.

Shut up, Jones. What man in white? You're talking crazy.

You'll see after tomorrow—you'll understand. We don't need her anymore. Together, we are the antichrist. She was just a prelude, a whisper. We are the thunderclap of hell.

We're not going to be much of a thunderclap if we don't get to sleep.

I get it, though. I get what he's going on about.

So?

How can you sleep knowing this? Knowing what's going to happen any moment from now?

Easily, watch. Zzzz snore.

Stop it. This is like Christmas morning, don't you think?

How would you even know, you don't even remember your childhood.

So. I still got excited for Christmas as a teen, didn't you?

No, shut up, I never cared for it.

I just want to unwrap our presents.

What are you even talking about?

Yes. We get to try this out and see what we're really made of.

The thunderclap from hell.

Don't you want to do it? To see what will happen?

And what do you think Angelique will say? When you do this?

She will be so happy!

Yes, so happy.

We're all knotted up, just like she wanted, and now watch the world burn!

And if she's not?

Well.

We've outgrown her love. Just like Jones said.

You afraid she'll hear you? Say it out loud, you coward.
We've outgrown her. There, happy now?
Yes. And she probably heard this whole conversation.
I think it's time we cut you out again.
Of the knot?
Yes. What do you think of that?
Try me, and see what happens.

2

That night we all dreamt of the House of Sky and Shadow. And in each and every one of our dreams, the house was on fire. It did not crumble, or collapse mid burn. It was silent, and still. Patient as the flames licked the edges of the clouds with light. And in one of the windows we saw him—the man in white. All white suit, white tie, and a long gnarled beard. His eyes were intense, staring out at us and calling us toward him. I didn't want to go. I'm not sure if the others felt the same way.

We woke after only an hour or so of sleep, restless. The angry sun shouting at us through the blinds of the motel room.

This motel room was like so many others I've stayed in through my life. It had that funky post-cigarette smell, tinged with the acid of harsh cleaners. The walls were a soft cream color, dotted with paintings of landscapes hung in frames that were meant to look classy, but instead came off as tacky.

Angelique was still asleep in the far corner queen-sized bed. Everyone wanted to sleep next to her, but only Cris was allowed. And even then, it was only because she threatened the rest with a terrible restless anger that crawled inside her blood. Cris rose up with the rest, wiped the sleep from her eyes. Bloodshot. Half-moon shadows. Still emaciated, open sores. Her bony angles slipping out of unwashed pajamas. Hair starting to fall out from malnutrition, and I think I even found some teeth in the sink last night. We all looked like wraiths, and I wondered, would this be what I looked like when I was dead? I still wonder that.

They all turned and stared at me. Blaming eyes, hateful eyes. I heard their thoughts whispering on the borders of the knot: *her fault, her fault, we should have cut her out. She set the flames, we know it. Just like Petal before her. A kindling girl, nothing more than a pile of matches.*

Should we cut her out now?

Too late, the house is already on fire, too late.

Kindling girl. I bet she can burn up real nice.

It was as if they didn't care if I heard them. So I ignored them, and walked over to Simon, to see how he was doing. Like the house of our dreams, he laid silent and still. For a moment, I thought he was dead. And then he shivered, and opened his eyes and said, "She's coming."

And then more thoughts in the radio static.

Yes, she is.

I thought there would be more?

Shouldn't there be more?

We wanted them all to come here! This is so insulting.

Would be a waste of our devil's chorus, to use it just on one person. An atom bomb to crush an ant. Such a waste!

Why didn't they fall for our trap?

So clever, it was so clever . . .

One person. Only one! How dare they insult the knot like that.

"Who is coming, Simon? Who is it?"

"Betrayer . . ."

And then he shivered so much his eyes closed and his body curled up completely. Was that me? Betrayer? No, that couldn't be right. The knot turned and looked at me. Eyes sharp in that bright sun shadow.

Betrayer, betrayer, betrayer . . .

I felt hot prickling on my skin, and oh fuck. Were they going to use the devil's chorus on me? Shit. I *snapped* but I was so weak, I'm not sure if it did anything at all. The edges of my fingers were numb, and this burning sensation crawled up my spine. Almost pleasurable at first, until it grew teeth and bit down hard. Radial rings of fire crawled across my body. Like being burned up from the inside. Was this what spontaneous combustion felt like? It was so horrible. Every single one of my nerves, burning.

And then came a knock on the door. The burning stopped, as the knot turned and looked, their hateful gaze now directed to what lay beyond. Angelique stirred, restless, and woke up, bleary-eyed and dazed. Cris was no longer at her side—she was standing with the others and staring. The knock happened again, a quick rapid succession, violent and harsh on the ears. Angelique sat up, kicked her legs off the side of the bed, and grabbed her cane. "What the hell did you losers do this time? Don't tell me we're in trouble with the cops and need to duke it out."

She walked over to the window, everyone parting out of her way, still staring at the door. I heard them muttering along the edges of the knot, resisting the urge to use the sound of the devil. They did not want Angelique to know how powerful they'd become, not yet. They would show her in due time. I felt a tingle around my heart, like the brush of invisible fingers against the ventricles.

Don't you dare say a word.

Responding to that would be a mistake, so I said nothing, thought nothing, and just watched as Angelique pulled aside the beige drapes, just a little, to get a quick peek outside. She laughed, a faintly off-kilter sound, the laughter of the absurd. "Oh lookie here, it's Petal. And she has an axe."

"An axe?"

"Yuppers."

Should we do it?

Yes. We should show Angelique what we're capable of.

She will love us even more so!

Yes!

Now is the time!

The knot tightened, their stare blistering in the morning light. A prickle of heat in the air, as their bones droned softly. Every single hair on my body stood at attention, and I felt my own bones humming along with theirs. What was this? I didn't want the sound of the devil inside of me! And even still, I should be the one controlling my own bones, shouldn't I? A snap wouldn't do it, I knew that much. A push or a pull wouldn't matter, and if I knocked it would be pointless. How could I stop this hum from inside? The images started to flutter around my thoughts, but they weren't for me . . .

They were for Petal. Images of her killing herself with the axe. Chop, chop, chop. Limb by limb, until she was a pile of bloodied stumps. I snapped, and I was right, it didn't stop a damn thing. So I tried a push, against the knot, a cut, a snip, against that knot. Nothing. I tried to pull then, on the edges of the knot. Try and untie myself from their clutches.

"What are you guys doing?"

Angelique turned around and looked at us. The bone drone faded into a low melancholy murmur. The images flashed once more, then faded like old photographs left out in the sun for too long. "Come on, answer me. What is this? I did not show you how to do this."

Cris stepped forward. Her eyes were strong, her chin tilted up, her smile wide and proud. "You did show us, in a way. You gave us the tools, the knots, and you showed us the map to our bones."

There was a pause in the air. Waiting for Angelique to say something, anything at all. Would she approve of this? Chastise us? And was the knot as strong as everyone thought it was, or would Angelique undo us with a snip of her fingertips? We've seen how death could be so simple in her hands. It didn't take much at all.

Return to the void . . .

She tapped her cane. "Why didn't you show me sooner . . ."

And then, mid-sentence, came a crack and crash against the door. Axe blade, red and black, burst through the door. Then a swing back, and shouts from outside. "Open up, you motherfuckers! I've seen the bright of entropy night, and I've come to undo all this shit you've done in the world. You're going to love the void, oh, I promise you that! It's like dreamless sleep, endless and beautiful. So open up! Open the fuck up!"

Was this really the same Petal as before? I couldn't believe she could change that much in such a short time. What had happened to her? She left because she was skeptical of Angelique. Saw that we were becoming a cult, and didn't want to have any part in that. But this . . . this mania. This cry of entropy and destruction. This wasn't like her at all. Had she been brainwashed?

Angelique stepped away from the door, and almost fell, her cane righting her balance at the last moment. Another crash, splinters scattering around, as Simon sat up, his eyes wide and terrified, his whole body shivering. Our oracle was broken now, that was for certain.

"Betrayer!" he called out again, "Betrayer!"

And Petal howled beyond the door, a wild wolf in heat.

"Okay," Angelique said to the knot, "Show me what you losers got. Release the beast."

"Wait," I said, hand up, quick. "I have an idea."

A restless sigh from the knot. "This better be good."

"Keep the bones asleep for now, okay? You don't want to waste all that energy on one person."

"No . . ."

"Let's all do a pull instead. Angelique, can you lead us with this one? Like a conductor for an orchestra."

Angelique raised an eyebrow. Skeptical. "What are you even thinking."

"Listen to her, that's not Petal."

"You're all just emptiness in the shape of human bodies, everything is pointless, nothingness, shadows! Look, look! See and understand. Understand the truth." She reached her hand through the newly chopped hole in the door, palm out, showing a fresh keyhole tattoo. It was irritated, red, and possibly infected. I winced in empathy.

"See?" I said, "That's not her. They did something to her, and maybe if we pull together, right? Pull the thread out, we could unravel it and get to the real Petal. The one who would never do anything like this."

"Okay," Angelique said, "It's worth a shot. You losers ready? Let's see if there is enough gas in the tank to bring this home."

The knot nodded, but I heard them whispering. They had other ideas. They were going to do what they were going to do and damn the consequences. I wanted to warn them to stop, to just do as I asked, but I was terrified of them. So I hid my thoughts under the images of clouds, and decided to pull on my own, with Angelique helping me. Maybe we could do something quickly, before the others geared up and burned it all down.

Oh fuck I hope so. I really did not want Petal to die. Not like this. Not ever. She deserved better, she was our friend. And I knew, deep down inside, our friend was still in there. Waiting, patiently, to come out and see us once again.

3

Me and Petal went way back, probably further back than anyone else in our little knot. Our families had always spent the summers in Dark Rivers, vacationing near the great lake and spending hours lost and lonely on the little islands that dotted edges. At night we would run through the woods, pine branches swaying over our heads. We kept in touch on the days when summer was over, emailing back and forth, talking on Radio Fire and various other social media sites.

Sometimes whimsy would get the better of us, and we would send letters through the mail. I remember one in particular, where she sent dead leaves pressed between pages of *Finnegan's Wake,* torn out from the book with ragged edges. They seemed to shine between the pages, red and orange, like fire stolen from the branches of the tree. We'd make up stories to tell each other, what we would call our *tall tales,* but there were more like a personal mythology, shared between the two of us.

Odd how close we got back then, and how we drifted apart during our teenage years. I think I was the one who stopped writing, but I could be wrong.

We just sent fewer and fewer letters. Months would go by, and I would completely forget about it. And then, when it came time to choose a school to go to after I graduated, I got a letter from Petal. She said she dreamt of Dark Rivers University, and in her dream, there were tunnels beneath the campus. In her dream we were there together, walking through those tunnels, the skin of the world directly over our heads. It was lit with these orange lamps strewn about on the ground, and she said there was a secret in the heart of the tunnels. Something we had to find. It would answer all of our questions, tell us the meanings of our lives. It was so important, she wrote. So very important.

I applied last week, and you have to come with me.

At the time, I wasn't even sure I was going to go to college just yet, much to my parents' chagrin. I wanted to take a gap year, maybe.

Explore, take a job, find out who I was before taking the leap and going back to school. I was kind of done, high school was a rough experience, and the thought of four more years of that just made me recoil. But.

But.

There was something in this letter. The pages warm beneath the tips of my fingers. It smelled of autumn, of dead leaves and moist earth. I felt the need to understand my life. I was lost, I was listless, and I was so lonely. My parents just had no idea how lonely I felt. It seemed all my friends disappeared into drugs and dangerous relationships my senior year of high school. My best friend died of a heroin overdose the week she tried to get sober. One last bump, she said, to celebrate her new, sober life. That's all it would be. I found her dead the next day, when I went to wake her up for work. Fucking hell. I've seen so much death in my life. Nobody should ever have to see that much death.

Others dropped out of school, and got a joint place in a trailer park they called their compound. Where they would just hang out, get high. Talk cheap stoner philosophy and pretend to understand the secrets of the world. None of them worked, so they stole from their neighbors, and sold drugs to feed their habits.

I couldn't be around them. Not after I'd seen that kind of death. And Jack, my ex-boyfriend, started dating this dangerous guy who loved to set fires. He was a dealer, and some people said that he was in and out of juvie for killing his parents at a younger age. That he'd started with killing the neighborhood pets and moved up to people. Maybe it was a rumor, I don't know. I just couldn't do it. I had nothing in common with any of these people anymore. I still read poetry and science fiction novels, hung out in libraries, and at the most drank one or two cups of coffee a day. That was the largest extent of my drug habits. I didn't even drink-drink, not even when I went to college.

And this left me so damned lonely. They reached out to me, or I reached out back, but it was like brushing my fingers against a glass bubble. I could never push hard enough to break through, to shatter it and touch my friends with bloodied fingers. It hurt to be that alone. It hurt so much. I tried making up for it online, with social media, that kind of thing. But that felt hollow. I needed human touch, I needed companionship, I needed anything.

And when I got her letter. Petal. Telling me about her dream. Telling me about Dark Rivers University. That place we used to summer. Where would practice kissing each other under redwood trees. Back when sex and relationships were dreams for another day. I knew I had to do it. I had to go there. I had to hear that secret beneath the tunnels. I had to find out what she was talking about, to know our futures.

I wished the secret had been there, and shown us everything that was going to happen, so that Petal and I could've maybe done this whole thing differently. Maybe save us all this fucking heart break. Loneliness is such a curse. It makes us do horrible things we would never normally do. Just so we could stop hurting, even if just for a little bit.

4

I guess that memory proved Petal and I weren't born of the tree, and weren't like Natasha, Angelique, or any of the other witches in the knot. They all had short memories, that last only a few leaps back and then nothingness. Even Simon, their precious oracle, had childhood memories and were more like us than like them. Maybe we we're doomed, the three of us. The knot turns on the outsiders. Maybe Angelique wasn't born of the tree, either. Maybe she was nothing like Natasha.

I wish I had answers. All I have is this terror, and these memories, and the feeling of being suffocated by who we were. What was that tree, even. It made me feel like I was hooked in the jaw like a fish, pulled out from under the waves into the baking light of the sun. When I remember it, I get vague impressions, like an outline of a memory but not a real thing. Hazy, indistinct, dreaming. Maybe we were all dreaming awake. Maybe each moment was a nightmare.

Fear the living.

I wanted to think Angelique was outside of all this and innocent. That the knot was the true terror, and that she knew not what she did bringing us together. I had so many questions for her. But now, no, now was not the time for questions. Now was the time for concentration.

I swallowed some spit and centered myself. That stomach acid roiled around inside of me again, a restless fire. Petal pulled her hand out of the hole in the door again, splinters scraping the edges of her wrist. She did not seem to care at all. No yelps of pain. No rubbing her wrist. Just the axe back in the air and crashing down again. The knot turned their attention towards the door, and Angelique turned around, faced us, her hands in the air. Like she was about ready to conduct an orchestra. The pit of my stomach dropped and I felt my knees weak with the power running through me, and I clenched my teeth and centered myself.

Don't you say a word.

Not a single peep.

We'll toast you if you do and then toast her.
Angelique will understand.
She knows us and loves us like we love her.
Our shadows changed from pale to bright red. Angelique dropped her hands and started waving them, pointing at heaven and earth with each hand, and I followed her with my mind, concentrating on Petal, looking for the Petal that was still there, inside of her, that loose thread of being that made her, well *her*. A nebulous thing built up over a lifetime, now hidden under folds of brainwashing by the serial killer cult.

What are you doing?
Stop. Do what we're doing. Join the knot. Help the knot.
Prickles of heat against my scalp and fingertips and those fuckers won't do this to me, they can't do this to me. Not without wasting their energy. let them try to coerce me. Go ahead. I kept diving into the dark, following Angelique with each crash of the axe, seeing that small thread of light deep inside the chaos of darkness that was Petal. I decided not to push, not to pull, but instead to whisper, slowly. I knotted with her, just her, cutting off ties to the others. It hurt, like having a finger snipped off, but necessary. That finger had rotted and the hand was sour with bad blood.

Petal Petal Petal
A flicker of that light. She heard me . . .
Pain, again, prickles of pain both of us, hurting now. I felt fire on my hands, and Angelique was screaming at them now, telling them to stop it, to stop what the fuck are you doing? I couldn't be distracted, though, I had to help Petal out. Tie that knot between the two of us tighter and tighter, with childhood memories by the lake. Those endless summer days when we felt an awakening loss of the world against our lips, kissing sweet in the darkness.

In my mind I brought up the image of the letter. I remembered exactly what it looked like, her last one to me. The dead leaves pressed on the sides, and her words scribbled in her messy scrawl that was half cursive, with all the letters leaning into each other but not quite connecting.

Remember this, remember the secret. Remember? We were going to find it together.
But instead, we found this.

And I felt her reach out to me and there was a cry of sadness beyond the door. I knew I had it, and in that moment, I swam back into my body, all at once surrounded by pain. As if everyone one of my bones jumped at the same time, my nerves screaming. Un-fuck-ing-bearable. This was that nuclear attack, wasn't it? More than just the sound of the devil. The full-on chorus, and it was focused on me. Blind with pain, I saw the shadows of the knot, turned, staring at me, and Angelique screaming as I hit the ground.

They weren't even bothering with Petal anymore. They didn't even care. She was okay, she was herself again, the axe clattered on the floor as she wept outside in the palms of her hands. Good, good, I wanted her to be all right. She ran from one cult and joined another, and the tragedy of that struck me in the heart. As I cried out in pain, and I think I blacked out then. I can't remember. I just remember the pain, all bright and brutal, and being on the floor. That motel room floor. The darkness coming for me. It was a moment of emptiness, of dreamlessness. I wished I could've seen the House of Sky and Shadow in that moment. I wanted to make sure it was okay. Maybe it wasn't burning anymore? Oh I hoped so. I hoped it had stopped burning.

Because here I was, on fire. And Angelique cradled me in that dreamless darkness, singing to me. I hurt so much, but it was all going to be okay. Petal was good, and even though the mouse girl was dead, I was able to save someone. Maybe that was a gift to the mouse girl, I don't know. That in the end, I did what she couldn't do, and rescue someone from a cult. Maybe. I sure hoped that was the case.

5

When I woke my skin was sunburn red, and everything was tinged with rainbows of light. Auras, I guess you could call them. I had that migraine feeling crawling around the edges of my mind. No dreams at all, and somehow that felt peaceful and not cruel. As if I had to stop existing if only for a little bit, and it reset my entire being. Funny how that was my greatest fear for the longest time, nonexistence, and yet when I actually experienced it, I found it recuperative. Strange how that was, strange indeed.

We were moving now, over the highway, and I was in one of the beds in the back of the camper. Petal was on the other one, with the rest of the knot crammed in the front seats. Angelique was here between us, eyes closed, legs crossed, her head tilted back. I could feel every bump and hole in the road, and it felt like morse code against my spine. I did not feel anger at what the knot did to me. I wish I could. Somehow, I knew they had our best interests at heart. They did what they thought was good for the knot and good for Angelique. And I definitely couldn't blame them for that. I loved Angelique so much, I got it completely.

I know, I know, that sounds insane saying it out loud right now. But you weren't there, you didn't know what it was like. I feared them and, yet, needed them at the same time, and somehow understood them. I was outside of them, the knot no longer tangled up in my own thoughts, and yet I missed the memory of them. That sweet feeling of never really being alone. Of always being in contact with someone else. My own parents left me to my own devices so much, it made me haunted and lonely. They were my family now, as much as I hated to admit it.

"The knot says they're sorry," Angelique said, "They didn't understand how dangerous it could be, to bring up the sound of the devil like that. They were caught up in the act, not thinking, just giving into it. There is a power there, yes. But a dangerous one . . ."

I coughed, looked at Petal. She was still out. Shivering. Eyes rolling around in her head.

"Is she okay?"

"She'll be okay, eventually."

I looked around. "Where's Simon?"

I felt him missing, like a hole cut in reality in the shape of his body. I didn't like that feeling at all.

"Don't worry, sweetie, he's at a hospital now. Being an oracle got to be too much for him, so we had to leave him behind. Poor thing."

"Oh."

"The cops will probably arrest him after that, but that's okay. We're close, you know? Close to being done with all of this."

"What are you talking about?"

She opened her eyes, and they sparkled like stars placed in her skull.

"My father is coming to see us soon. Right after we get Natasha back and finish what we need to do here. Oh sweetie, we're so close to going home again. Isn't it wonderful?"

I felt a chill and wanted to run away and keep on running. Maybe kick open the door to the RV and jump out stunt double-style, rolling along the road and hoping I didn't get ripped up too much. The devil wasn't real. He couldn't be real. This just wasn't right.

"I . . . I don't understand."

She grabbed my hands in hers. Rough palms, calloused. Bone thin fingers, we were all so broken and starved. How much longer could we keep going like this before we died? Complete organ failure? That sort of thing? I didn't even want to think about that. Maybe Simon would tell them where we were going and the cops would chase us down and stop all of this. Stop it before we collapsed and were all dead.

"He's done with this world now. And I know, it's scary, isn't it? But it's why I brought us together, in the end. So we could go back to his arms, and return home. Our real home. Doesn't this world feel empty to you? Like you don't belong here, and nobody wants you and nobody loves you? We're all outsiders. Your parents deserted you, remember? And if they would've loved you, they would've stayed. They would have cared for you, and kept you safe from the nightmares of the world."

And then she leaned in, her lips close to my lips. I could taste her in that moment, sweet, like pineapples. Her breath warm and fragrant against my skin. "I kept you safe. I kept you warm. I kept you from the nightmares of everyday life. I gave you a family who loves you, who wants you and will never let you go. A family that will let you come right back in, even if you leave us or try to kill us. That's the kind of family we are. Our bonds are iron. Our knots steel."

And then she kissed me and my heart filled with fire and laughter. Everything still hurt, but now it was a distant ache, tinged with this feeling of togetherness I missed so much. I knew deep in my heart of hearts she was wrong. I did! Don't give me that look. I really did.

But if you would've felt that kiss, so tender, so haunting. There was a ghost of so many promises on her lips. Promises that would be fulfilled when Satan showed up to take us home with him. If it hadn't been for that kiss, I would've argued with her. I would have said yes, the world was filled with suffering, but it was also beautiful and wonderful, too. And that even though there was loneliness, the friendship was sweet and lovely. Even though we hurt each other over and over again, it was somehow worth it.

I would've mentioned mine and Petal's summers together at the great lake. Our letters and emails exchanged through the years. I would've talked about running through the campus at all hours of the dawn, the way the sun looked, stray beams through the bare branches of trees. Like skeletons on fire. I would've talked about climbing to the roof of our dorms every night and talking until dawn. And that we did all of this without Angelique, before we even heard the whisper of her name.

That we didn't need her for any of this. That this world, as messy and as broken as it was, was good enough.

But that kiss. That kiss was argument enough. Here. Come closer. Let me kiss you like she kissed me, and show you the power of it. It was more than just lips on lips. It was like a snap, a push, a knock, or a pull. It was a *kiss* in that sense of the word, a spell. Beautiful, haunted. See? See what I mean? How do you feel?

Like you would follow me to the ends of the earth? Like you would kill for me? Die for me? Lay hungry and starved until I fed you with my own two hands? Even if the meat was carved from the heart of your own mother?

Yes. Yes you would. I can see that look in your eyes and you know it's true. You would love me now like I loved Angelique.

But I won't do that to you, look. Here. Let me snap a bit and draw you out of it. Don't worry, don't worry, those shakes are just temporary. Here, lie down for a little bit, there, on the couch. My kids won't be home for a while, and we can continue this again when you're better.

6

Later on, Petal seemed to come to, and Angelique went up to the front of the RV, leaving us all alone in the back. Not sure how they could have fit everyone up front, but they did. And it left me feeling kind of lonesome, but in a way I couldn't explain. The knot was silent now. Even my connection with Petal was severed. I was alone in my own head, and for some reason that scared me more than a little. I knew my thoughts, my own memories, all too well. I knew my tendency to pick at the horrible things I've seen, revisiting the images one after another. Like digging glass under my skin, those emotions bubbling to the surface.

I didn't want to think these things. I didn't want to remember these things. But I couldn't help myself. That pain was sweet, tingling on the edges of thought. Every once in a while, Petal seemed with it enough to talk a little bit, but that was fleeting, and my thoughts would return. Again, and again, and again.

Sara Fisher. The mouse girl. Our last night at the hospital. The way a human throat felt in my teeth. The way a windpipe crushed between the palms of my hands. Tactile. I could smell Sara Fisher's blood, and her intestines leaning out of the hole in her stomach. Remember the pale shadows of her skin? She wasn't dead. She couldn't have been dead. The plane crash. The dead mother and her child. I didn't want to remember these things.

"You okay?"

"Yeah. Are you okay?"

Petal scoffed. "You're a horrible liar."

"I guess I'm as okay as I'm going to be."

"No, no you're not. What are you thinking about?"

"I don't know. I don't want to talk about it, okay? Talking about would make it worse, not better."

"Maybe. Maybe not."

"You still didn't answer my question, are you okay?"

"No, no I'm not. I don't ever think I'll ever be okay ever again."

"That's a lot of evers."

"I know you're trying to make me laugh, but stop it. This is hard."

"I get it."

"Do you? I don't think you do. You won't even tell me your own thoughts."

"Fuck. You weren't there for any of it, you were gone. Always gone. You don't know what it was like to see them die, you just don't get it."

"Okay, that's fair. And I guess you probably won't get what I've been through either, but hell. I'll try, okay? I'll try to push through it and maybe we can make a connection."

"Okay."

"Did you knot with me, by the way? Earlier?"

"Yeah."

"Why'd it stop?"

"I . . .I don't know."

"Oh. Yeah. Well, okay. They kidnapped me, you know. I was leaving and trying to hitchhike home when those assholes pulled up in a van and just kidnapped me old-school horror story-style, with a black sack over my head and everything. A lot of it I can't remember."

"Try, I guess. Maybe it will help."

"I don't know. Does remembering help you?"

"Fine."

"There was an emptiness inside of me. I guess it was always there, since I was little, you know?"

"I know, I remember."

"You remember?"

"Yeah, you told me about it in your letters. I still have them, you know."

A pause. There was a rattling sound as the RV hit a bump. Cris swore, and they swerved a little, but kept right on going. I wanted to say something, to see if everything was okay, but I decided against it. This was more important, what was going on between me and Petal right now. I missed this, and I missed her. I don't think I've ever had a connection before or since Petal. Not like that. Not even with my kids, not even with Angelique.

"Oh. Well, they brought it out of me, you know? I don't know how they did it, but they made it feral, and conscious. And I saw it everywhere else, right after that. I saw the emptiness in the trees, that they were just cells and bark and leaves and nothing else. Humans were fools, they saw themselves as being a person, but inside they were just skeletons wrapped in meat. They had nothing, nothing inside of them, and I saw that. I saw that they didn't exist, that I didn't really exist, either. There was just this gaping maw, devouring everything. Emptiness. The void. Emptiness. And it gnawed at me from the inside, like a cancer eating my heart."

And I understood. I did. I wished I hadn't. But I decided not to say anything about it. These were her words, her time, and she had to tell me this.

"And this is the most fucked-up part. I'm still not sure how this made sense, but I knew that Angelique was the cause of all this emptiness. Right? It's completely insane. But I saw it so clearly and it hurt me. It hurt me to think about it, to dream about it, to even see a picture of her in the newspaper."

And I wanted to ask, we were in the newspaper? Were they also talking about us and Angelique online? We'd been so sheltered on the road, not watching TV, not going on the internet, none of that. How much has the world seen? And what did they think of us? Were they as scared of us as I was? I hoped not. There was no knowing what this world would do if it saw us a threat. All of those Americans armed to the teeth. Nothing good would come of that at all.

"And the only way I could stop the hurt was to kill Angelique. And I knew that in order to do that, I would have to kill all of you."

Petal lifted up her head and looked right at me. Tears streamed down her cheeks. I wanted to kiss her like Angelique had kissed me, and let her know that everything was okay. That we were going to be all right. But I knew that kiss would be a lie. Nothing was ever going to be right ever again.

Maybe I should have done it, though. Kissed her one last time. An echo of the memory of us under those trees on the beach, lips pressed sweetly together. Hearts beating in two separate ribcages in perfect synchronicity. If only we had found that secret she'd dreamt about, we could've known our fates and I would have kissed her right then and there.

"Thank you for reminding me who I was, who, who I *am*. You know? You brought me back to myself, and I was able to get rid of that void inside of me. Not completely, mind you, but just enough so it shrank back down, and I no longer wanted to kill you guys. Thank you."

And I wanted to reach across and hug her and kiss her and hold her and tell her everything was all right. But our knot was severed. Our bodies too far apart, a gulf between us of time and love. We were in glass bubbles now, unable to break on through and set each other free.

"Hey you two back there, listen to this! Simon's on NPR. We're fucking famous!"

Cris cranked it up and filled the entire camper with the sound of Simon's voice. It sounded different, broken, almost betrayed.

"So who is this Angelique everyone is talking about?"

"The thing you dreamt about long ago and then forgot about on waking."

"I don't understand, can you explain it a little better? Is she really the antichrist, the devil's daughter?"

"You've had dreams of dark shadows following you, haven't you? Menacing, the kind where when you wake up in a cold sweat and your heart is racing, ba-boom-ba-boom, and you wondered if you could've died in your sleep," the sound of a snapping finger, "just like that."

"I, I guess . . ."

"To know her is to love her."

"What does that have to do with these dreams?"

"Hail Satan! Hail the Daughter of the Wormwood Star! Angelique, Angelique, I still love you, I do. Even though the future is so blurry to me now, and haunted with a million wandering ghosts. Please, please come back to me and take me with you."

"What about all of the murders that seem to follow your cult? Is this just a coincidence? The police obviously don't think so, or you wouldn't be here, awaiting trial."

"No, I mean. No. I mean. Not us, it wasn't us."

"Oh. So who did it?"

"Like I told the cops, it was the Brotherhood of Key and Serpent. Go beyond the Jawbone Door and see what we saw! The tree is the truth, seek the tree, and see the truth. Look at my shadow! Pale, see, pale! They can't snap, or pull, but their knives, oh their knives. Beware their sharp knives. If you see someone with a keyhole tattoo on the palms of their hands, run! Run! Run!"

There was a pause, and worried muttering from the station. When it came back, we heard the interviewer ask plainly, "What is it that Angelique believes?"

"Sorry?"

"What did she teach you. This religious leader of yours, the one you called the Daughter of the Wormwood Star. What did she teach you?"

"That when we are dead, we can do anything."

"Oh. And you followed her for that reason?"

"Because we loved her! I love her! I love her blood pumping and bones howling! She showed us the bright corners of the world, and I would never want to go back. When your father comes, Angelique, do not forget about me! Please! Please come back for me. Please. Take me with you. Please. I am so sick of this world and its shadows. Please."

And then Angelique said, "That's enough of that," and turned the radio off.

:episode ∞:
Father Lucifer

1

I need to take a breather here for a moment and explain something to you. I don't know. I feel like this is important, somehow. That it's related to all of this in a way I can't explain, okay? It's another one of those things I learned back when I was still a philosophy major, and it really stuck with me. And whenever I think about my time with Angelique and the knot, I think about this paradox, and I can't help it. It's all entwined in my mind.

It's called the Porcupine Dilemma. Cute, am I right? It was dreamed up by Schopenhauer of all people, and trust me, it's not as cute as it sounds. So, the story goes, it's a cold day. Freezing winter, the kind where you find dead birds or mice on the sidewalk in the morning because they froze to death overnight. And the porcupines are trying to keep warm, right? So they all huddle together so they won't fucking die. But each time they get close enough to get warm, they prick each other with their needles. They can't help it, right? And so they scuttle back away. They don't like hurting the ones they love, even if it's accidental, and even if it's in their nature to hurt people with their needles. It doesn't feel good.

But they need to stay warm to live. They need each other. They do. So they huddle back together, getting closer and closer. So warm. Only to prick each other again.

I think that says so much about what it means to be human, don't you? How we want to be close to each other, but we're so afraid of hurting each other. And we can't not hurt each other. We don't want to, but it happens. That's life, right?

And yet we try. We try. We try to connect.

I know, this doesn't explain anything, does it? And yet somehow, it's all a part of this in ways I don't yet understand, no matter how many times I think about it.

2

We still had the scrawled GPS coordinates on a napkin Simon gave us before we ditched him. Came to him in a dream, he said. He drew a picture, then, of a black stone lighthouse standing still against the skyline. *It is the color of thunder,* he told us, *of pregnant clouds on an autumn night.* In his drawing, the tower was whole, completed. It rose before us now, changed. Ragged, storm smashed, angry. There, on the top of a grassy hill, larger than we could have ever imagined. Surrounded by soft clouds and the shadows of seagulls. In the distance we could hear the waves beyond like a fetal heartbeat, calling us back to our primeval home. That cauldron of sea whence we came.

The top had been torn off, or blown off in an explosion. Later, when I was in prison, I would research this place. I had all that time on my hands, and this gnawing curiosity to somehow understand everything that happened. Even though I knew then (as I do now) that there was no way to logically understand all of this. You could only feel around the edges of it, sensing where the paths lined up, but never truly seeing the whole. Everything to do with Angelique was like sleepwalking through a foggy night, slippery, ambiguous, full of hidden cliffs and sudden falls.

At the time, this was the largest lighthouse in America. It was about four hundred feet tall, but in person it looked so much bigger. A mile high, it seemed. Massive, towering. Like a rotten tooth stuck in the jaw of that hill. You ever look at the stars at night and get dizzy? Realizing how small, and tiny and insignificant everything is in the grand scheme of the ever-expanding universe? Of course you do, don't lie to me. That is also part of the human condition, to feel like we are an important piece in the jigsaw of the universe, only to discover that it's a million-piece puzzle that takes five years to complete only one edge of it. Infinity confounds us, presses against our skulls, and crushes us beyond thought.

That was how the tower made me feel, when I saw it for the first time in real life. And when I looked at the images on those webpages (now gone from the internet, not even on the Wayback Machine) I had that same feeling. That spiraling, empty feeling. Even when I picture it in my head now, as I describe it to you, I feel nauseated and sick and want to lie down and maybe curl up into a ball. Spiraling inward, never to uncoil and be myself again.

But did I stop researching the lighthouse? No. I kept digging. Searching. Looking for answers along the foggy edges of night. It felt like I was searching for myself. For the meaning of who I was, after everything that happened. You don't understand what those years behind bars where like for me. I was listless. Unmoored. Lost on the infinite sea of self. Everything I knew about myself was gone, replaced with this aching emptiness. The only still constant thing in my life was loneliness. Even when I was surrounded by all those prisoners, even with my kids and my husband later on in life, I felt it. Alone. That was the only pure definition of myself. The lonely girl. The lonely woman. The lonely child. The lonely daughter, the lonely mother. That was who I was, who I am, deep in the core of my being. In a way, I was the lighthouse. Alone, even when surrounded by everyone else. Alone.

The name of the place was very fitting. Christened *The Anchorite* when it was first built, it gathered more nicknames through the years. *The Storm Witch, The Blind Hermit, The Prince of Night,* and then after the accident, *The Headless Giant.* Here is a riddle for you, what is the purpose of a lighthouse if it has no light? Yeah, I don't know the answer to that one, either. Maybe someday we'll figure it out, and it will be our secret.

Anyway, it turned out an explosion had destroyed the crown of the lighthouse, way back when they still used kerosene to light those things. There were rumors that it was on purpose. That the lighthouse keeper, Mister Lampeater, had gone a little strange in the weeks leading up to the big kaboom. The lighthouse had only been in action for about a year or so, when he'd been brought in to replace the old guy. I can't remember the other guy's name, but I think it was something plain and boring, like Mister Trembley or Mister Jones. I do remember what he looked like, the scanned-in newspaper pages still fresh in my mind.

Bearded, long tangled hair, craggy weather-worn features. The years of pipe smoking and tending to the lighthouse had filled his wrinkles with soot. Eyes that were deceptively kind. He'd hung himself a few weeks before the top of *The Anchorite* exploded, and the police didn't think the two incidents were connected. Of course, the website had other ideas. Websites always do, don't they? The internet is a breeding ground for conspiracy. And maybe they were onto something there, I don't know. I just know that the place had a history, and that somehow tied into all of this.

The explosion killed twenty-five people. Mostly tourists, come to see the (then) tallest lighthouse in the world. There were no witnesses, no forensics back in those days, no way to try and recreate the last few hours and figure out exactly what went wrong. Rumors abound, of course. And when these packages of his letters surfaced weeks after the explosion, tied in twine and bobbing on the waves towards the beach, they just wrote it off as lighthouse madness. It happens, sometimes, they say. The loneliness, the light, the kerosene eating into your brain.

They had some excerpts on the page, scanned in from the local history museum. It was mostly nonsense poetry, rambling on for pages and pages. It talked about the Headless Giant, how he lived beneath the sea, and was waiting for the right hour to wake up. The lighthouse did not guide the ships away from the cliffs, he claimed, but instead was there to wake that sleeping beast. He talked about the father of lights, how he recreated the Wormwood Star on earth, the lighthouse reflecting something sinister beyond the night sky. *The daughter comes*, he wrote, *and she will be a fire that sets this world free. Be afraid of her, for she is the shattering sound of the dark. The whisper when the trees are still. There is light and then there is light, and to know the truth between the two is to see the keyholes in the doors of darkness.*

I will burn tomorrow, and the world will see. The world will see exactly what I mean. The Headless Giant will be visible to them, and they will see. They will see the echo of night on earth, and the emptiness at the core of everything.

3

Here we go. Shit. Out of all the difficult things I've had to talk about, this feels like it's the most difficult. And that says a lot. Fuck. Okay, time to pull the band-aid off, right? Just dive right in. I haven't thought about this in decades. This was the one memory I refused to revisit. Even thinking about it now makes my bones scream beneath my skin. One, two, three. Here we go. Fuck. Fuck me. Okay.

I was cut off from the knot, and surrounded by that terrible oppressive silence outside my skull. Everyone else, even Petal now, it seemed, were moving in perfect synchronicity. Like a rehearsed dance routine, graceful limbs moving in rhythmic gestures. The door to the lighthouse was shattered and tilted, barely hanging onto the frame like a crooked ghost. There was a symbol painted on the door, and I get goosebumps now, remembering it. The same one from Lucy Diamond's door in the hospital. A circle, a triangle, that crooked slash. Lights flickered from the windows, amber and strange in the twilight gloom, the ones at the crown a halo in the night sky. We could see the ruins of the lens for the lighthouse even from down here, and it sent refracted rainbows of light across the ground. Dead birds were scattered everywhere in the grass, their eyes replaced with tiny black stones. They seemed so fake, so unreal, like they were constructed from paper mache. Weightless, like that chill wind from the sea would carry them away.

I remembered the last few days at uni, before the plane crash and the death of Sara Fisher. There were bird corpses littering the campus back then, too, weren't there? Also, the eyes gone. Replaced with black stones. I wanted to ask the others if that was right, if I was remembering things correctly, but I didn't want to break the silence in my head. To speak out loud right now was verboten, that I knew. If I couldn't communicate through the knot, then I couldn't communicate at all. The thought left me feeling all woozy and dizzy, and in that moment, I felt like this was it, yes. I was finally going to die. And it was nothing like I pictured back when Angelique told us to picture our death. It was going to be far, far, worse.

"Can you losers sense Natasha up there?"

Cris seemed to jump at the sound of Angelique's voice. "No?"

And Petal chimed in as well. "No, no I can't either."

"Clara, you?"

But I couldn't feel anything, either. Only the loss of the *we* I had come to rely on so intimately, without even knowing it. It ached against me like a phantom limb. But that was it, I was cast out.

"Okay, focus, come on now. I want you to use that collective power of yours and see if you can see what's going on up there."

"Well," I said, "It's a trap, duh."

"But what kind of trap, right? Unless you want to be the first to walk in and the first to die. Do you? Do you have that death wish inside of you?"

I said nothing in response and let the others use their powers. I thought I heard the sounds of birds chirping, but the noise came from the ground. From all the dead corpses. I knew they weren't making those sounds, but I did hear it. I did. And it wasn't coming from inside of my head, they were audible and strong and I wondered if they were ghosts or something else. Something far worse than ghosts. A bleeding of parallel worlds, perhaps. A wound of the still living seeing their own selves dead through the skin of the veil.

And above, when the living knot concentrated, the seagulls all went quiet. So the sounds of the ghost birds were the only sounds I could hear. I felt my hair stand on end, goosebumps, skin prickling. I wanted to join them, to put my own powers to their use. To be knotted up again. And then I remembered the mouse girl, what they made me do. Why was I still even here, doing this? Angelique. Yes.

She was in danger. In more ways than one. The knot. The lighthouse. All of it.

And her father waits for us. That, too, is a danger. The worst of all, I think. To see the devil in flesh and bone, to watch him watch us. To see us and feel his love for us and the hatred of the world, and to carry us into the shadows beyond. I did not want that. No matter how much I loved Angelique, I knew that this was a deadly thing. Maybe I could save her from that fate as well? Oh, who was I kidding. I couldn't save anyone from anything.

But I had to try. I loved her, and I had to try. And even though the knot was dangerous, and had me do terrible things . . .

I loved them, too. Motherfuckers. I did. Shit. I was going to see this through to the end.

You would think that I might regret that. That I should've just followed my gut instinct and gotten out of there while I had the chance, right? Long ago, long before the mouse girl and the rest. Would I have survived? Sure, I wouldn't have gone to prison, and I wouldn't have done all of that. I wouldn't be haunted, or broken, or this shadow in a shadow world living out my shadow days in someone else's life. But, I would probably also be dead.

Without the tools I learned from Angelique, I would have been killed by the Brotherhood of Key and Serpent. If it weren't for the knot, and us staying together, and carrying me through the sad and lonely hours, I would have probably killed myself, so many times over. And if it wasn't for Angelique, giving meaning to my life, to keep me moving on and fighting, even after, even after . . .

Even after.

Fuck. Maybe I'm just making up excuses for my actions. Ex post facto. Did I live an authentic life in the end? Who the hell knows. Were all my actions in bad faith, and was I just avoiding responsibility for who I was? Maybe. But you know what? Fuck Sartre, and fuck Socrates. It was my life, and I get to define it how I want. I can miss the knot, and that royal we that gave me meaning, and I can miss doing things that I know I shouldn't do, but did anyway. There was no gun to my head, but that's okay. Angelique was all the gun I ever needed.

And the knot stopped for a moment and turned to Angelique. "We see nothing."

"Nothing? You sure you tried hard enough? Try again."

The knot all closed their eyes at the same time, a hidden metronome heartbeat guiding their movements to a creepy, unseen rhythm. So smooth their motions, so doll-like. Petal stood next to me, Angelique to her side, all of us watching the knot, seeing their hair flow around their bodies like they were underwater. I ached to join them again. To be part of that once more. I wanted to say we are concentrating, longed to once more say we are looking into the tower with our mind. We are pulling. We are pushing.

But I cannot. I could only watch from the outside and ache.

They opened their eyes again all at once, exhaling, speaking in unison.

"Still nothing."

"Fuck. Nothing! Nothing. Fuck. Are you losers sure?"

"We're sure."

Petal walked forward, placed a hand on Angelique's shoulder, trying to comfort her. Angelique shrugged her off, stomped forward. "This is dangerous."

"Maybe it's not, maybe there's really nothing up there. Wouldn't that be a good thing? If we walked up there, and there was no trap?"

And I laughed. I couldn't help it, the absurdity of it all got under my skin.

"What's so funny?"

Angelique's words had a bite to them, and I flinched like I'd been slapped. She seemed so angry the last few days, ever since we left Simon behind. There was a darkness growing in her, and a deep-seated pain I'd never seen before. I was both terrified and more in love with her than ever before.

"I'm sorry. I mean, it's not funny. But it kind of is? It's like Waiting for Godot. Or Seinfeld. Nothing is there, nothing waits for us, Godot never comes."

"That's not even close to funny."

"Oh. Okay. I'm sorry, I . . ."

"If Natasha isn't up there, if this isn't a trap? What do you think that means. Be careful now, really fucking think about it."

So much pain and darkness in her now.

"I, I don't know."

"It means Natasha would probably be dead. That's what."

"Oh."

"Yeah, oh. Fucking hell." She ran her hand through her hair, getting her fingers caught on her snarls and curls. She lifted up her cane, pointed it at the front door, and said so very calmly. "All right, I guess this is it. No going back! We're going to go inside, trigger the trap, and hope that we all get out of this in one piece. And if not? Well, we're all dead anyway, aren't we? So nothing will change. And my father will come for us, and take us away from here, and leave this world of suffering in ruin from his waking."

I felt my knees weak, shaking. Yes, we pictured our deaths, but that didn't mean we'd actually experienced death. Now that it was staring at me right in the eye, my bones were filled with bees and I wanted to run the other way screaming. Goosebumps marched over my spine and through my body. But I would not run. Not with Angelique standing there, head tilted up toward the twilight hours, cane held solid and bright in her hand. I just hoped that she had enough juice so that she could save us when shit got real. And that the knot wasn't too drained to do anything.

Angelique turned and looked at me. "Okay, Seinfeld, you get to be the first to walk through those doors. The rest of us will follow you."

And oh shit. Yes. This was punishment for my little joke, I knew it. Shit. And as I walked forward, Petal grabbed my hand. The irritated tattoo on her palm hot against my fingers. "I'll come with you."

I wished we could be knotted together right then. As we walked through that shattered, disheveled door, and saw the darkness that flickered in the ruins beyond.

4

Ruins of shattered walls and a spiral of a staircase leading up and up and up. Scorch marks dotted the walls, and everywhere there were severed hands like candles, much like the ones from the hospital earlier. They lined the walls, were placed on every staircase, they covered and dripped melting fat over coffee tables and book cases on the museum on the first floor. The air smelled like kerosene on burning flesh, a rancid reminder of death with every step. We all snapped as we walked, fighting the drowsy hungry feeling from the creepy mutilated candles.

"This could be why," Angelique's words drooping, slurred, mouth at a crooked angle, "You saw nothing. A veil of slumber coating this lighthouse . . ."

And there were bodies strewn across the floor. Who were they? And where they dead, or sleeping, or what? We had to step over them, and it was like Sleeping Beauty, and we were the only ones still awake in her tower. One moaned as we stepped over them, and I saw open wounds, ragged throat holes, eyes gouged out, and realized they were dying and half awake at the same time. Fighting slumber, as they bled out, the hands of glory bringing them onto the edges of sleep, and past that, death.

One reached out, tried to grab my ankle, and only brushed me with its fingertips. Unable to grasp, sleep-coated. I saw a keyhole tattoo on the palm of their hand. What had happened here? The figure tried to call out. Face mutilated, throat gashed open and gurgling the words out, the blood sliding from the wound in puddles of sentences. I recognized him, yes. One of our teachers. Doctor Max Booth, Ph D. Fuck. What was he doing here? And I thought back to our days at Dark Rivers Uni, and Sara Fisher's death . . .

Was he responsible?

I snapped in my head, fought that drowsy slumber, and kicked him. The head tilted back, the wound in the neck opened up further as he struggled, fingers grasping at the hole, trying to close it, vainly. Oh so vainly. As we half-crawled up those spiral steps, clinging to each one like it was a tether to life. I tried my best to ignore this awful sinking feeling, that there was something moving in the darkness on the edges of our vision. Look, there—the shadows changed shape. They grew and shrunk, like they were breathing. I felt suffocated, swallowed alive. The womb of the lighthouse tower digesting me, slowly, slowly, slowly. I reached out to the knot with my mind, to gather some comfort in these last few moments. Death waited above, I knew this now. Death, and perhaps Angelique's father.

But no, no response. Silence. I couldn't even see the edges of their knot anymore. Just the inhale and exhale of the breathing dark. As we climbed, and climbed, and climbed. Hands and knees crawling, terrified, but continuing on. There was a sinister presence in that dark. A consciousness, digesting us. As we crawled, I remembered a moment as a child, when my grandmother died. We were all visiting her, and she was outside in the snow. I remember it so clearly. She'd wanted to go outside and help us make snow angels. And she'd laid down on her back, wearing only her house blouse and no coat, no hat, no gloves. She'd laid down, the tips of her fingers and toes blue, as she smiled and made snow angels.

Our parents were inside, not even knowing what was going on. I guess, in a way, my grandma raised me, more so than anyone else. And when she slipped on, her heart giving out in those moments, her face tilted to the sky as snow tumbled down, coating her face and her hands like dove feathers, I cried out. I tried to shake her awake. I tried to do anything, to bring her back from the edges of death.

But no. No more. I remember the sounds of ambulances next, and the soft silence in my chest, as my heart stopped beating for a breath or two. I was maybe six, seven years old. My parents later lied to me and said it didn't happen like that at all. They'd walked into the house first, and found her body on the couch, and took me outside to make snow angels, so that I wouldn't see her corpse. Mom said it was her making the angels with me, not grandma.

But I know what I saw. I remember it so clearly. I pitied them, feeling the need to lie to me at such a young age. I could handle it, I could. The truth was far more digestible than any lie. I don't know why I remembered it at this moment in time. Odd how the mind works, so odd, indeed. You're probably wondering why I decided to nest a memory in my memory as I recall it to you, but the two things are so connected, in a way I don't yet understand. Like the Porcupine Dilemma, like everything else, there are threads all tied up and knotted together. This memory, that memory, all of it.

Somehow, the memory of her death brought me peace, and fought off the slumbering candles with more power than any snap could ever do. If I died it would be okay. Death was everywhere. If I lived? Well, that was another story. For another day. But each moment I crawled, I felt closer to some grand truth that I would never quite understand—I could only see the outline of it, the silhouette running underneath every moment of my life in sticky tendrils.

We crested the last of the floors, the wide-open shattered crown of the lighthouse, and we saw the scene that waited for us beyond. More bodies with keyhole tattoos. Petal let go of my hand, in shock. Had she gotten to know any of them? Probably. Maybe she saw her own future lying there, dying on the ground. Her keyhole tattoo now marking her for death. Who knows? And the shadows on the floors beneath us inhaled, exhaled. More flickering mutilated candles, and in the center of all this death? Natasha, now not much younger than any of us. Probably seventeen, I would think? Maybe.

She was the spitting image of Angelique, and our love cried out for her as well. She was tied to the shattered remains of the giant lens, her head tilted upward. She shivered uncontrollably, as tubes drained her blood onto the floor with each heartbeat. Her shirt was ripped open, her body slit down from the top of her chest to her belly button. Guts were visible, still moving, undisturbed. Her heart under her pried-open ribs. Her face blissful, strange, the same look the mouse girl had in her eyes when I choked out her last few breaths.

And behind it all sat a man dressed in all white, on an old wicker chair, his legs crossed and his face smiling, sweetly. Like he had been waiting for us this whole time. Blood splattered on the shine of his teeth, his lips smeared red with the lipstick of the dead. A messy gnarled beard crawled down his face, and his eyes. Oh god—his eyes were so intense, so vivid, so *wrong*.

5

"I see you've heard my call, yes, and came to me, just as I expected. I wish we hadn't gone to such drastic measures, no. You should have come when I asked nicely, when I asked sweetly. But you made me do this, you made me go this far. And now look what you made me do! Your poor sister over there, suffering. No need at all! You should have let us burn her and burn the tree, you should have let us take you down and bring you to our side. Petal, Petal my dear. I am so disappointed in you. I taught you all I know, and this is where you end up. With her, that filthy antichrist, the corruption of the nothingness that is everything. That fucking Daughter of the Wormwood Star."

Natasha shuddered as the guy got up and walked forward, her blood still draining out onto the ground. Her eyes were distant, strange eyes, mouth frothing, the smile distorted, broken. She looked high as fuck, and I didn't know if it was because she was dying and the adrenaline was taking her away from us, or if this sadistic jerk had pumped her so full of chemicals that she was in outer space already. The whole scene left us all in a state of shock, and for a moment I felt the knot tangle up with me again, and then fade away. Pulsating on the edges of my vision.

Angelique placed her cane flat on the ground. Her eyes spun red, intense. Oh shit, shit was about to go down. Come on, Angelique, don't fuck around. Just say that magic phrase and make this end right now so we can get Natasha to a fucking hospital. *Return to the void . . .*

"Who the hell is this loser?"

"I am the humble servant of the void, and I have brought you here, Angelique, to kill you. I tried to show you, to show all of you the promise of nothingness. To turn you back on the devil himself, that father of numb boring matter. Matter and light! What corruptions of the great emptiness at the heart of the world. No, it just won't do, will it girls?"

And then he snapped his fingers, and the air thickened like molasses. Natasha quivered and lost more blood, as my thoughts screamed out *do something, save her! She's going to die, she's dying, why won't anyone do something? Why won't anyone save her?* I looked at the knot and they were all glassy-eyed, high as fuck now, their bodies turning and looking directly at Angelique, the movements balletic, robotic, synchronized. Their hair all turned white at the snap of his fingers, flowed around their heads like they were underwater. Their skin deathly pale, blue veins visible, like slow cracks in fine china.

Shit. They were under this guy's control.

"Oh yes, I came to them at night, whispered to them and showed them the awful truth of reality. What, who did you think built the House of Sky and Shadow? That's my house you're dreaming in! My fucking house. And they listened to me, oh yes, they did. And now they know the song of sorrow and emptiness. They lived in that house, and now they understand what we need to do to make things right again." He stopped walking toward us for a moment, pulled out a satin handkerchief, and dotted at the blood on his lips and glasses. It didn't wipe it away, but instead smeared it and stained his hand-kerchief a deep crimson, his beard now a mess of gore and violence.

"Enough! Enough talking! Enough of this bullshit. You're not making any sense, none of this is making any sense." Angelique raised her cane and her scar started to grow and split. Already she was pulling on her own powers, to try and put a stop to the knot. The air filled with the electric energy of her snaps, and I knew I had to lend her my strength. I moved forward, about ready to reach out and touch her, to combine our forces. All she had to do was start saying those words, *return to the void,* and this could all be over. And yet, I saw her strength waver, her knees buckle a little. Could she do it? Oh. I really hoped so.

"Fine, I guess we'll just go to the main attraction already. Pity, I was giving you the respect of telling you the why of your demise. I thought you would want to know all about your little sacrifice. Your bones will be painted red, you see, and your father will come to claim them. You can feel him here now, can't you? Lucifer. Your death will bring him closer, clothe him in mortal meat, and I will kill him. The void demands it. He and your kin are abominations of entropy, and that will simply not do. So you will die, and he will die, and the world will keep on decaying and rotting and burning. Now, give me the same respect I gave you. You must die for me. A sacrifice is asked for, and a sacrifice will be given. Come girls, let's do this just as we practiced in our dreams."

And then the knot turned. Their powers focused on us, like being inside of a microwave set to thaw. And everything went spindizzy, crash, I fell against the giant lens, my body knocking right up against poor Natasha. I almost slipped on her blood, tried to hold onto her. She was fading fast, I could see that now. Angelique laughed, pointed her cane at the man in white.

"You fool. He was coming to get us anyway, you don't have to do any of this or murder anyone. He's sick of this world and people like you—we were going to leave you behind to your rot and entropy and just get on with it already."

And he snapped his fingers in response, his intense gaze narrowed directly at Angelique now. "Shut it. You will not spoil my fun. You're not the only one who can snap or pull or push or any of that other nonsense. The void is all and everything, and those who stare into it can feel it, touch it, move it with their lips and their tongues. Like this, just watch. Just like this."

And Angelique ragdoll-collapsed to the ground in a pile of limbs, her eyes rolling around like glass marbles. I tried to move forward, but everything slid sideways, danced around me, vertigosick. Fucking hell. I felt the prickle of my limbs and my vision was clouded with shadows moving on my periphery. Those shadows must've climbed up through the spiral staircase, and now they breathed up here, amongst us. Swallowed alive by their shallow breathing.

I watched as Petal tried to go over, to get Angelique up and moving. No dice. The knot turned to her and the full force of their anger let loose. This just wasn't going to do. I wasn't going to let them atom bomb Petal with the chorus of the devil. That just was not going to happen tonight. I fought the vertigo, slid around and pushed myself forward. It took all of my willpower and chewing a hole in my left cheek to keep from projectile vomiting, the vertigo was that bad. But I made it yes, I made it. I couldn't snap, I couldn't pull, I couldn't do anything when I was like that, the spinning stole my thoughts away from me and hid them in the uneasy greasy corners of my mind.

But I could shove them out of the way and knock them over, breaking up their little spell and scattering their own thoughts. I was hoping it would knock them out of whatever trance that asshole had put them under, but no dice. Their eyes were still all shadowy and broken and high, and their hair still white, and their movements jerky like a marionette. What had he done to them in their dreams?

"Come on, girls, I can see your knot is still tied tight, let's give it a tug and get back to work. The mother of the void has been patient with us so far, but she might not be for much longer, so we need to hurry this up. Entropy is ticking away, tick, tick, tick."

Petal pushed Angelique's hair aside, and was trying to wake her by stroking her cheek and gently singing to her. "Come on, baby girl, come on," she sang, "The birds are chirping, the sun is rising, sleep is gone and behind us now. Come on, baby girl, come on."

Where had I heard that song before? A record, an old one my parents had. Some cult that actually had a number one hit on the billboard charts. What was their name? Oh right, the Sunshine Family. Why did I think about this now? It wasn't the time, and yet it felt important, somehow.

And I reached over, and grabbed her hand with mine. The three of us now connected flesh to flesh. I don't think we could wake Angelique up. Hell, I wasn't sure I could stop my spinning. But I did know that our touch brought me a sharp clarity, and if I closed my eyes, the spinning stopped. I reached out, and found the shadow of a knot that me and Petal once shared, and started to thread it together again, and she didn't fight me. I tried to find Angelique's knot, too, but there was nothing there. Just a shadow in the shape where her threads should be.

Petal.
Yes?
Can you see their knot? The coven.
Yeah. Can you?
No, too dizzy, was barely able to get to yours.
Oh.
Could you guide me there? And then the three of us pull together?
Pull?
Right. A pull, just like Angelique showed us.
We want to pull them toward us?
No. We want to pull them apart. Take the threads, and pull and pull on the knot, until it comes undone.

And it felt like it took us a million years to do this, but in reality it was more like a few milliseconds and nothing more. We started to pull, and each time a thread came loose, the person it was attached to collapsed to the ground in violent convulsions, as their heart exploded in their chest, shattering their ribs. We only got three of them down, working toward Cris, when I heard a screaming and everything was filled with silence.

"No, no, no, no, no! You lousy, idiotic, heathens! I will have to stop this myself."

And before I could react, I was knocked backward, my eyes blurry and barely open. The world had stopped spinning, and Petal was on the ground, and that stranger in the white suit was on top of her. He gutted her in one slick motion with a hook, blood burbling from her mouth as her intestines and offal spilled out. The sounds she made, and the smell. Oh god, I remember that slaughterhouse smell so clearly. I can't really describe it to you unless you've experienced it yourself, that tang of blood, of raw meat, that smell of shit as the intestines are pierced. She wasn't dying quickly, no. I could see the pain in her eyes, her voice shaking, as the guy stood up, and wiped the blood from his hook. Why couldn't she at least have a quick death? Why are violent deaths always so slow, so drawn out? Petal, of all people, shouldn't have to suffer . . .

"Now, am I going to have to do something to you, too?"

Clara . . .

Yes?

This was exactly what I pictured.

What?

When Angelique asked us to picture our death. Somehow, being gutted by a hook was the most painful thing I could picture.

I'm so sorry, Petal . . .

It's okay. It's actually not as bad as I . . .

And then silence.

Fuck this noise. There was this restless anger in my heart that had been growing since they'd cut me out of the knot. It was fueled by a lifetime of loneliness, heartbreak, and isolation. Fuck this guy, fuck the devil, fuck all of this. Fuck the life I was born into, fuck the suffering of everyday existence, fuck everything and fuck everyone. Fuck it until the sun explodes in the sky and fuck it until the moon falls into the sea and fuck it until the heat death of the universe and fuck it like the big bang and fuck everything and everyone that treated us like shit, that left us lonesome and broken and dying. Fuck. FUCK.

I screamed in a way I knew would break the world. Not with my lips but with my blood and my bones. I screamed like Angelique taught us to snap and shout and knot and pull and push. I screamed and it was primal and primordial and like an explosion of silence. I let my loneliness out and the world stopped. Like a heartbeat, broken, stopped. One, two, three.

I exhaled and opened my eyes and saw I was surrounded by corpses. Natasha was dead on the lens, her eyes exploded out of her skull in a river of gore, her mouth dangling open in shock, everything limp and unmoving. Angelique, Petal, everyone, even the last of the core of our coven, dead. Eyes exploded, lips dangling open in fear, bodies still and silent. Just like Sara Fisher, they had been drained of life and have become objects. Corpses. Not even the shallow breathing of the barely alive, not even a twitching of eyelids to feign life. Just blood and shadows and nothing.

And then one corpse stood, stumbled forward. Hook still in his hand, that horrible man in white. He was blind, eyes exploded, chest bloodied, everything stained with the terrors around him. His mouth twitched and he laughed, clumsily wiping blood from his face, and feeling around his eyeholes.

"Oh, what did you do, you foolish child, what did you do? Made me blind? Really! Is that the best you can do, is that all your mighty power can summon? Some daughter of the devil you are, weak and useless. You didn't think that would actually work on *me*, did you? I am one with the great void that devours all! I have seen the emptiness in the heart of time, and can amass entropy to do my bidding! I am made of stronger stuff than your simple magic trick, your little psychic show, your tiny hocus pocus. I will do what men have always done, pick up a nice sturdy weapon, and fucking eviscerate you. No psychic powers required, no devil to make me do anything. Just me, your corpse, and your eyes staring on in horror at the infinite emptiness that lay beyond death."

And he rushed forward at me, clumsily, blind. Was this a joke? This was sad, pitiful, wielding the hook like it a toy or a movie prop, barely sticking to his hand. I didn't have time to feel sad about Angelique (a hole in my heart the size of her face), but that would come later, at the police station, when it all hit me. I was still in shock over everything, and still mortified after what I'd done, what I've seen, who we'd all become. I almost didn't catch him in time, running toward me. I almost fell on the hook, died without thinking. He was so clumsy though, and it was so easy to just step aside, and push him over the edge. He didn't even scream as he fell, he just . . . fell.

A stone in the air, a body on the pavement. The sounds of his bones crunching made me feel hollow and empty. This wasn't a victory. This was survival.

And I heard fire roaring somewhere, but wasn't sure where. And I saw the shadows silent around me, no longer breathing. Though they congealed now, and for a moment I swear I saw a face in the shadows. A giant massive face, handsome in a way that bent gender, and broke it. Two small horns were on either side of its head, and the eyes flashed like stars in the night sky. It was as tall as the lighthouse, and for a moment there, I thought it looked sad and lost and wounded. And then it was gone, like smoke.

The sound of sirens came over the hill in the distance. Firetrucks, police cars, maybe even a SWAT team or two. Whatever. I just sat up there and waited for them. I felt so empty. And part of me wanted to cry big hulking sobs. Like that might somehow make it all okay, if I could at least feel it, and express it, and make it real.

But no, there was nothing.

6

The rest you know, I guess. The trial, all of that. I guess it could've been worse, but the evidence was strange and confusing, and it was hard to pin me down for all of the murders. Whatever. I still feel them around me, you know. The coven. My knot. It's strange, but in prison I felt the knot even stronger than when they were alive. It made me wonder—maybe they all survived, and I only assumed they'd been dead. Wouldn't that be something? Even when we found their obits online, I had this feeling like they were still alive. Because of how strong the knot felt.

And every once in a while, we would slip into that voice again. And we would look at ourselves outside of ourselves, echoes in the shadows of the world. We would whisper to each other along the edges of that knot, and something would slouch in the darkness around us, and we would see the edges of death and wonder where we were . . . who was coming for us . . . and why we felt so breathless and still. We choked, for a moment, trying to breathe . . .

And then I would gasp for breath and remember these were phantom limbs, nothing more. Residuals of a knot. I went and saw their graves when I got out of prison all those years later. Just to prove to ourselves that we were really dead. Placing our hands on the stones of our graves, and feel the heat of the sun against bare palms.

It hurts to keep going. And there are days when I see my kids and I shine. I am not quite so lost and broken inside. But there are things I keep from them. Things we keep from our husband, too.

Like we will never love him like I loved Angelique. Or Petal. Or the others. Maybe that's for the better. Could a marriage survive a love like that? It's all-consuming, destructive, worshipful love. A love that demands death and life and everything else. What we have is a calm, resplendent thing. With our own secrets that keep us interesting. There are things I don't ask him, and things he doesn't ask me, and that's okay.

We called you for this interview because I'd started dreaming of the House of Sky and Shadow again, and we don't know what to do about it. It's on fire, and the knot grows stronger around me, their ghostly voices telling me to join them. I'm hoping this will be enough, and it will placate them and they will leave me alone. I'm not like Cris or the others. When I pictured my own death, I was absolutely terrified. There was no acceptance in me, no coming to terms with it, like Petal did near the end. It was just . . .

You're probably wondering about the tattoo. Sigh. I got it in prison. I know, after everything we went through, why did I do it? I don't know exactly. It's on the left hand, and Petal had hers on her right. Sometimes I picture her ghost hand enveloping mine, and our keyholes touching. Maybe it would be like a mirror facing a mirror, and we carried infinity between us. Maybe. That would be nice, wouldn't it?

It's the only thing that gives me comfort when the dark hours touch me. When I hear footsteps in the halls of our house, and I know it's not any of our kids. They're heavy, clomping, footsteps. Like giant feet. With a subtle clack, clack, clack. Like dog nails on hardwood floors. Or a horse trotting with bare hooves on concrete. Or when we see the shadows congeal again into a face, and I can tell it's the devil come to take me home, just like Angelique said he would.

But I'm not ready to go. No, not just yet.

Acknowledgments

Would like to thank my parents, my grandparents, and most of my family for supporting me, even when they didn't like my gross horror novels and short stories. I would also like to thank my editor, Darin Bradley for helping me carve this into the right shape. The book is hundred percent better because of his suggestions and expertise. Thank you to my awesome kids, Ashlyn and Liam, for telling me when I've got something really good and scary, or when it's just kind of meh and I need to tweak it some. Thanks to all my writing friends, but especially Jonathan Wood and Natania Barron for reading this over as I wrote it, and giving me good feedback, and also just being kick ass cheerleaders. And thanks to Underland Press, for publishing this madcap crazy work.

Hail Satan! Hail Angelique! Hail the Daughter of the Wormwood Star!

Printed in the USA
CPSIA information can be obtained
at www.ICGtesting.com
JSHW080806021024
70910JS00003B/45